GODS' Warrior

Preacher Spindrift series

Derek E. Pearson

First published 2018
Published by GB Publishing.org

Cover Design © 2018 Tillier Designs
Cover Illustration by Anita Clark

GB Publishing.org
www.gbpublishing.co.uk

For Sue, it's about time she had one to herself

Acknowledgements
Thanks to George and the team at GB Publishing who
welcomed Preacher Spindrift onto the world stage and saw
him become finalist at the *Foreword Indies Book of the Year
Awards* – twice. Here he is again.

CONTENT

[1] (Foreword) Old friends and a funeral

Caleb Sawyer died peacefully on his porch as he always believed he might, and I attended his funeral. He had been a popular man in his neighbourhood, and deservedly so. I had learned to love him and respect him decades before as a good friend – and as a staunch ally in my fight against the enemy of everything I hold worthwhile.

I have been a long time on this Earth. A very long time. I've seen civilisations thrive and fall, great men forgotten, and wicked men prosper. I have also learned that nothing can replace the value of a good heart; no, not for all the tea in China.

That warm September day when his neighbours gave Caleb a true Shafter send off was an honest celebration for a fine man. Children left little posies for the friend they called 'Gramps'; a man who always had time to praise their victories and sympathise with their troubles – and could always find fresh, cold buttermilk and a few cookies for a hungry mite.

That porch of his was a place filled with laughter and simple wonders, a place where children felt safe and were treated as equals.

I watched his funeral service with Caleb's second wife, Alice, at my side. She had left him alone a year before he died because she loved him too much to watch him fail from the cancer that took him too fast and far too soon. After he was committed to the ground she returned to her river and disappeared back to her own life.

I would meet Alice again in the halls of Scytaer Faehl, the city between the worlds. Ever changing and beautiful beyond the telling of it, Scytaer Faehl is the home of the fey, elemental sprites who move between their wonderful city and the place humankind thinks of as home as easily as we walk through a door from one room to the next.

I was taken there by Pel-osen, a prince of the race of air sprites. I had met him when he was still known as Colin Cahoon, a captain with the 11th Regiment of Engineers and one of the first American troops to go face-to-face with the German army during the desperate days of the war in 1917. He had become involved in a support operation after the battle of Cambrai, a failed allied advance using tanks.

What had started so well got bogged down and within two weeks the Germans had regained every foot of Flanders taken during the lightning allied advance. Colin got himself blown up during the recovery action, and I

1

nursed him back to health. I was both regimental padre and medical surgeon for the American Expeditionary forces in the region.

Colin helped fill the vacuum Caleb's death had left in my heart, but then I discovered he was much more than the remarkable man I believed him to be. He was a prince of the elementals who had been abducted as a baby by his jealous uncle and abandoned to his fate on the bleak Texan plains.

The story of his return to his family and what we did to defeat another vile offshoot of the enemy of all humankind has been told elsewhere. Alice heard that her friend Spindrift was in town and sought me out after Pel-osen's wedding to his true love, the earth elemental Rowan. We had a fine reunion. The elementals are heart-breakingly beautiful people, full of compassion and mischief. I could easily have spent the rest of my life with them and let the world go hang without my ministrations.

Then it was 1918 and the world was still at war, men were killing each other in unprecedented numbers. They had invested a huge amount of their scant resources in building bigger, better, and ever more powerful methods of destruction.

People starved while tanks, guns, aircraft, submarines, and ships rolled off the production lines and stalked out into the arena of war to kill, kill and kill again. Some men became heroes and some cowards; but too many lay down their lives fighting for King and Country, for their President, or their Kaiser.

Captain Cahoon, had been reported as missing, believed dead. He had escaped the madness and the horror of the trenches. However, he, like me, knew that the true enemy was not the man in the uniform of another country. They could only kill and maim. The true enemy would not rest until every man, woman, and child on the face of the planet had been subsumed into its vile body.

If one country was the victor at the end of the European conflict humankind would pick itself up and start to rebuild its civilisation. The baker would bake his bread once more, and the teacher stand before their class. Once devastated streets would return to normal; and people would lay down their arms to work together and rebuild their lives.

The dead, those lost legions of the once living, the wasted youth, what of them? They would be honoured and remembered in glory, while the spectre of their rat gnawed, bloated bodies floating in the blood, the mud, and the shit, that would be forgotten. The blundering blind stupidity of it all, the insanity, cruelty, and the waste, all that would be put away at the back of the cupboard and monuments to the fallen would be erected in its place.

It was so tempting to remain in the city between worlds, where I had been made so welcome. I could leave humankind to its folly and only visit when it found civilisation and sanity once more, if it ever could.

However, I couldn't do it, it would fly in the face of everything I knew.

Humankind was one the Eden-borne races, races that contained the unique souls of a lost and noble people. They were the transplanted children of a lost world, children I had helped create and watched evolve into the sophisticated killers they had since become.

Eight million years is a long time to waste on a failed project. No matter how foolish it seemed I decided I must keep my promise and protect them from the true enemy, GODS' enemy, the Sha-aneer also known as the ancient wise worm of the deep earth. I had been called and must answer.

The Sha-aneer was hunting again, and this time it was in China. I must go to the ancient city of Lijiang and then the village of Shuhe. From there my hunt for GODS' enemy would begin once more.

[2]

He stood out in the crowd along Square Street like a dark beacon; but then, he would have stood out anywhere. He was one of those charismatic people. For a start he stood head and shoulders taller than the people around him, and he was leaner than most.

He was dark for a white man and looked extremely capable, broad-shouldered, and well-centred, but he was attracting more attention than was healthy for a foreigner in recent years. He was one of those whom the locals might politely call a wàiguórén to his face, which means foreigner in the formal tongue, and less politely a gwailou, or white devil, behind his back.

Most westerners tend to hunch down a little when walking amongst the Naxi, or Nashi, people who were the principal ethnic inhabitants of the old town. On average they were shorter and more compact than us, and we tried to compensate for it by bowing our heads a little.

Not the Germans of course, they either tried to become invisible or did their best to look invincible, which drew adverse glances from townsfolk who considered them merely boorish and uncivilised. Quite a few of the Kaiser's people had been assassinated in China recently, some of them top-knobs. I could easily understand why.

Officially, I supposed, I must consider myself at war with Germany. My homeland, England, was, as were the French and now the Yanks. In fact, half the planet seemed to be taking sides in the war, as if it was the only game in town and they wanted their piece of it.

Yes, I guessed I would have to include myself as an ally against the Germans if the need arose, but before I could pocket the King's shilling I first pictured myself as a roving soldier of fortune and had gone a 'wandering, adrift across the wide world. My hands were available for hire. If Heinie had the money and needed my help for anything less than martial combat, I'd pitch in on his behalf.

I'd heard rumours that the Chinese republic had also declared war on Germany, and that Japanese invaders were supporting it with cold cash. No sign of it here, cash or war. To me the ancient town of Lijiang looked the way it had always looked, and I'd put money on the fact that if old Kublai Khan himself was to walk down those bluestone streets he'd feel right at home.

The tall stranger was leading the biggest, blackest dog I'd ever seen, and both were looking around Square Street like they'd never seen a town before.

Behaviour like that marks you out as a target for the more unscrupulous members of the fraternity, and I had already spotted a few shabby types taking notice of the man. I made my move before they could, ploughing through the crowds towards him like an iceberg eager to keep its appointment with RMS Titanic.

He turned his dark gaze on me and smiled as I approached. His unconscious pat at his right breast told me where he was stashing his wallet, if I had been light-fingered enough to do something about it. The Chinese pickpocket could easily lift his bankroll before he felt anything amiss, and they'd be using chopsticks. He needed protection, I told myself. Damn it all, the man obviously needed my help.

Lijiang was an ancient centre for culture and history, but although I appreciated culture to the point where I was beginning to enjoy the distinctive plangent sound of Naxi music, my gifts lay elsewhere, and a chap needs to make his living anyway he can.

I thought of myself as a general factotum, a labourer when work is available, and an ambassador suited best to the succour of the unwary, and I charged very little. The price of a good meal is usually enough; and just looking at that tall man made my belly rumble. I could almost taste my next meal of pork and black beans. I grinned back at him.

It was springtime in the Old Town of Lijiang, the central town of the Lijiang County in Yunnan Province. It was a beautiful place that recent history seemed to have forgotten, which suited me fine. Eight-hundred years old, its nine hundred acres of tightly packed streets are hemmed in by gorgeous flaring tiled roofs, the whole located on a plateau nearly eight thousand feet above sea level.

It nestles in a sheltered lee, protected by the tree-covered Lion Mountain in the west, the Jade Dragon Snow mountain range nine miles away in the northwest, and the Elephant and Golden Row Mountains in the north. Vast fertile fields sprawl across the southeast and fresh streams and rivers of clear, icy meltwater run through everything.

Lijiang is clean and smells fresh as any place I've ever seen, but because folk think the old town looks like a big jade ink slab they call it 'Dayanzhen' or the 'Big Ink Slab'. I must admit that sounds better than 'The Smoke' which is what people justifiably call my home town of London. It had been years since I was last starved of fresh air in the soot-blackened old town of my birth, but the stench from any noxious bonfires would bring back memories and tug at the old heartstrings like a fishhook to a harp.

'The name's Whittaker, Nathaniel Whittaker. Glad to meet you, sir. You look as if this is your first day on the Ink Slab. Care for some company while I show you around?'

I stuck out my hand which he shook firmly. I felt a jolt of something surge up my arm as soon as he touched me. I don't know what it was, but it brought me to my toes and put some *wiggle-waggle in my two-step*, as the man sang in the dance hall. I was still hungry, but I felt wide-awake for the first time on that fine spring day.

'Spindrift,' he said. 'Pleased to meet you, mister Whittaker, and right glad of your company.'

'Nathan, please,' I said. '*Mister* Whittaker is making old bones back home and strangers get on much better without the formalities. What shall I call you?'

He nodded his agreement, 'Wise head on young shoulders, Nathan. You sound English, what brings you to Lijiang?'

I noticed he hadn't answered my question or offered me his birth name, but I chose not to pursue the matter for the time being.

'Curiosity and a relay of oilers brought me to Asia. Wind filled my sails and blew me along the old Silk Road from the Med through India to Tibet and all points in-between. Fetched up on the Ink Slab and liked it here enough to seek my fortune. The streets are paved with bluestone instead of gold, but as they say, hope beats eternal in a young man's breast. And what brings you here, mister Spindrift?'

He opened the neck of his long black coat and I saw his dog collar and gold crucifix for the first time.

'I go where my Lord wills me, Nathan. Christians are suffering persecution in China at present, and an American mission house in the village of Shuhe has become strangely silent over the last few months. I'm on my way to see if I might assist my brothers there. If they are dead I will mourn them, if not I shall at least discover the cause for their silence.'

I had become increasingly aware that the pair of us and Spindrift's big dog standing together were like a rock in the millrace of that busy street. We were causing plenty of annoyance among people who had places to be and wanted to get there without cutting a path around a couple of gwailou and their animal. I came to a decision.

'I can take you to Shuhe, mister Spindrift, or should I call you, Father? It's about four miles from here at the base of the Jade Dragon Snow mountain range, you can see it over there in the northwest. But I think we need to get ourselves out of this street and somewhere a bit quieter, so we can talk.

'I can show you a place where two can eat as cheaply as one and the food is really good. Sorry, but my stomach's growling so loudly I can't hear myself think. And I'm sure they'd find something for that excellent hound of yours. What do you say?'

'Call me Preacher or Spindrift, please, Nathan. And I say lead on. Consider me safely placed in your capable hands.'

Once I had got myself around a bowl of pork in black beans with white rice, and the Preacher had eaten a good portion of chicken with noodles, chased down with Huangjiu, the local yellow rice wine, my body's clamour for food quietened at last. I was able to concentrate on my new companion.

He had a military bearing that clashed with his religious status, and a lean muscled face that commanded notice. He carried himself with a quiet confidence that would easily stake his place in any room. When he unbuttoned his coat to take a seat at our table I saw a revolver holstered low at his hip. He looked ready to deal with anything. I wondered what he expected to find in Shuhe.

[3]

It took just over an hour to walk northwest from the dining house in the Old Town through the outskirts of Lijiang to the lower stretches of the forest that contained the ancient village of Shuhe. The thirteen peaks called the Jade Dragon Snow mountain were shrouded in cloud and lowered like frost giants over the treeline.

I had once climbed a fair way up the tallest peak, Shanzidou, with a party of musical Frenchmen out on a spree. We had reached the point where it was glacial enough to chill their champagne properly and admire the view south to Lijiang where they had cooked a meal, drank their wine, and then we climbed back down.

They sang loudly at each other until we returned to the village, which sobered and quieted them for some reason. They were odd fellows, but I was well paid, so who was I to judge my paying guests? But I will say that they were not seasoned mountaineers, and that Oscar Eckenstein's sterling reputation as a climber had not been threatened by our little jaunt. There was no way they could have followed 'the trail.'

Entering Shuhe, known as the 'hometown of the springs', is like stepping back in history to a quieter place and time. Walking along the well-preserved flagstones of Sifang Street, the short main thoroughfare, you can almost hear the hoofbeats of the trade caravans following the ancient tea route. It was so peaceful it was impossible to imagine anything or anyone threatening a religious house there.

When we reached the Black Dragon Pool at the end of the street I turned to the Preacher. He was gazing down at the fat, silver fish that clustered at the surface waiting to be fed. The bubbling sounds of running water were loud all around us. It was the only noise we could hear.

I asked, 'Do you know where to find your mission house?'
He said nothing, but instead walked to a broken stele beside the pool. He picked up a handy stone and struck it twice, producing sharp, musical notes. He looked around expectantly. When nothing happened, he struck the stele again.

'Who you want?'

The querulous voice issued from the steps of the Sansheng Palace, a nearby temple and one of the largest buildings in the village.

'Who you want?'

I saw a reed-like figure in traditional robes. It was almost bent double with age and it was only his sparse beard that convince me he was a man.

'Who you want?' The ancient thin voice rang out again. Spindrift answered in dialect. This caused the old man to pause and consider the Preacher with keen regard. He straightened up and the years fell away from his body.

'Will you take tea with me, reverend?' He asked, his voice now strong.

'May I bring my young companion?'

'Of course, and your wolf. Follow me, please.'

He strode away, and we followed along colourful streets. I could smell pungent evidence of leather workings. Fast flowing streams were culverted beside the lanes and the man eventually invited us to step onto a small stone slab that took us across a stream to an open door. We found ourselves in a neat small room decorated with ornately carved redwood panels.

The man drew a brightly coloured curtain across the doorway and bustled to the other side of the room where he opened a screen to reveal a long and narrow window that looked out across a river.

He indicated the arch of a mottled span of stone that crossed the river. It looked beaten by time and the elements but still stood proud, framed by bright green willow trees.

'That is the Qinglong Bridge,' he told us. 'Called the First, it is the most important bridge in Lijiang. I tell you this, so you know you are in an important place. Most wàiguórén think of us as a charming backwater on the northern edge of the Old Town, a waystation as it were, but they are wrong. We were here first. This is the oldest Naxi settlement and many of our cultural treasures, such as that bridge, were built by the Mu family of sacred memory. Now, sit, sit, I'll make the tea.'

He brewed the tea, muttering to himself while he did so. Then he brought fine bowls to the table where we sat, and a steaming pot on a tray. He filled the bowls and raised his to us.

'Chin, chin,' he grinned, then blew noisily into his bowl before taking a sip. We followed suit. It was delicious, and I told him so.

'Longjing tea, called Dragon Well, is manufactured in the West Lake district of Hangzhou. I think it is a match for Heaven Pool tea. You may argue they are equal, but tea is a matter of taste, like all art.'

We sipped again then our host placed his bowl carefully on the table and folded his fingers together under his chin. I was constantly correcting my estimate of his age, eventually plumping for the mid-fifties to late-sixties. His eyes were clear as Shuhe's famous spring waters but were embedded in a nest of finely lined leather. He obviously smiled a lot.

Spindrift introduced us both and we learned our host was called Junjie, which he happily told us meant 'handsome hero'.

'My mother was an optimist, but I take after her father rather than mine. Shit happens. At least I can be grateful I got his brains as well as his ascetic physique. Not bad for a man of eighty-three, if I must say so myself.

'Now then, what's this about an American mission here? Are you talking about the padres who live in Songun Village just south of here? They took a house near the Stone Lotus temple by the cave. Was that a mission? They never preached the gospel that I know of, but I met with some of them. They were more like archaeologists than priests, though they wore the collars and the little man on the cross around their necks.'

He indicated the crucifix at Spindrift's throat, then continued, 'There's a small church in the Old Town but nothing here. We Naxi have our own beliefs that we brought with us from Tibet a thousand years ago, and some of them make for great discussions over a glass of beer. Your people's mission never got started, my friend, but I can take you to their house, if you wish? It is a brief walk, perhaps fifteen minutes. Shall we go?'

I complimented him on his command of English and he shrugged as if it was nothing.

'I speak English, German, and Portuguese, and three different Chinese dialects as well as Mandarin and Naxi. I am blessed with a talent for tongues that has paid for my house with its view of the First Bridge and put food on the table. I write books and poetry too, and I've written a few songs, but I never could sing a note without setting all the local dogs to howling. I would love to be able to sing, but please, don't ask me to prove how bad I am.'

He lead us back out into the street and chatted amiably until we arrived at a narrow white house with a traditionally flared roof but unusually austere windows. Instead of a curtain the entrance held a stout looking door. Junjie rapped smartly on one of its panels. Silence greeted us. He rapped again.

This time we heard a whining voice through the wood. Our guide answered with a short barking phrase. The door was thrown open and a young woman stood on the threshold with mouth and eyes wide open in shock. She flung herself at Spindrift and fell to her knees before him.

'I keep house nice, father, you see. I keep house nice for the gentlemen, you see.'

We would later learn that her name was Nuo, which means Gracious. She ushered us into the house like royalty, firing words at Junjie all the time as if he was an inspector she needed to impress, while insisting to us in broken English that she was a good woman of faith.

When Spindrift spoke to her in her own tongue I thought she was going to faint. She fell back against the wall and grabbed at her throat as if trying to remember if she had said anything untoward.

Junjie calmed her down and told her we would be staying for a while if that was all right with the gentlemen? She smiled and nodded, pointing at us and then herself and saying she would 'make welcome for all'.

'I no ask gentlemen' she admitted. 'They no here, not for weeks, months.'

'Where are they?' I blurted.

She shook her head, 'They go look for something and never come back. Oh, father,' she said to Spindrift. 'I think they dead! I think they all been killed.'

[4]

A man's fortunes can change a lot in twenty-four hours. I had woken up that morning in a mean flophouse cellar room that I split with a party of working men who smoked the opium pipe. It was a poor billet but at least I could just about afford the scant comfort of a shared pallet and a daily bowl of rice. Don't ask what I shared the pallet with – my hide still itches at the memory.

That evening I had the promise of a comfortable bed in my own room after a good washdown and a better meal. Nuo had prepared a more than competent dinner for the three of us – Junjie had accepted Spindrift's invitation to join us for a meal and he proved an excellent companion at table – and while we ate we pondered the fate of the world and the missing mission fathers.

Nuo had insisted on taking my clothes while I was bathing before dinner. She had pulled a sour face when I drew near, and she chided me, 'You need wash! Dog smell better than you!' I knew not to argue.

The house had a proper bathroom with a tub *and* showers at the rear on the ground floor; it even had a row of three water closets through a door to one side. I could get comfortable in a place like that but warned myself not to become too accustomed to such luxuries.

I was employed as Spindrift's guide at best and would be accepted as no more than a temporary guest in the house. As sure as night follows day, I knew that once he found his mission men I would be out. Back on the street and scrounging for my next yuan. I decided to make the most of it while I could.

So, I found myself freshly bathed and wearing the fine robe and slippers Nuo had provided, and I was sitting at a well-stocked table listening to one of the most erudite dinner conversations I had heard in a long, long month of Sundays.

They discussed the European situation and events in North Africa, the ferment in Russia and the Sino/Japanese fear that the Bolsheviks – a new word to me – might have plans to cross the northern Chinese border.

Junjie smiled archly, 'Let them come. Russia is a big place, but China is bigger with more mountains. By the time the Bolsheviks reach Beijing they will have become Chinese and I will have to learn yet another new dialect. Politics is like a wind that blows through the field and ruffles the crops for a while. When the wind drops the field remains. In the same way the face of politics changes, the people remain.'

He leaned forward, 'I have never left Shuhe other than to visit Lijiang, I don't need to. The world comes here to me along the Silk and the Tea roads. We make sure we learn the languages of our visitors, so they never need to learn ours. We hear what *you* are saying while we can speak freely and say whatever we wish without being overheard. It is a rare man who understands our tongue so well, as you do, Preacher Spindrift. Are languages a passion of yours, as they are mine?'

'Languages and history, and what Dr Freud calls psychoanalysis. Everything that touches the mind and the heart of man, anything that helps me understand my fellows better and break down the barriers between his mind and mine. No man is an island, Junjie, but if we can't talk to each other we might as well be oceans apart.'

'History? Yes, Confucius said we should study the past if we would define the future, but he also said that the man who knows all the answers has not yet been asked all the questions. I think he smiled a lot when he said stuff like that, and people interpret his words to suit themselves. Life, he said, is really simple, but we insist on making it complicated.'

The old man nodded, deep in thought, 'One thing is true, my friend. If we can consider another man a stranger and different from us he's easier to kill. Once we can talk to a stranger we learn how similar we truly are and that might stay our hand, but not always.

'Did you know that the Kaiser once wrote to his uncle and complained about the bureaucratic procedures for appointments of men to the British embassy in Berlin? His uncle was Edward VII, the British Emperor and King. Little Kaiser Willy is one of Queen Victoria's grandchildren; she considered him both a problem child and her greatest failure.'

He shrugged, 'This terrible situation in Europe might almost be considered as a family's failure to communicate around the dinner table as we are here.'

Junjie stood and walked to the window, which he opened.

He continued. 'Listen to that. Can you hear the war? The conflict in Europe is said to have touched every point of the globe, but for us here in Shuhe the fighting might as well be on the Moon. Confucius, Master Kong, he held that the purpose of war is defence or to find unity and peace, but if you send men to war without first training them you throw their lives away.

'How many of those men in the trenches are properly trained? Lives are being wasted over there, while we sit in peace and eat a good dinner. Listen, can you hear so much as...'

The explosion directly outside the window blew him off his feet and filled the room with dust and the sulphurous stink of gunpowder and cordite. What followed was to be my first taste of Spindrift – the man of action.

He leapt to his feet and ran to the window shouting to me 'Nathan, see what you can do for Junjie.' Then he dived headfirst through the shattered frame. He didn't even hesitate.

I hurried to the old man's side. He was breathing, which was good, but his face was bleeding as were his hands, and his clothes were blanketed with grime and powdered glass. I was at a loss as to what I should do.

A shadow appeared at my shoulder and I turned to find Nuo's tender cheek almost pressed to mine. She touched my arm and scurried from the room. When she returned she held a soft brush and a dustpan. She began to gently sweep the glittering glass from Junjie's clothes and leathery skin.

'We can't touch him,' she said. 'We cut our hands badly if we touch him. This is terrible business, who would do this?

A voice like steel answered her in dialect. We turned. A man stood in the doorway behind us with an old navy service pistol in his hands. It was pointed at us and he was using it to order Nuo to get away from me. He barked instructions at her. She whimpered like a cur and shuffled towards the man on her knees, mewling broken words as if she was begging for her life.

The man ignored her, he just grinned at me and raised the barrel of his gun directly towards my face. I saw him thumb back the hammer and tighten his finger on the trigger. Everything after that happened in slow motion.

Nuo uncoiled like a snake and whipped the contents of her dustpan straight into the man's eyes from close range. He cursed and stumbled back, his free hand at his face. The pistol discharged harmlessly into the wall. I didn't have time to think, I just ran at that villain and thrust my shoulder hard into his belly. He crumpled with an explosive shout of expelled air and I scrabbled for his gun.

He was winded but not down yet. Instantly his clawed fingers grabbed at my throat and began to squeeze. I was desperate to break his grip around my neck, but I needed both hands on his wrist to stop him turning the pistol back in my direction. It was a quandary for a man of peace like me. He was crushing my windpipe and I knew he was stronger and more ruthless than me. I was out of options and feeling groggy from lack of air.

Then with a gust of foul breath the assassin screamed and took his fingers from my neck. I slammed his wrist onto the floor and his gun clattered from his grasp. I rolled away from him and staggered to my feet, the pistol firmly in my hand. It was then that I saw the carving knife we had used at dinner jutting from his arm; blood was soaking his sleeve. Nuo stood to one side, another knife ready in her hand.

The man screamed abuse at her and grabbed at the knife to draw it from the meat of his arm. I cocked the pistol and shouted at him to 'cease and desist' or some such rubbish. He sneered at me as if he knew I'd never pull the trigger, and with a gush of blood he had the knife firmly in his paw and lashed out at Nuo. He had decided she was the more dangerous of we two. On the evidence of that evening I would have to agree with him, but I couldn't let him hurt her.

I shot him in the arse and he howled with pain and disbelief.

'I think I should take that, please, Nathan.'

Spindrift's calm voice had never been more welcome. I handed the gun over to him with a sense of relief. Junjie had recovered consciousness. He climbed gingerly to his feet and beat at his clothes, which emitted a cloud of dust and glittering shards of glass. He regarded the shattered window with a sour expression and firmly bolted its shutters.

'We don't want to invite them to throw bombs into the room,' he explained. He jutted his chin at the bleeding, scowling intruder. 'Who's the dog?' He asked.

[5]

I helped Nuo tidy the room while Spindrift first examined Junjie and then the sullen stranger. I wondered if I might have a better opinion of the attempted assassin if I spoke his language, but I didn't think so.

Spindrift fired questions at the man while he tended to him. The Preacher's hands were gentle as a surgeon's, but his barked words made the assassin cringe. Even so he maintained his silence and his burning eyes promised grief for everyone in the room.

I responded to a pounding on the street door and opened it cautiously, Nuo at my side. It was late, and the street was dark, but I could clearly see the platoon of uniformed soldiers with their rifles at the ready. The men looked around as if expecting an attack at any moment. The officer in charge saluted me and removed his cap. When he spoke, you could have knocked me down with a feather.

'Evening, old chap. Do any of your people speak English?'

Before I could answer Nuo pulled me to one side and planted herself front and centre.

'Who want to know? This private house, very proper. Not call for soldier boy, go away, chop, chop.'

Her English had gone from very reasonable to cod pigeon at the drop of the man's hat. I was impressed. The officer gave a curt bow.

'Very good, miss. You see, we've had reports of a loud explosion in this vicinity. Apparently, someone set off an explosion strong enough to knock a hole in a wall, and we've got orders to look into it.'

Nuo looked him up and down. 'You want to go look into hole you go do it in your own house. Who you, anyway?'

'I am lieutenant Shropshire, late of the Royal Fusiliers and now with the Yunnan Province militia. We are the local police, my dear.'

'I not your dear. What you want?'

'Can I help?' Spindrift's quiet voice made Nuo jump like a startled cat and she landed in my arms. It was a complete accident and she pushed me away almost instantly, but she made a nice armful all the same.

Shropshire introduced himself again, and as he did, so his men crowded forward into the light from the doorway. In a night already plump with surprises I saw they were all dark-skinned, bearded, and tall. They wore turbans. They were Sikhs!

Shropshire seemed relieved to be dealing with a man instead of a cantankerous woman. He explained about the explosion again and highlighted the local concerns. Spindrift let him have his say, nodding sagely, then he opened his coat to expose his dog collar and crucifix.

Shropshire gazed at him in surprise. 'I'm sorry, father. I didn't realise. I'm afraid you must be aware that there is a certain element currently abroad in China who are taking arms against anyone associated with the mother church. Have you had any problems recently?'

'Well, I guess we have. Got a fellah in there who attacked my young assistant with a gun not a few minutes since. He's saying precious little to me, cat got his tongue I guess, but I'd be right grateful if'n you'd take a poke at the miscreant and find out what got him so darned riled.'

Spindrift's American accent had come oddly to the fore. It made him seem even more foreign and vulnerable, a stranger abroad in a strange land. Shropshire looked him up-and-down judgementally.

He nodded, 'Right, you leave the bounder to us, father.' He indicated his Sikh fellows. 'Two of you chaps with me. Let's fetch the devil before he causes more mischief. Come on.'

They hustled past Spindrift and Nuo and disappeared into the house. Several minutes later they emerged dragging my attacker by his arms. Shropshire stopped at Spindrift's side.

'He's been roughed-up pretty soundly, and somebody stabbed him in the arm. Was that you?'

'No, lieutenant. It was my housekeeper.'

Both men regarded Nuo. The officer nodded at her.

'My deepest respects, ma'am. You did a man's job of work there I must say.' He turned back to Spindrift. 'And was it your housekeeper who shot the man in his behind?'

Spindrift grinned, a white half-moon in the shadows.

'No, that was an accident. My assistant wrested the gun from his assailant and it went off.'

'A sound shot. Hit the bugger in the meaty part of his left buttock. Missed everything vital. Well done there. And who cleaned him up? Somebody did a neat job of it I'd say.'

'Thank-you. I am a trained surgeon.'

'Are you? Are you, by God? Do you know anything about tropical diseases? Are you free now? We have some cases come in that have our quack completely baffled. Could you take a look?'

17

Spindrift looked suddenly tired. 'And so, it starts. Nathan, please, wash your hands thoroughly and come with me. Nuo, please, stay here and look after Junjie. Lock the door behind us and don't open it to anyone until we return. Lieutenant, give me a few moments to get my bag and I'll be right with you.'

'Preacher,' I said, 'what about my clothes?'

Nuo shook her head. 'Still wet, Father.'

'You'll be fine in those robes, Nathan. Nuo, have we more suitable footwear for our young friend?'

And so it was that I found myself clattering through the stone-clad streets of the Old Town dressed in robes like a monk and wearing robust wooden sandals that added an inch to my height. The Preacher and I must have made an odd couple, cutting through the streets at a fair clip with an armed guard and a bound, limping prisoner.

We learned that the sick men were in isolation, that their condition was 'Pretty frightful' in Shropshire's opinion, and that the militia doctor refused to go near them. They were a party of four men brought in by two Sikhs who were now sharing their isolation.

'The disease spreads like lightning,' explained the lieutenant. 'And it has the most God-awful effect. Poor bastards seem to be melting, and the smell! Never smelt anything like it.'

'I believe I have,' said Spindrift, solemnly.

'What? You know what it is?'

'Yes. If I'm right, it's called Sha-aneer and it is the most dangerous infection on this planet. How much further? We must reach these men as soon as possible.'

'Not far. Just around the corner here. This Sha thing, is it fatal?'

Spindrift looked bleak. 'Hopefully,' he whispered.

Militia headquarters proved to be a walled compound with a large brick building at its centre that had a square, European look about it. Shropshire's men hustled the prisoner away while the lieutenant led us down some stairs to a storage area. He pointed towards a barred door furthest from the stairs.

'In there. They're locked in there. Medico wanted the victims kept as far away from the men as possible. He thought it might be a form of haemorrhagic fever and contagious as all hell.'

'He did well. It is deadly and transmitted by touch. Sha-aneer is like no other infection.'

He looked around. 'These walls are stone?'

'Well, yes.'

'Good.'

That was when the stink hit me like a physical force. I reeled back from it as if I'd been struck by a fist and put my hand to my nose. Shropshire held a handkerchief to his face. Spindrift paused, his eyes glittering.

'Smoke, mirrors, and scare me jacks. Carrion crows, magpies and foulness.'

Then he intoned something that sounded Latin and the worst of the stink subsided.

'Lieutenant,' he said, 'would you be so good as to wait here and keep everyone away, please? Nathan, I've seen one example of your marksmanship. Are you handy with a pistol?'

I hit what I aim at and I told him so. He handed me the assassin's pistol.

'Very good. Shoot where and when I tell you and be quick about it.'

He took a deep breath, 'What we are about to do is done in God's name,' he said. And we stepped closer to the storeroom's barred door.

[6]

Spindrift reached out his hand to raise the bar across the door. The men on the other side must have heard us. The door jarred and juddered in its frame as if a heavy body had slammed against it, and as if with one voice we heard them scream.

Satan, SATAAAAN! Satan is here! The Eden beast is amongst us! The host shall kill it and eat its little toy. We shall devour its soul, we shall suck the juice from its sweet and tender sooooul!

This last was a drawn-out, unnatural sound. The voices dripped with malice and terrible hunger. I looked sideways at Spindrift and he raised his eyebrows at me. His eyes were dark pits in the craggy shadows of his lean, muscular face.

'I have to deal with this, Nathan,' he said. 'But you can join Shropshire by the stairs if you wish.'

I thumbed back the hammer of my pistol.

'We're going to kill something, aren't we?'

The door shuddered again. There came the sound of splintering wood. Spindrift dipped his hand inside his coat and pulled out two crystal balls, each about the size of a baby's fist. They glowed with a cool, silvery pallor. He drew his own pistol with his left hand.

'This will happen fast, Nathan, so be ready. I will open this door and throw these globes in the same instant. You must shoot them in mid-air. I'll cover you. Can you do that?'

I nodded, too tense and scared to speak. I looked back down the corridor and saw Shropshire. He had also drawn his gun and was holding it ready at his side. He gave me a thumbs-up and I attempted a smile. I felt sick.

Spindrift began to chant something that seemed both profound and musical. It had the sound of an old Gregorian chant to it but was also somehow uncanny and melancholy. It stirred something in my heart, and I felt the hollow in the pit of my stomach fill with longing for a finer life. I suddenly saw the truth of the drab, mundane nature of my existence and wondered at how far I had fallen away from the dreams I had once had as a child. Tears stung my eyes and I knuckled them away with my free hand.

Behind that barred door all had become silent. Spindrift leaned forward, his hand outstretched to the locking bar. He glanced at me.

'Ready?'

I nodded and held the pistol in the two-handed grip my father had taught me.

'Ready,' I said.

The Preacher flung away the locking piece and the door instantly burst open. He threw his globes into the room and I fired automatically, even though my mind was numb with shock.

Something reared up in that windowless room. *Something* shrieked like a stuck pig and lashed out at us. I froze at the sight of a creature made of grey mottled flesh that filled the doorway with nightmare. At that same moment my bullets shattered the Preacher's crystals and the world erupted before my eyes. The crystals exploded with a white glare and doused the creature in blinding flame.

It fought the fire and reached out like an opening maw to engulf me in its burning grip. I was frozen in place and could only watch in shocked disbelief while it spilled towards me.

Spindrift reached out his pistol and fired twice into where the creature's belly would have been in a sane world. He simultaneously held his right hand out flat and barked 'Clausum!' The heavy door slammed shut on the twisting, screaming inferno.

'Nathan, quick man. Help me put the bar back. Let's get this door properly sealed. Come on, man, move!'

I was galvanised into feverish action. I grabbed up the short plank and we slammed it down into its steel hooks. Just in time. The door bowed like a belly, and strange, guttural, oily voices shrieked and howled, calling upon Satan like furious demons before the dark, majestic throne of Hell.

'What happened to those men? What was that thing?'

Shropshire had left his post to join us by the door. He was pale and wild-eyed, quivering with shock. I suspected I looked very much the same. Not the Preacher. Like a pillar of stone Spindrift stood facing the storeroom where a monster burned and screamed with spiteful fury. Then there came a sound like a big bucket of slops thrown against the wall and the door bulged for the final time. I heard a faint crackling sound, like fat bacon in a hot pan, and then silence.

There came a hubbub from the stairwell behind us, and we turned to see a small group of anxious Sikhs cautiously descending to the corridor. Their fearful eyes were large in their narrow, bearded faces, and scanned swiftly from side-to-side. I wondered at the courage of these men who had heard nightmare sounds emanating from the stairwell and yet still came down to investigate.

They fixed on us and then Shropshire. A spokesman stepped forward, but I noticed that none of them had yet taken that final step from the stairs. They stood poised, ready for a speedy retreat.

'Sir,' said the lead man to Shropshire, 'We heard a dreadful commotion and have come to your aid. What would you have us do? Are these fellows causing you a problem? Shall we arrest them?'

Shropshire seemed to rouse himself from a dream. He turned from the Sikhs to us and then gazed at the barred door. He shook his head.

'Ajaipal, could you and the chaps fetch Dr Fisher here, please? I think he might want to see this. There's a good fellow, quick as you like.'

'Very good, sir.'

The men climbed swiftly back up to ground level and left us alone.

Shropshire holstered his gun. 'I should be very grateful for an answer to my questions. What did I just see? What *was* that benighted thing? What did you do to it? What happened to the men in that room?'

I too was trying to reconcile recent events, but only felt confident of one fact, I had nothing sensible to bring to the conversation and would be better keeping my mouth shut. I took a step back and left the Preacher in the limelight. Spindrift put a hand to the door and he too holstered his pistol. He held his hand out to me.

'The gun, please, Nathan. You have no need for it now. The problem is resolved.'

I reluctantly handed it over, instantly missing its comforting weight. Like Shropshire I was keen to hear some answers, but I didn't have his talent for firing questions, and after the last few minutes I was very much in awe of my new employer.

I had one question the lieutenant hadn't asked. What strange hold did this man have over me? What had stopped me from running screaming back up those stairs at my first sight of the creature? My policy had always been to show danger a clean pair of heels, and that had kept me breathing for nearly twenty-three years of travel and adventure.

I know some men try to make themselves look good – even in the cannon's mouth. But it is pointless. Personally, I prefer a hot meal and a comfortable billet for the night when I can get it. I had never put myself in harm's way on purpose before; what on Earth was I doing down there in that cellar that night?

Spindrift hefted the door bar from its hooks, placed it carefully against the wall, and then took a grip on the door handle. He paused for a moment as if in prayer, his head bowed, and then he pulled, and the door swung open easily. I had expected to see blackened walls and charred furniture but everything in there was intact, except it had been coated in a thick layer of fine grey ash.

I looked for the cremated remains of the great beast. The creature had been huge, I thought, there must be some remains. Something more tangible than this drift of pale dust. But there was nothing.

The room was as cool as the corridor and contained a row of beds plus a table and a few chairs. A cold lamp sat on the table, and the chairs were scattered randomly around the room as if thrown there. Other than the lamp there would have been no light source in that room. I realised that whatever had happened to the stricken men must have happened in darkness, which made it seem more terrible.

'Shropshire, you sent for me?'

A balding man with a large moustache burst into the room and then stood stock still, his face a picture of shock. He looked around wordlessly and then sputtered, 'In the name of all that's holy what happened here?'

Shropshire turned to Spindrift, 'That's exactly what I want to know. Well, Father, are you going to tell us?'

7

I had been looking forward to spending the night in a comfortable bed. A night spent sleeping in the rare privacy of my own room, but the prospect began to seem increasingly remote. Dr Fisher invited us to leave the choking, dusty atmosphere of the storeroom and we had followed him and Shropshire up to a pleasant, book-lined study which was evidently also his examination room and surgery.

The tools of a surgeon's trade were neatly stowed in one corner of the room. Saws, knives, and probes glittered in the mellow light of wall sconces. The air was sweetly perfumed by good pipe smoke, and his chairs were deeply buttoned leather Chesterfields. An exquisite carpet muffled our footsteps.

We could almost have been walking into the fine consultation rooms of a Harley Street surgeon in London and I mentally compared it to the bleak, Spartan place below ground where six men had met their terrible deaths that evening.

Fisher got busy with a decanter and we were soon nursing large glasses of a commendable claret. The doctor's attitude had performed an abrupt about-face when Shropshire had introduced Spindrift and me as a surgeon and his assistant.

Fisher's face had lit-up when the lieutenant explained that Spindrift, 'who was also a padre, don't y'know' was a specialist in tropical medicine, particularly the treatment of exotic infections, 'Including' he said, 'the Sha thing our men had caught.'

I sat comfortably in my chair and sipped at my wine, feeling like a child remaining silent while the adults talked grown-up business. I was fascinated to hear whatever Spindrift had to say, otherwise, truth to tell, I might well have fallen asleep. It had been a long day.

Spindrift complimented Fisher on his wine and his room, and then he broached the subject about which we were all most eager to hear.

'The Sha-aneer is certainly the most wicked and ancient infection I have ever seen. It brings together the very worst aspects of other diseases such as haemorrhagic fever and leprosy, as well as blistering conditions such as bullous pemphigoid, dermatitis herpetiformis, flesh-eating necrosis and pemphigus vulgaris.

'In certain circles the disease is called God's enemy due its terrible physical effects on humankind, which, as you know, is made in God's image. It is a transformative disease, as I think you saw, lieutenant Shropshire.'

The man looked startled at the mention of his name. 'Wait,' he said. 'Are you telling me that, that beast in the storeroom was made up from one of those poor men? What did it do, eat the others? Really? Somebody, wake me from this nightmare, please!'

Spindrift leaned forward in his chair. 'Once infected the victim's physical condition becomes fluid. They change and become monstrous, and then they merge. All six victims became one Sha-aneer and its only purpose was to infect more victims. That's how it grows. But, in a way you're right, lieutenant, those men *were* devoured by their infection. They would have been completely subsumed by the disease.'

Fisher grimaced, 'Is it fatal?'

'No, I'm afraid not. The infected person loses all semblance of humanity and becomes consumed with a terrible hunger to infect more people, but they don't die. The only treatment is to burn the infected victims with phosphorous or any white-hot flame. I know of one man who cleansed his body by plunging a white-hot awl into a Sha-aneer blister on the ball of his thumb. It burned out the infection but also took his arm to above the elbow. To my knowledge he is the only man to date to survive infection.'

'This is horrible! There's no other option? We must burn the poor victims?'

'None other, Dr Fisher. Fire is the kindest way, and the safest.'

'Why haven't I heard of this vile infection? I would have thought the medical papers would be full of it.'

'There are two good reasons why it hasn't been reported. Thankfully it is quite rare, and its effects tend to be localised. To date there have been no cases reported in a large town, and where it has been found we have managed to contain it.

'That reminds me, Dr Fisher, there is one important thing you need to know. Once infected a victim becomes a living vector, it will seek to touch and infect everybody it can reach. It also becomes a fruiting body and seeds its surrounding area with small red and black striped worms. They are very distinctive and deeply infectious.

'Once touched the worm instantly penetrates deep into its victim's flesh and the whole process begins again. You must ask your men to search the compound, look everywhere, even in their bedding.'

He held his hand up, his thumb and forefinger perhaps half an inch apart. 'The little worms are no longer than this, and might be coiled into a circle, making them appear smaller. You must tell your men that despite their size these worms are deadly, I cannot stress this enough, they must not touch naked flesh. They do not kill, but death is infinitely preferable to infection.'

Shropshire finished his wine and leapt to his feet. 'I'll get the chaps onto it straight away. You're a Godsend, father. A real Godsend.'

'Bless you, lieutenant.'

Once Shropshire had hurried out Dr Fisher refreshed our glasses.

'And what is the second reason, Dr Spindrift?'

'I'm sorry?'

'What's the second reason the medical profession knows nothing of your Sha-aneer? You said there were two.'

'Yes, of course. But it must be obvious to a man of your sensibilities, Dr Fisher...'

'John, please. No need for such formality between professionals. And what shall I call you?'

'Spindrift will be just fine, John, or "hey you" if you prefer.' He grinned, 'There's no mystery to it, John. I never liked my name from the day I was given it. Folks call me "Spindrift", "Doc", or "Preacher", as the fancy takes them, and I pray you do the same.

'But you asked about the second reason. Fact is, most folks who butt heads with the Sha-aneer get infected, and those few who survive don't know how to describe it. Any doctor who tries to treat the victims will end up infected, as certain as the sun rises in the morning...'

Shropshire burst into the study with a Sikh in tow. The man's eyes were rolling in terror.

'Prem here found one of those worms and went to pick it up, despite everything I told him. He swears he didn't touch it, but it's disappeared. Do we burn him? What do I do with the idiot?'

Spindrift barked, 'Get away from him, Shropshire. That goes for all of you, don't go near him. Now, you, Prem, stand very still.'

The man was quivering with fear. 'Please, sir, don't burn me. Don't burn me.' He was cradling his right hand in his left.

'Shut up. Now, breathe out for me.'

The man did as he was told. I instantly smelled the unmistakeable reek of his infection. Spindrift moved closer to him.

'We may still be in time. Prem, you must trust me.'

'Sir, please, sir, don't burn me.'

'Quiet now and hold still.'

I know what I saw him do, but I can't explain it. I saw it clear as I see my hand before my face now. Preacher placed his right hand over the Sikh's heart. He began to chant in a low voice, some of it Latin I think, and some of it God alone knows what.

And then he pressed hard with his right hand and used his left to grip his subject's shoulder. The Sikh jerked like a gaffed fish, his mouth and eyes wide open in shock. His legs buckled, and he almost sank to his knees in a faint.

Just before the Preacher moved slightly to cover his actions I swear I saw his hand sink into the Sikh's body. I'll swear it on a stack of *Bibles,* or any other holy book you want to put in front of me. The whole time the poor devil held firm in his grip was shuddering and panting like a wild thing, his hands grasping at the Preacher's arms as if trying to push him away or hold him closer, it was difficult to tell.

Shropshire was like me, he wanted a better view and he leaned forward to get closer to the action. Preacher almost snarled at him. 'I told you to stay well clear. Get back!'

And with that he wrenched his right hand away from the Sikh's body and he stepped back until he was clear of the man, who promptly fell to his knees, his fingers clutching and probing at his chest in shock. He gazed at the Preacher and uttered a stream of fluid sounding words. I guess he was speaking in his native tongue because I didn't recognise anything he was saying. He might have been praying or cursing, it was hard to tell.

Preacher ignored him while he studied something struggling in his right hand. I only saw it for a moment, but it looked like a malicious, skinned rat, and its black eyes scanned the room with evil intent. It glared at me and opened a hole in its face that must have been its mouth. Then Preacher covered the thing with both hands and pressed them together, grunting with the effort.

There came a flash of light from between his fingers and a sudden choking stink like boiled vinegar and something else, something carthy, caustic, and stale.

Preacher opened his hands like a stage magician and a thin trickle of fine grey dust fell from his palms. He took a handkerchief from his pocket and he wiped his hands. Then he reached out for his glass of claret and he drained it to the dregs.

He sighed deeply. 'Cheers,' he said.

8

The Old Town was practically empty of street traffic at that time of the morning. Our footsteps echoed in the silence. We had stayed with Dr John Fisher and Lieutenant Shropshire for another hour – and more wine – after the episode of the infected man called Prem.

Pressed for information, the Preacher had explained how he had pulled what he described as a 'seed worm pod' from the victim's body, and that he had not been affected because he was 'blessed' with a natural immunity to the disease.

He also explained that, unlike the little worm itself, the seed worm pod was very reactive to oxygen and could not survive long outside its host's flesh. It had burned away completely in the air, 'Like the highly volatile elements rubidium and caesium'.

I saw Shropshire nodding his head as if he understood everything. But his eyes had nearly rolled back into his head while the Preacher was talking, and I could see he was out of his depth and sinking fast. However, the questioning watchfulness of Dr Fisher's eyes told me he was of my own opinion about what we had just heard. He, like me, was convinced that the Preacher was only singing half the mass.

And now we were making our way back to the mission house and our welcome beds. We had promised to join Dr Fisher for lunch later that same day. I believed the Preacher would face further cross-examination about the worm and what had really happened to the man Prem.

My own head was crowded with questions, but there was one prickly concern that kept coming to the fore and I had to fight hard to bite it back before it could escape.

Preacher regarded me with hooded eyes and chuckled, 'Out with it, Nathan.'

'Out with what, sir?'

'Out with that question that's burning a hole straight through the tip of your tongue. You're a great man for the listening – I've come to appreciate that much about you – but you should never let your curiosity go hungry. Feed your curiosity and you feed your mind. So, please, ask your question.'

We walked a little further before I said, 'Well, two things, really. That thing back in the storeroom. You told us it was the bodies of its victims subsumed and transformed by the disease, that's correct?'

'Succinctly put, Nathan. Yes, that's correct. And, so?'

'And so, why was it speaking English? I've never heard of a cancer having a conversation with a medical practitioner before. I think this Sha-aneer is much more than a disease; I believe it to be an intelligent form of life that has an agenda. At least, that's the way I understand it from what you've told us.'

'Very good, Nathan. And what's the second thing?'

I took a deep breath. I was tired, and I wanted my bed, but this next question might see me back on the street before morning and heading for the flophouse once more. But I had to know. I thought about finding a way to couch what I said next in a more delicate manner but decided to just blurt it out as a bolt of whole cloth rather than cut it into prettier pieces.

'Forgive me, sir. But I think it knew you and was calling you by name. I think you are the Preacher Satan Spindrift, and I believe there is much more to you than a dog collar and a crucifix.'

'And a medical shingle.'

'I'm sorry, sir, but I don't know what shingle is, except pebbles on the beach.'

He laughed at that. 'I have spent a long time in the company of Americans, I forget myself sometimes. By shingle I mean the brass nameplate outside my medical practice, Nathan.'

'I understand, sir. But, am I right?'

'Yes, my bright young friend, you are right. And now, here we are at the mission. Before we rouse the house, I have a few things to say to you, and please, listen closely. You now know my name, I ask you not to use it when others are present.

'It's too late today, but I will soon explain to you not only how the worm knows me, but also what the creature truly is. It is an ancient enemy of mine, and yes, it has an agenda. And lastly, I believe I know what happened to the ministers from this mission house.'

'And, what was that, sir?'

'I regret we may have burned them in the storeroom of the militia compound last night. If I'm right we must find out where they became infected, and then we must go there and cleanse the site before the next poor devils stumble across it. Enough of that, for now, let's seek our beds. I wonder if the good Nuo has remained sentinel for us?'

It was Junjie who opened the door to our discreet tapping. He placed a finger to his lips and led us inside.

'The girl is asleep. I told her to go to bed. The days are long gone since I could entertain one such as her for an entire night, if I ever could except in my imagination.'

Spindrift examined his face, 'How are you feeling after the explosion? Any side-effects? Dizziness or sickness?'

The old man laughed, 'I've felt worse than this after a bottle of rice wine. I'm fine.'

'That's good. Then why are you still awake?'

'Insomnia! It's the curse of the aged. You wait until you've put a few more decades behind you, then you'll see.'

I saw the gleam of the Preacher's half-moon smile in the darkness.

'I'm sure you're right, my friend. Well, we're going to bed. Why don't you choose a room and at least get some rest before the morning? Then you can join us for breakfast.'

'I shall with pleasure. But I must tell you that I haven't wasted the long night. I think I know where the ministers went when they left this mission. I've been reading some of the notebooks in the library. One man named Pallant, Gregory Pallant, kept very comprehensive notes on everything he did. I can share what I've learned with you at breakfast. I shall see you later this morning.'

You would have thought that after the H. G. Wells scientification kind of day I'd just had I would have lay down in my bed and spent the night haunted by nightmares and cold sweats. But instead I slept like a baby and woke to birdsong – and the large watchful eyes of Nuo. I suspect she had been examining me while I slept, but when I awoke she quickly turned away and continued folding my laundered clothes with an air of intense concentration.

'Good morning, Nuo. How are you?'

She turned to me and bowed, and as she did so her natural elegance made the action an exquisitely lovely gesture, almost a dancer's move. The shutters of my bedroom window were open, and she was bathed by pure sunlight. I could clearly make out the silhouette of her slender body through her plain dress. She was a work of art.

For the first time in a long while I was inspired to take up my drawing implements. I wondered if my new post with Preacher Spindrift would last long enough for me to afford some. If I lived that long.

Nuo dimpled at me. 'Good morning, lazybones, sir? Not for much longer, the morning is already grown quite old. The father and master Junjie are at breakfast and they invite you to join them. I have your old clothes here, or you may wish to wear this fresh robe I have found for you. What you wore yesterday is covered in dust and smells like a sick cat. I shall leave you to get ready.'

She left my room and took the shine of the morning with her, but she threw me an impish smile before closing the door and that was enough to set a spring in my heel.

Faced with the prospect of lunch hosted by Dr Fisher in just a few hours' time, I happily joined my boss and our new friend at table but breakfasted lightly. The coffee was hot and strong, so I poured myself a large bowl of it and sipped with relish.

My mind's eye was busy examining that slender female form so recently displayed by gentle sunlight, I was too distracted to hear my name until the Preacher had repeated it three times and I gave him my full attention. He smiled at me, but Junjie laughed aloud and slapped my shoulder.

'I bet I know which little bird is nipping at you, my young friend!'

I felt my face glow hot and apologised, 'Sorry, I'm not really awake yet.'

Junjie grinned, showing big brown teeth. 'At your age I could dream like that all day if the girl was pretty enough. It's natural for we poor foolish males.'

Preacher arched a brow, 'True enough, but first to business. Junjie, where do you think the mission fathers went?'

The old man shrugged as if the answer was obvious. 'They've gone hunting,' he said.

9

Junjie hustled off to the library, still munching on a hunk of bread. He returned in moments with two leather-bound notebooks that he placed on the table beside Spindrift's plate. The Preacher gazed at them like a basilisk, his face expressionless, then raised quizzical eyes to the Chinaman.

'Am I to read both from start to finish? Or are you going to tell me what you found and save me some time?'

We were greeted by a mouthful of Junjie's big stained teeth again. He had a disconcertingly intense smile that involved every inch of his face. Over the years he must have found many aspects of life amusing, and after a while his face muscles naturally settled into that broad grin whenever they relaxed. That was the only way I could explain the complex web of laughter lines etched deeply into his face.

He said, 'Some men prefer to discover their own paths, while others are content to be led by those who have gone before. Like you, my friend, I sometimes choose the latter, but I would always give a man the choice.'

He lifted the top book. 'I suspect Gregory Pallant would be a very boring dinner companion, he is a veritable grindstone of an author. He grinds everything – even the wittiest story – into the finest minutia. Then he grinds it again until all that's left is dust with no substance.

'He is a man who would have to pick at a loose thread or be tortured near to death by the sight of it; and he would have to cross-reference and check everything you told him rather than accept the smallest discrepancy on face value.'

He nodded at the books, 'Pallant was an unforgiving pestle of a man, he could only have become a Christian. The Buddhists wouldn't have him, he has no sense of humour, he is too unbalanced for Taoism, and Confucius would consider him a fool. In fact, I believe even your Jesus would soon be forced to show him the door if he turned up for supper.

'You know, I always admired that young man for turning water into wine. I, however, have never got further than turning copious amounts of wine into water, but I'm pleased to say I have always taken more pleasure from wine than it has from me.'

The Preacher reached for the notebooks. 'Perhaps it would be quicker to read these for myself after all.'

Junjie smiled woefully. 'You are right, I am become garrulous, but I know why. Most of the people with whom I share a table have the erudition of small children but none of the charm. I am excited to be in the company of fellow travellers in the land of knowledge, and yes, I include you, my dear Nathan. But the mission men, you ask? Where are they, yes?'

He picked up the first notebook and leafed through it. 'My reading tells me they planned to hunt a dragon in the caves of the Tiger Leaping Gorge, but first they sought clues in the cave by the Stone Lotus Temple.'

'What kind of dragon?'

My question sounded so sudden and so loud that it surprised even me. Preacher and the Chinaman both looked at me as if they had been reminded I was there. Junjie handed me the book, open at a specific page.

'One that looks like that.'

The preacher and I put our heads together to study the drawing taped into the book. I have always admired oriental art, and this was a very fine example of Chinese draughtsmanship.

Junjie pointed at the creature in the book. 'That is one of the Imperial dragons as described by Wang Fu, a scholar who lived during the Han dynasty. If you look at the drawing you will see the nine characteristics he listed. See, there is the camel's head with cow's ears and a deer's horns, all perched on a snake's neck.

'The body is a traditional mixture of a clam's belly, an eagle's claws, a tiger's paws and exactly one hundred and seventeen carp's scales, most of them yin and a few of them yang. Those beautiful eyes are meant to be those of a demon. Can you imagine Satan has such wonderful eyes?'

I looked at the Preacher to see if he had something to say on the subject, but beyond a slight smile he didn't react at all.

Junjie continued, tapping the page as he spoke. 'There is a total of nine species of classical Chinese dragons, of which only the Imperial dragons have five toes. All others have four. This beautiful specimen is the Underworld Dragon, in Chinese, the Fu-ts'ang Lung or Fucanglong. He is the guardian of precious metals and jewels buried in the earth.

'The dragon's nature is said to be rough and fierce, and yet he likes beautiful gems and is fond of roasted swallows. He is afraid of iron, but, as you know, most spirit creatures are. Legend says he is also afraid of the wang plant, centipedes, the leaves of the lien tree, and five-coloured silk thread.'

I blurted, 'But why's it afraid of five-coloured silk thread?'

Junjie grinned, 'Why the wang plant and the leaves of the lien tree? I suggest you ask a dragon next time you see one.'

He pulled back his sleeve to expose his wrist. On it was a band woven from five coloured silk threads. He shrugged and grinned.

'Better to be safe than sorry. I wonder if the mission men wore such bands? Perhaps they didn't, and the dragon mistook them for roasted swallows. I do hope Pallant tasted better than he writes. One would need strong seasoning to compensate for his dry reasoning.'

Preacher interjected, 'What makes you think they went to Tiger Leaping Gorge? That's over fifty miles from here. And why?'

'Reading Pallant's notes is like wading through wet sand, but he is very comprehensive. The motive, of course, was money. Our American friends were men of God, but they choose to enjoy life in style. You can see the evidence all around you; this fine house, the bathrooms, the comfortable beds. Even little Nuo has been chosen with a cultured appreciation for the finer things in life, as Nathan has realised.'

I swear I heard the muffled sounds of female laughter and wondered if our housemaid was listening at the keyhole. My cheeks felt hot.

Junjie chuckled at my discomfort then continued. 'We need to go back to the Han dynasty and the seventh in line, Emperor Wu, who reigned for 54 years, from 141-87 BC. It is impossible for a modern person to imagine the power wielded by the Han rulers. They were like gods on earth. And they held the wealth of a nation in their hands.'

He sipped his bowl of coffee and smacked his lips. 'Good coffee, Nuo,' he said without raising his voice. I heard that quiet, bell-like chuckle again. Junjie leaned towards the Preacher.

'And now we reach the crux of the matter. Emperor Wu commissioned marvellous sculptures to celebrate the principal four dragons in mythology, these were Tianlong, The Celestial Dragon, Shenlong, the Spiritual Dragon, our friend Fucanglong, the Dragon of Hidden Treasures, and Dilong, the Underground Dragon.

'The celestial dragon protects the palaces of the gods, while the spiritual dragon commands the winds and rain. As we know, the dragon of underground treasure guards wealth, while the underground dragon is responsible for geological events on Earth.

'One year, Emperor Wu decided his people should be allowed to witness his incredible wealth, so he sent these four sculptures on a tour of the country. Each dragon had been manufactured by the finest craftsmen of the age and was worth an Emperor's ransom. Wu sent an army of troops to protect them, but unfortunately greed is not a modern failing.'

Junjie punctuated his tale with a slurp at his coffee bowl and sighed with pleasure.

'At least some good things come from the west. Now then, where was I? Yes, that's it. The general of that army conspired with his officers to steal the dragons and use their wealth to usurp the imperial throne itself. And he almost succeeded. He would have gotten away with his plan too if one of his officers hadn't been more loyal to his Emperor than his general. He foiled the attempt and saved three of the dragon sculptures. His troops brought the three dragons back to the Western Han capital of Chang'an, now Xi'an, in the Shaanxi province.'

Junjie shook his head. 'The general and his co-conspirators escaped with the fabulous Fucanglong sculpture and they headed towards Tibet and the lands to the West. They followed the silk road and it brought them through here. That dragon would have given them all a good life, a better than good life. However, greedy men always want more, and they fell out with each other.

'Weapons were drawn, and blood was shed. Men died, and the general was mortally wounded. With his last strength he managed to carry the sculpture to the only haven available to him. He hid it deep in a cave. I suppose he thought that if he could not have the treasure nobody could. We're told his bones are still there, acting as guardian for that great Han treasure.'

He lowered his voice, 'The Han dragon would be worth an unimaginable ransom if one were to find it today. The others have all gone the way of such things, broken up into pieces for one reason or another, probably to fund wars or buy expensive concubines. Fucanglong is said to be the only survivor, and it is probably worth enough money to buy a decent-sized country. And so, in brief, this is what Pallant's notes are all about. Your mission men believed they had discovered its location.'

The Preacher took a deep breath and tapped the book.

'Tiger Leaping Gorge?' He asked.

'A cave in Tiger Leaping Gorge' Junjie nodded. 'And that's where the problem starts.'

[10]

The streets of the Old Town were seething with humanity. I wondered that the sky held enough air for them all to breathe. I felt pressed in and battered by the sheer weight of people about me, appalled by the sheer numbers. This aversion to crowds, my panic at being just one more beast in the herd, was what had finally driven me from London.

In the Smoke the air was tainted by the effluence of industry, home fires, and the stink of too many people in too small a space. Such was not the case in Lijiang, the air was fresh and clean. But I still felt my precious individuality being leeched away, felt myself becoming just another drop of life in the floodwater, another mindless piece of flesh amongst the faceless masses of humanity.

I was tugged along in the Preacher's wake like a small boat towed behind a steamer, walking fast towards the militia compound and our appointment with Dr Fisher. Perhaps it was his height, or perhaps it was the sheer force of his personality, but the crush of people seemed to part before the Preacher and he moved through the host like a shark through a shoal of sardines.

I lacked whatever quality he possessed, and even following close on his heel I had to twist and turn and shoulder my way between people who seemed hell bent on getting in my way. I was glad when we finally reached the compound and Preacher showed the guard the note Dr Fisher had given us the night before. We were escorted to the doctor's study where he greeted us like old friends he hadn't seen in ages.

We were a little early, he said, so there was a chance for a, 'Glass of cheer and a chinwag before we go to the mess.' As I expected he wanted to learn more about the strange infection that had taken six men in so horrific a fashion. The Preacher diverted the conversation. He wanted to know where the troopers had met the victims.

'And another thing. The infection develops very quickly,' Preacher explained. 'But you tell me the four men and the troopers were still coherent when they reached the compound. So, how did you get them into isolation without anyone else getting infected? I've seen it take hundreds of men in a matter of hours, what did you do?'

'Marched them down to that storeroom at gunpoint, old man. Kept them away from every other bugger in the place. Didn't like the look of them at all. The troopers showed little sign at first, but the other chaps were shivering like palsied lotus eaters and their skin looked odd. I didn't like it, so, I

36

thought, better safe than sorry. Shame about the troopers, stout, honest chaps, but they'd been exposed, and I couldn't take the chance of infecting the whole compound. From what you tell me I did the right thing, what?'

'You did, John. Not just for your fellows, but for the whole town. It would have taken Lijiang in days, if not hours. We're lucky the troopers brought them here to you, a man who knew how to deal with them and could quickly make some tough decisions.'

'Nice of you to say so, padre. I say we're bally lucky to have found you and those handy grenades of yours. Damned if I'd have known how to deal with the poor bastards if you hadn't rolled up. Still, I did what I did, and you did what you did, and your man there did what he did, so, here's to us! Mud in your eye!'

'Cheers.'

We appreciated the wine in silence, then the Preacher brought the subject back to where the troopers had met the men. Dr Fisher chewed it over. He shook his head. 'I'm the wrong man to ask. Best beard Shropshire when we join him for lunch, he'll have a better idea about rotas and the like. Should be a good table, what with today being Sunday. Be pleased if you'd say grace for us, padre.'

It was Sunday? I hadn't known. My life had entered an odd twilight phase. For me the days of the week slipped past without variety, always dancing to the same old tune. Raise some cash somehow, get something to eat, find somewhere safe to sleep. Stay out of the rain when it's wet, find somewhere warm when it's cold. The sun rises, the sun sets, and Nathan Whittaker grew another day older. Nothing else changed.

Then the Preacher showed up with his black dog and my days had a purpose once more. The dog! Where had the Preacher's dog got to? I hoped it hadn't got lost somewhere. Then I almost missed the question I had been asked because I was worrying about the hound.

'Sorry?'

Fisher grinned, 'A young man's head is a palace filled with fog and idle fancies. My blessed mother used to say *I* was always counting stars in daylight. I was more likely counting the hours to my next meal. Always bally hungry. Don't you worry, Nathan, a belly full of good food will set you up for the afternoon. I asked what brought you to the old Ink Slab? You don't look military. Are you dodging that fracas in Flanders? Can't say I blame you if you are, bloody frightful mess I hear.'

I shook my head. 'I was already over the hills and far away when the Archduke took the bullet. Sounds impossible but I hadn't heard anything about the war until I reached Nepal. I was working my passage on a tramp steamer and you don't hear much news in the bowels of an oiler rounding the Cape. Too busy losing your breakfast and being terrified of drowning to care about the political scenery.

'I guess if I'd taken ship to Preacher Spindrift's home in the United States I'd probably have been back in the trenches dodging sniper bullets long before now. Thing is, by the time I did hear about it, everyone was telling me it was all going to be over by Christmas – and I knew I couldn't get there in time. And anyway, my invitation to the party must have got lost in the post. So, here I am. I never aimed to be here, and it's taken a while to reach the place, but here I am. When the wild geese call again I'll be on my way to the next town or mountain, but just now I'm happy to be of use to the Preacher here.'

'What about your parents?'

'Mother died back in 1910 when I was seventeen, and father had forgotten to sign the marriage licence before he left. He was a soldier man, a sergeant, and between them he and my grandfather taught me everything they thought I needed to know. I can shoot a gun, field dress game, I've got my letters and I can play the piano. I also cook, and I have some skill as an artist. I decided I could find my way in the streets of the world as well as I could the pea soupers of London town, maybe better.

'I've put my hand to lots of things since waving goodbye to the Smoke, and I've never knowingly hurt another person. Proud to say I've always earned my bread, never stolen it, and I'll put my shoulder to any honest wheel. And that's my life in a nutshell. You might say I was brought here by the tide and it hasn't flowed out just yet, so I wait on the beach to see what comes up next.'

It was not like me to beat my drum so long, but I hadn't liked the inference that I was dodging my duty to King and country. The Preacher regarded me with silent interest. I supposed he was wondering where all the wind had come from. I don't believe I had strung so many words together since we had met in the street the day before.

Fisher slapped his hands on his knees, 'My boy, you have sung for your supper, sung like a nightingale.' He stuck out his hand and shook mine as if he was trying to pump water out of me. 'Right pleased to have met you, Nathan. Add storyteller to your Curriculum Vitae. I'd pay to read the full story, so I would. You should write it down.'

As I always do when somebody compliments me I felt myself colouring and my cheeks became hot.

'Most kind of you, Dr Fisher. Maybe I will, one day. But it would be a strange tale that has no final chapter, and maybe I'm worried that writing "The End" to the story would put a full stop to my life. Maybe when I've stopped floating around the world like a piece of driftwood I'll put pen to paper.'

'You make sure you do, my lad. I'd read it with pleasure.'

At that moment the door opened, and we were informed that luncheon was being served in the officers' mess. Plans for my literary career could wait, food came first.

[11]

It was a good lunch. The officers' mess belied its name by being a well-appointed room, tidy enough to my eyes, and the air was filled with appetising aromas. Shropshire stood up when we entered and waved us to the table he had reserved. White-coated Sikhs pulled out chairs for us and then tucked them in behind our knees before laying linen napkins on our laps with effortless flicks of their hands. I was not used to being fussed over and had to watch the others to discover how I was to act at table.

There was too much cutlery for one person and my plate had been set to one side. I was tempted to put it between the knives and forks where it belonged, but no-one else had done so, so I let it lie. Then one of the white-coated chaps placed a bread roll on the plate and another put a bowl of steaming soup in front of me. I was ready to set-to, but first I keenly watched the Preacher and the others to see what they did.

Preacher stood up and everyone else in the room bowed their heads. I did the same which just brought my nose closer to the soup. It smelt delicious. My mouth watered, and my stomach growled. Preacher thanked the Lord for our daily bread and asked Him to bless those present with His mercy. He also asked for His loving hand to reach out and protect those less fortunate than ourselves.

I silently prayed that the Preacher wasn't going to read out a list of the needy. That bowl of soup was becoming a mortal temptation. His 'amen' was followed rapidly by the delicate clash of spoons on china, and I discovered that I was to use the round bowled spoon to my right. This set the pattern for all four courses, five if you counted the cheese and port at the end.

A small fruit ice followed soup, and then roast wild boar and vegetables with gravy. My enjoyment of the food was metered a little by my constant examination of the other diners to ensure I used the right eating irons in the correct manner.

The soup for instance. This business of ladling the spoon forward through the bowl before lifting it to my lips took far too long. And nobody dunked their bread in the savoury broth, they just broke it into small pieces and ate it. I wanted to wipe up every delicious mouthful, but because no-one else did so I felt I couldn't.

I battled my way through that wonderful meal in an unnatural fret, my elbows pinned to my sides rather than out and flapping as they usually did, like the wings of a hungry vulture. I discovered that the tines of my fork had to be curved downwards and used like a spear, not upwards and used like a shovel, which in my opinion the tender meat deserved.

All the time they were eating, the diners conversed in an appreciative murmur, but rather than congratulating the Sikhs on such excellent food they poured praise on each other, as if *they* had done all the hard work of preparing and serving the meal. I had always thought I was a fair cook but compared to the kitchen for that officers' mess I was a novice.

When the waiter finally brought the cheese and biscuits and poured me a glass of rich ruby port I thanked him and asked him to congratulate the cook for me. He looked surprised but smiled and nodded all the same. I realised the Preacher was regarding me closely once more, an enigmatic smile on his face. I coloured again, perhaps I was speaking out of turn, but I believed I was right to give credit where it was due.

After the meal the lieutenant and the doctor invited us to enjoy a cigar with them in the garden. I didn't want to spoil the flavours of my delicious meal with pungent smoke and so I declined, as did the Preacher. But we joined them for what they described as 'a postprandial turn around the grounds'. We had barely gone a few yards before Dr Fisher crouched in the centre of the path and broke wind, loudly.

'Sorry about that,' he grinned. 'Pork always turns me guts into a pair of bellows. Still, always better out than in, eh?'

I felt betrayed. After torturing myself to do the right thing all the way through lunch my host had just acted like the commonest oaf imaginable. I would no more fart in polite company than I would openly piss on their well-tended flower beds. At that moment I was grateful for their cigar smoke, and a quiet voice in my head wondered if masking the side-effects of troubled guts after a good meal was the reason these fellows lit the noxious things.

After we had made our farewells, and accepted invitations to return, the Preacher asked me if I could face a longer walk as an aid to digestion. I heartily agreed but offered to take him wherever he wanted to go by some route that avoided the crowds. It looked to me as if every citizen of the Ink Slab had decided to promenade in their Sunday best, and I was already feeling suffocated by the numbers.

'By all means, Nathan. I would like to see the Stone Lotus temple in Songun Village near the mission house, but I'm happy to take a diversion. Luckily, pork doesn't affect me as it does poor Dr Fisher, but I prefer a good walk after a big meal.'

My opinion of Dr Fisher must have been plain on my face because the Preacher blessed me with one of his half-moon smiles.

41

'It is difficult to judge a man who has been tutored in all the niceties but spends too much time with his fellow men. Some coarse meal gets in with the grain. But you did well with the cutlery, Nathan. I watched you watching everyone else. By the way, between you and me I think that is a crazy way to eat soup. I say get down into it and enjoy. You should see an Italian peasant enjoying their food in the field after a long morning's work, that's the way to appreciate good food and thank the Lord for his bounty.'

I laughed at this and decided to forgive the good doctor. However, I also planned never to eat pork with the man, ever again.

Once we were away from the main thoroughfare the crowds eased, as I knew they would. The people of Lijiang were out to be seen, and there were too few eyes on these quiet back streets. But there were eyes, and they had spotted a pair of gwailou. Shadows flitted around us, keeping pace with us along parallel paths.

'Preacher...' I began.

'Yes, I've seen them. They're not as discreet as they think. Clumsy in fact.'

'I think they're dragging us down to the river. They can dump bodies in the river and be gone in seconds. I don't know if they plan robbery or just murder, but I'd rather not be party to either. It would ruin a very pleasant afternoon.'

'I see I must get used to the English sense of humour once more, Nathan. It is quite unique.'

'Well, I hope you get all the time you need to do so, Preacher, I really do.'

We reached the river and I took us left towards Songun. That was when a gang of four men armed with long knives walked out onto the towpath in front of us. We heard the clattering of feet behind us and I saw another three men racing towards us, these were armed with meat cleavers. I heard one of them laugh. The meal I'd eaten churned in my belly and I prepared to die fighting. I looked around for something I could use to defend myself and wondered if I had time to lever one of the cobblestones out of the path and use it as a weapon.

And then I heard a terrifying snarl of fury and I prepared to suffer the hot bite of razor sharp, cold steel. There seemed no way out. I raised my fists with forlorn hope.

[12]

A giant black demon threw itself into the midst of the bastards with the cleavers and they scattered like bowled skittles. I was given a taste of what they planned for us when one of them lashed out wildly and slashed his colleague's upper arm to the bone. He received a faceful of hot blood in return. Horrified eyes glinted whitely from his dripping crimson mask.

Another of the cleaver men toppled helplessly into the river and was carried swiftly downstream by the powerful current. That river was fed by pure snowmelt, and even in the heat of summer it was bitterly cold. With luck hypothermia might get him before he had a chance to drown. The slashed man clutched at his injured arm and scurried away, gibbering in a high-pitched voice. That left the bloody-faced villain to confront the sudden and terrifying prospect of the demon, Preacher's enormous and powerful dog.

The dog prepared to leap at our attacker who held his cleaver out in front of him with both hands. I felt the animal's low growl vibrate in the pit of my stomach. The short hairs on the back of my neck stood to attention in alarm.

Bloody-face drew back his cleaver and threw it at the great hound with all his strength. The dog snatched it from the air as if it was a ball and then held it firmly in its jaws. It wagged its great head from side-to-side as if testing the blade and then advanced on our attacker. The man's gore coated face crumpled in disbelief. He turned and ran, howling in fright. The dog turned to me and proffered the cleaver. I swear it grinned at me.

I thanked it and gingerly took the thing by the handle, expecting it to be wet with canine saliva. It was dry, but I was beyond surprise by then. I turned to see how the Preacher was coping with the four men armed with knives. The dog prowled to his side.

My employer stood like a deadly statue, pointing his pistol at the men with a rock steady arm. He was grinning at them as if egging them on to try their luck. I joined him and hefted the cleaver as if I was ready to use it. I was fooling nobody. Those things scared me when I saw cooks using them on ducks in soup kitchens, I doubted I could really use one on a human being. I desperately hoped I wouldn't have to find out.

Preacher thumbed back the hammer of his gun and aimed it between the eyes of the lead assassin. He asked a question with a voice like a grindstone on gravel. I guessed he was speaking in dialect, but it might just as well have been ancient Greek. The knifeman understood well enough. He spat an answer and then spat again at the Preacher's feet.

As if at a signal the four men rushed us, knives held forward and sideways in a skilled fighter's grip. These people were the true killers, the crew with cleavers had just been a distraction. In a state of panic, I extended my cleaver and waved it like a steel flag. The dog tensed, ready to leap to our defence.

Preacher's pistol barked four times and all four men were instantly disarmed, their weapons shot from their grasp. Three of them turned tail and fled back up the side street from which they had emerged, cradling their injured fists.

The fourth, the one I believed to be the leader, stood still before us. His eyes reflected none of the pain he must be feeling. Blood dripped in a stream from the fingertips of his damaged hand, but he ignored it. He said something to Preacher who answered with a slow nod of his head. The man said something else and Preacher nodded again.

Then the man bent to collect all the scattered knives. He looked hard at the cleaver I was holding and glanced at Preacher with a question in his eyes. Preacher shook his head. The man swallowed hard, spat once into the river, turned on his heel and walked away, folding what was left of his dignity around himself like a cloak.

When he had followed his gang up the side street and we were alone once more I exhaled explosively. I hadn't realised I was holding my breath until that moment.

Preacher quickly reloaded his revolver and holstered it. He put the spent shells in a little bag hanging from his belt. He ran his hand through his hair and gave a low whistle, then bent down to pet the dog. At that moment the four knifemen pounded around the corner and ran at us once more, screaming defiance.

Preacher loosed four shots in the time it took me to gasp once in horror. Three men went down, but that lead bastard was made of sterner stuff. He staggered forward until the Preacher was almost in reach. I wasn't thinking, I threw my hand out to push him away.

The weight of the cleaver I was holding seemed to surprise him when it sliced into his chest and across his shoulder. Preacher fired again at point blank range. The man was dead before he hit the ground. Blood geysered up and out of him in a curving spray and then pooled around his twitching corpse.

The towpath seemed impossibly still and quiet. All I could hear was the pounding beat of my heart and my ragged breath whistling from my open mouth. I had never killed a man before. I didn't count the monster in the militia storeroom as human – I didn't know what to think about *that* terrible creature – but I had opened the body of the man at my feet with a cleaver and the shock of that impact still reverberated up my arm. I felt faint and sick.

'Nathan, drink this.'

I found a polished metal cylinder held under my nose.

'I'm sorry, I couldn't face brandy,' I gagged.

'It isn't. It will help you feel better. Drink it.'

I cautiously sipped at the cool liquid, expecting the bite of raw liquor. What poured down my throat seemed to instantly evaporate and flowed up into my sinuses and directly into my brain.

'Drink all of it. You will feel better. Go on, my friend.'

I did as he bade me, and he was right. I handed the empty cylinder back to him and it vanished into his long coat.

'What was that stuff?'

'A tincture of my own devising. Let me look at you.'

He examined my clothes, hands, and face. He nodded, looking satisfied.

'You'll do. You're very pale and that's due to shock, but, thank the Lord, the worst of the blood missed both of us. We won't draw curious eyes. Shall we go?'

'What about these men?'

'They're dead. The world is a better place without them. They had their chance to leave but they couldn't keep their word. I invited the man to go in peace, but instead he chose to rest in peace. It was his choice.'

'Who were they?'

'I think we should best discuss the matter elsewhere, Nathan. We've made quite a commotion and that will be sure to attract attention. Let's go now. I don't have time to waste on helping the militia with a murder enquiry.'

As if on cue I heard running feet, feet clad in heavy boots. We ran from the scene and made our way into the maze of side-streets. Within minutes we were lost, and we stopped to catch our breath before continuing at a more sedate pace. The flared roofs of the one and two storied buildings hemmed us in on all sides so I couldn't see any familiar landmarks.

I had lived in Lijiang for just over six months and believed I had a good grasp of the place, but the location of these quiet streets escaped me.

'Which way, Nathan?'

'I'm sorry, Preacher. Truth is I need to know which way we're pointing and in these narrow streets I can't see the sun.'

He paused before answering, 'We're facing west.'

'Are you sure?'

'I have a well-developed bump of direction.'

45

'Then we need to head that way, north. That will bring us to the Black Dragon Pool and from there I can get us anywhere we choose.'

We walked for about half a mile before I found myself on more familiar ground and began to relax enough to ask questions about our assailants.

'Preacher, I've been here a while and I've never had any trouble with the locals. No offense, but I've known you for just more than a day and I've been attacked twice. What is it about you that upsets them?'

'Perhaps it is that I am a man of the cloth?'

'So, okay, who were those men back at the river?'

'I asked their leader that exact question. He said they were members of The Society of the Righteous and Harmonious Fists, survivors of what has since been called the Boxer rebellion of 1900. I'm not so sure, his accent was strange, and his face wasn't Chinese.'

'Whoever they were, what have they got to do with us?'

'That's a good question. I'm curious to know the answer too.'

A voice behind us said, 'Turn around very carefully and I might allow you to live long enough to learn your answer.'

[13]

The Preacher had spun and drawn his weapon in a single fluid motion before I could even begin to react. But instead of the bark of his pistol I heard him bark with laughter. He strode away from me and I turned around cautiously to find him pounding a tall and oddly dressed blonde man on the shoulder.

The man was wearing robes, but these weren't like the long coat, waistcoat, and loose pants some of the Chinese were wearing, or even the robe I had worn the night before. These were ornate and had a mediaeval air about them. I can't say why but they looked expensive and were patently handmade.

Some men are handsome and know it all too well, some aren't but act as if they are and get away with it. And some are plain pug-ugly and too bad-tempered for anyone to tell them the truth. The Preacher's friend was one of the best-looking men I'd ever seen outside a Pre-Raphaelite painting. He shone with an inner light and had a smile that would charm birds from the trees.

Beside him the Preacher looked like the negative version of the same species. They were the dark flame and the light standing side-by-side. I felt like the shabby poor relative.

'Nathan, I want you to meet a great friend of mine. Come over here.' He beckoned me. 'Nathan, this is... Wait, what should I call you?'

The man stuck out his hand, 'Colin, Colin Cahoon. Pleased to meet you, Nathan.'

He had a distinctive twang that I recognised as American, but I couldn't say from which part. It struck me that wherever he came from the natives seemed friendly, and any friend of the Preacher's was a friend of mine. I shook his hand and appreciated his firm, dry grip. I repeated my name and smiled at him.

He tilted his head at the Preacher, then asked me. 'Have you found life has suddenly got mighty interesting since you met this strange fellow?'

'We do seem to be attracting a lot of attention.'

'Yes, well, Satan has a way about him. He's a trouble magnet, true enough. But he fights on the side of the righteous and I have been proud to stand with him in a few tight spots. Tighter than the fat lady's whalebone corset at the circus.'

He chuckled at a memory, then flicked a curious glance at the Preacher.

'Has Nathan met the enemy yet? The worm?'

Preacher nodded, his mood suddenly sombre.

'Six men that we know about so far and it could have been a lot worse. We were lucky. Now we must find the original site of the infection and destroy it before it spreads. This city has a population of tens of thousands, it would be catastrophic if they became subsumed. A disaster for all Asia and then the world.'

'And the mother worm?'

'I don't know. The men we saw must have been infected by a seed worm, the mother would have completely absorbed them as you know. They were still in the mobile stage when we released them.'

'They're at peace?'

'Ashes to ashes.'

'Amen.'

I was beginning to think they were using a secret language to deliberately exclude me and the meek rabbit in my soul changed to a snippy fox. This happens when I believe people are openly lampooning me – which is to say taking the piss. When all a man has to his name is his dignity it becomes a precious thing and mockery bites hard. I know, I have many bite marks from such bitter encounters, and in my time have earned plenty of bruises because of my hot responses.

'Excuse me butting in, gentlemen,' I said. 'But are we talking about that infection, the Sha-aneer thing? If so I would appreciate a little more clarity on the subject. What is this mother worm? What are you chaps talking about? Hmm?'

I stood arms akimbo and glared. I know, I'm tough as the skin on a custard and look about as threatening as a dormouse, but I can't help it. When I think my chain has been given a tug I demonstrate the poor temper of a fool and I start to yap like one of those annoying small dogs. The fact that one of these men was my employer and the other topped me by half a foot or more didn't hold me back. Yap, yap, I went, yap, yap, yap.

The preacher fought back his grin and held his hand up before me.

'You're right, Nathan, and if I am to invite you to become one of God's warriors you'll need a clearer understanding of what we're up against and who I am. That way you'll be better placed to make the choice – fight with me or walk away. Do you know somewhere we can talk in private and get a friendly drink? I think we've already had enough excitement for one day, let's get out of the spotlight.'

I led them to a nearby Portuguese bar I knew that had private rooms at the back, rooms kept free for professional women and their customers so long as they ordered wine and little plates of hot meat and fried bread.

We chatted about nothing much until the waiter brought our order and had closed the door on the way out. Preacher's dog lay down in front of that door and pressed its head against it. After a few moments it looked up and made a huffing noise.

'Okay,' said the Preacher, 'we can talk.'

He kept his voice low but what he told me could as easily have been shouted at the top of his lungs by a frothing lunatic. He told the tale of a dying planet and a noble people who sent out great ships to seed the most promising species of distant worlds. He explained that we, mankind, were the result of this project on Earth.

He told me that the gardeners who planted the seeds in our forebears were long-lived and still walked amongst us to protect what he described as the Eden born. He also told me that the worm, the Sha-aneer, was an ancient creature, older than the earliest slime in the sea. He explained that it wanted to wipe us out because it believed we had stolen its home planet and it wanted it back.

If the Sha-aneer infected a human they became part of it, part of the 'host'. Their flesh became part of the beast as I had seen in the militia storeroom, and their soul was devoured. The worm took a man's body and his immortal soul the way we had eaten pork at lunch. What remained was assimilated, making the worm strong and powerful.

Preacher took a drink of the sharp Portuguese Douro wine. 'The mother worm is immense, truly immense, and it is always underground. Deep underground. It seeds the area around it by sending those little red and black maggots out and they burrow into the victim's flesh and infect the poor devil. It eats the mind, drinks the soul and alters the body.

'Bring together enough victims and a new worm calf makes its nest. It will divide and spread or lay and grow and wait. I have travelled the world looking for these worms and I have destroyed them. Colin nearly died fighting one of them with me, in France.'

He gazed at me with haunted eyes. 'Nathan, I must have a human with me when I confront these creatures. It's the way it has to be. So, I ask you, will you stand with me or not?'

'Can't Colin join you? Isn't he human enough? Aren't you?'

'No, Nathan. That's the thing. *You* are the only human in this room.'

[14]

I wouldn't have been more surprised if he had told me he was my father. In a funny way I guess he was. According to what he had just said he was my great grandfather so many times removed I would have needed the biggest telescope in the world to see him as a speck on time's most distant horizon.

That was a tough enough rind to chew. But if he wasn't a man what was he? And what was Colin? I decided the best option was to keep quiet, drink the wine, nibble on the warm salty meat, and let them talk. I could add nothing of value to the conversation.

The two 'men' regarded me with evident curiosity. They had expected some sort of outburst and received silence instead. What did they want me to say? I chewed the fat instead. I wasn't hungry, but the meat and fried bread made the wine taste better. And I was being asked to swallow more than I could digest at a single sitting.

The dog gave a warning growl and moved away from the door. There followed a brisk knock. The Preacher called out, 'Come in.'

A round, sweating man opened the door without entering.

'Gentlemen,' he performed a twitchy little bobbing action which seemed designed to show off the top of his fleshy head. All the while he was wiping his hands on his grubby apron, swiping at his nose and scratching something flaky from his ears. I remember praying that he wasn't the cook, because if he was, for the time we remained on the premises I would only put wine in my mouth. I didn't fancy eating anything those busy fingers had touched. It was okay, he was the manager. He told us so.

'Gentlemen, I am Luciano, the manager. Forgive me but I have the militia here on my premises. They are in the bar, here, in *my* bar...'

His hands tangled and coiled together like copulating snakes. The image revolted and amused me in equal measure.

'Senhores, there has been bloodshed by the river. Men have died. They have been shot, it is terrible. The militia want to know if anybody has come into my bar since the last hour, and there is only you. Sorry, senhores, I had to tell them the truth, they...'

The brusque order from behind him silenced his wheedling voice.

'That's enough, Luciano, get to one side. We'll take over from here, off you go.'

50

The manager was shoved to one side and Shropshire strode into the room. His expression was belligerent at first but once he realised who we were he beamed at us with genuine warmth. He indicated the table.

'I say, you chaps, didn't we provide you with enough potage at the mess? Still a bit peckish, are we? Should have said; there's always another scrape or two of cheese in the larder.' He smiled at Colin, 'Pleased to meet you, sir. Any friend of these chaps; well, you know the drill.'

Colin stood and shook the lieutenant's hand firmly, Preacher performed the introductions. Shropshire cast a fleeting glance over Colin's robes. He said nothing, but I could see the mental shrug in his eyes. He probably thought the circus was in town. Then he told us about an event he described as 'the massacre' down by the river.

He continued, 'It's a quiet stretch of water so no witnesses for the killings despite all the gunshots. In fact, wise folk would have made a point of avoiding the place while chaps were taking pot shots at each other, and who could blame them? People told us about a blood-soaked man seen running away from the place, but there seems some confusion about whether that was before or after the shots. There were also reports of a running man bleeding heavily from a wound to his arm and shoulder. Probably the same chap. Difficult to tell.

'Witnesses are always the same, you know what it's like, "He was a tall short man with dark blonde hair and a pale brown complexion". If you've got six witnesses, you've got six completely different versions of events.'

He eyed the Preacher. 'I hate to ask this, padre, but may I see that pistol of yours? Just a formality, you know.'

The Preacher stood without a word and unholstered his gun. He handed it to Shropshire butt first. The lieutenant sniffed at it and raised a quizzical eyebrow.

'This gun has been fired recently.'

'Yes, you were with me when I fired it earlier this morning. At the compound.'

'So, you did, yes. So, you did. Silly of me. How could I forget?' He handed the gun back. 'Did you chaps hear or see anything of the fuss down by the river?'

Preacher nodded and then pointed his thumb at me. 'I thought I heard gunshots, but Nathan told me that the locals like to set off firecrackers to ward off evil spirits when a baby is born, or a house is blessed. He thought that more likely than guns.'

51

Shropshire agreed. 'He's right. We don't see much in the way of guns in Lijiang, it's not the Chinese way, not usually. The dead men were armed with knives and one of them had been shot then slashed open by a blade.'

He touched his chest. 'Right here, across the heart, deep enough to expose the ribs. Shot *and* stabbed, classic case of belt and braces. Whoever did it wanted to make sure the man was dead. Must have really pissed someone off, pardon my French.'

Shropshire shook his head and offered a rueful smile. 'To be honest if we finally catch the killers I'd like to shake their hand and buy them a pint. Those dead buggers were known to us. They were prize troublemakers, members of a gang involved with prostitution, extortion and theft, and not above a bit of murder themselves. They were part of the black-market opium trade, and they also ran a nasty line in trafficking virgins. The Ink Slab is a lot cleaner without them.'

He took a deep sniff, 'The air's fresher already. Anyway, I better get my boys out of here. Luciano is losing business with us in the place. Hope to see you again soon, and under more pleasant circumstances.'

He held out his hand to the Preacher who shook it firmly. 'As I say, I'd like to shake the hand of the man who killed those vermin. Did the world a favour.'

He turned to go but paused in the doorway. He nodded at me.

'Best to get some soda water to that blood on your sleeve, young fellow. Must have cut yourself shaving I expect. Soda water will see it off, best thing.'

And then he was gone, and the manager reappeared to see if he could get us anything. Preacher asked for another bottle of wine and a soda siphon. The portly man waddled off and our waiter brought the order within a few minutes.

Shropshire was right. The soda water dissolved the small streak of blood on my sleeve and removed another spray from my collar. I used the Preacher's handkerchief to dab away any residue, then he helped me get some out of my hair. Colin grinned at us.

'You guys didn't fool that officer for one minute, he knows you did it. What's the betting he's called the search off and put the killings down to a spat amongst gang members or rivals? Strike four bastards who deserved it and chalk up a rare victory to the good guys. He'll be buying you a beer, Satan, I'd put money on it. He looks like a guy who keeps his promises.'

Preacher smiled. 'He's a smart man for a limey. Telling us how to get rid of the blood on Nathan's clothes was his way of telling us he knew we were guilty, as was the handshake. And there's more, he's a Freemason. His handshake told me he was in the Craft, and I replied in kind. We're almost brothers now, as far as he's concerned.'

I piped up, 'Can't you let him be your token human in the fight against the mother worm? He looks a lot more capable than me.'

Preacher and his friend laughed aloud at that. They looked at each other, their eyes dancing and then back at me.

'Behold,' said Colin, 'the reluctant hero. You're an honest fellow, Nathan. I think that's what Satan values in you most. And are you a God-fearing Christian of good faith, one who prays to the Lord?'

'Not every day, but when I enjoy a good meal, see a beautiful sunset or a lovely girl I thank Him for His bounty in my own way. I certainly don't think of Him as Preacher's ship from a distant planet, nor do I see Him as a big beard in the sky.

'I also can't think of Him as a servant who runs around picking up after me when I make mistakes or punishes me if I upset someone. He was my creator, but now it's down to me to sort out my own fate. I enjoy being alive, long may it continue, and I will fight for my right to enjoy good meals, sunsets and pretty girls for as long as I've a breath in my body.'

Preacher put his hand on my shoulder.

'So, then, are you with me?'

I offered him my best look of wide-eyed innocence.

'Isn't that what I just said?'

[15]

The wine at the Portuguese bar had combined with everything else we had eaten and drunk in the militia mess at lunchtime, and I was feeling more than a little queasy. I was also still suffering from the shock of the attack by the river. I hadn't known I was carrying the man's blood in my hair, that bit of information didn't help calm the acid bile rising in my throat.

I felt a lot better once we were out in the fresh air and doing something, rather than sitting about in that stuffy room yapping about spaceships and mother worms. My steps were more than a little unsteady thanks to the drink and an overfull belly, but my sense of direction didn't fail me. I soon had us on the right track for the Stone Lotus temple.

The locals had once believed that the mouth of the cave at Songun Village looked like a snarling tiger, so they built the temple there to appease the spirit of the beast. We were close enough to the mission house that I fully expected Junjie to pop up from the shadows and take over as guide in my place, and he would have been right welcome. I was more in the mood to take a nap than take a turn around the old temple and breathe incense smoke.

I needn't have worried; the Preacher was more interested in the cave. As we approached I could see what the locals meant about the snarling tiger, there was something feral about the cave mouth. The garlands of flowers piled around it couldn't dispel the sense of threat that permeated the place.

I noticed Colin hesitate before entering the cave. He gazed up at the sky with intense longing before he ducked and walked into the shadows. I was reminded of someone taking a final deep breath before diving underwater. He wasn't human, the Preacher had said, then what was he? I followed him into the cave, sharing his foreboding.

From such a wide mouth we soon reached a narrow throat just a hundred yards or more back from the daylight. The cave was the size of a chapel with a short nave, and once I had adjusted to the dark I found it had a quiet, contemplative air.

Buddhist students used to come into the cave to read their scriptures, and long before that early humans had lived here. Some of the cave interior had been carved into seats and benches over the years. The place would have been cosy as a nest in winter and cool in mid-summer when the humid rains came.

A beam of bright light shone like a spear from the Preacher's hand and the cave came to life in blocks of light and dark. He was studying a fissure to the rear of the cave and the lamp he was using made it brighter than a moonlit night.

I had seen some of the new electric battery handlamps in London, lamps made by the Efandem Company in Wolverhampton, but they were damp squibs in comparison to the beacon in the Preacher's hand. I guessed it must be a Swiss device or perhaps German. They were clever engineers and made wonderful things, that bright light was a sight to behold in that gloomy place.

That was when I first smelt something rank in the air. It was like decay and open sewers but combined with an odd, pickled vinegar stink that twisted the nose. I had said Lijiang was a clean town, cleaner by far than London, but that stench out-stank old Father Thames himself. It was a gut-wrenching reek.

The Preacher switched his handlamp off and hissed 'Get away, both of you. Get back towards the cave mouth.'

I needed no second invitation. That stink was playing merry hell with my tender belly and swimming head. Making for fresh air was a very sound idea. I crouched low as I could and felt my way back to daylight.

And then, from back where I had last seen the Preacher I heard voices; strange, oily voices from people who seemed very satisfied with their lot. I listened.

Light in the cave, yes, light in the cave. Who is it? Is it more of the Eden beasts come to join us? We are so hungry, always hungry for more. They melt on our beautiful flesh. We grow, we grow. We shall be ready to divide soon, divide and send out hatchlings.

We shall move amongst the filthy Eden seed and eat them. The Host sucks the sweet juicy souls from their tender meat, brings them into the host, melts their bones and blood into pure Sha-aneer goodness.

Haaaa, yes. The Host shall grow strong here, strong enough to quicken the Mother in the deep earth. She waits, she waits, oh, she waits. Soon, soon we shall give her the juices of the Eden seed and the meat of men made fine and wholesome.'

Shall we become the precious Mother? And shall she become us?

We are the host and she is the Mother. We shall become what she makes of us. She is the first and she shall be the last when the world is finally clean of the bastard Eden flesh, and the land is ours, ours once more.

And then a host of hissing voices repeated *ours, ours, ours...*

There followed an unpleasant gurgling sound like foul water trickling into a drain that I realised with disgust was laughter. I had never heard any sound of joy that seemed so intensely evil. My stomach tightened, and gooseflesh crawled along my skin. I had heard the phrase 'mortally afraid' before, and now, for the first time, I truly knew what it meant.

Dread played its fingers along my flesh and squeezed at my heart. Something crawled through my scalp. I was frozen in place by helpless fear.

Then a calm familiar voice said, 'That was all I wanted to hear.'

After the sounds of the Host the Preacher's voice rang out in that cave like a clean breath in a charnel house. His handlamp sprang back into life and in silhouette I saw him throw a pair of his globes into the fissure. His pistol cracked once and then was still, and it was then I realised with horror that he hadn't reloaded after the Boxers' second attack. If this single shot should fail, we were all trapped in the cave with the worm and had no means of defence.

Something bulged from the crevice and sent out long, elastic appendages that blindly searched for him, for me, for all of us. *He's missed,* I thought. *And now that thing is going to suck the juice from my body and swallow my soul. Fuck!*

I hadn't believed I had an immortal soul until that day. It's a sad thing to discover that there really is a God, but that you're never going to die a clean natural death and have the chance to meet Him. Death in that cave was going to be too cruel. And final.

And then I saw a flare light up from within the crevice and those tentacles whipped around like wild reeds in a hurricane. The voices screeched like Irish banshees, shrieking his name. *SATAN! SATAN! SATAN!* An ear-splitting whistle began to build, sound piled upon sound, and the ground under my feet trembled as if the whole cave was sick with fever.

A strong hand gripped my arm like a vice and pushed me towards the light, Colin yelled loudly into my almost deafened ears.

'MOVE, Nathan. Run, man. That worm's going to blow, and it'll take this cave with it. Now RUN!'

I tried to run but, in my fear, I stumbled on a rocky outcrop and sprawled headlong to the ground. I fell hard, so hard I was winded, and my right shin was badly bruised. The sound of the worm was now so loud it was a physical force.

Its flesh was melting from the crevice like burning fat, splashing towards me. The floor bucked under me, writhing like a living thing in agony. I was thrown into the air and slammed down again. More bruises were added to my sorry collection. I knew how the nail must feel when the carpenter hammered it home.

And then I was flying, lifted bodily from the floor, and thrust like a sack of wheat towards the cave mouth. In a daze I realised the Preacher had me by my jacket and the seat of my pants, carrying me as if I weighed little more than a child. The cave was crumbling under the force of the worm's mortal agony, if we didn't get out soon the collapsing roof would trap us, seal us in with the thrashing beast.

It seemed hopeless. The heat was intense, and fire sucked all the air from my lungs. If we weren't crushed, we would surely burn. I shut my eyes and prayed that the end would be swift. I didn't want to burn to death, it would be the most terrible way to die. I felt my hair crisp on my head and heat seared my open mouth. I had no breath to scream.

And then sweet coolness drenched my skin like a blessing and I opened my eyes once more in time to see us shoot out into the light like a bullet from the Preacher's gun. Behind us the mouth of the snarling tiger slammed shut in a gout of white flame and I croaked in elation. *We're out,* I thought, *we're out, we're safe!'*

But we weren't free of danger yet. The worm hadn't finished with us, not yet.

[16]

The earth beneath our feet bulged skywards like a swollen belly then tore open to reveal a deep and twisted crevasse filled with boiling fire and molten stone. The cave collapsed into it with an ear-numbing roar and the four-hundred-year-old Temple of The Stone Lotus tumbled like a falling house of cards. Streamers of burning liquid boiled and sprayed around us in snakes of poisonous orange flame.

I was dangling like a rescued lamb, limp and stunned in the Preacher's hands, while Colin hovered beside us in mid-air. Back in the Portuguese place these fellows had told me I was the only human in the room, and now they were proving it with a vengeance. I felt myself caught between the devil and the fiery furnace, and I prayed this fallen angel didn't live up to his title.

Colin yelled, 'Is this going to be a repeat of France?'

The Preacher shouted back, 'Not as large, I think, but we need to move. People are coming to look at this mess. We must get back down to ground level where we can't be seen. We can't stay up here. Follow me, this way.'

With me in his arms he swooped down towards a treeline several hundred yards away. The effects of the blazing worm were being felt as far away as there. Treetops were lashing around as if caught in a storm and the ground seemed to ripple eerily. I had never seen anything like it before – but just recently that seemed to have become my mantra. I blearily wondered what I had signed up for and felt my heart pounding like a fist in my throat.

We landed, but when the Preacher put me down I was almost instantly thrown off my feet. The ground under those trees was bouncing like a trampoline, even Colin staggered like a drunken man. Preacher stood firm with his knees slightly bent and pulled me back upright. The trees started to fall around us. We had to escape, so, with our arms outstretched like high wire acrobats we staggered out into the relative safety of the open.

The fire and pandemonium of the worm's great eruption blistered the sky to the east for another half hour at least. The air became thick with a fine grey ash that fell and swirled all around us. My mouth became terribly dry and tasted horrible. I tried to spit the stuff out but instead set myself to coughing like a tubercular dotard sitting too close to a smoky fire. I bent double and found it hard to draw breath. My vision grew dark.

'Nathan, drink this.'

Preacher held a life-saving flask of clean water to my lips. I gulped at it like a man who had just crossed a desert. The first mouthful was a thick, unpleasant slurry and hard to swallow, but the second went down easy as ice-cream on a hot day. The third made me feel like I could outrun a cheetah. I tried to rise from my crouch to thank him, but Preacher held me bent forward at the waist.

'Wait just a few more minutes, Nathan. Cover your nose and mouth and lean down out of this filthy dust. It will soon clear. Then we can go look at what's left of the cave and temple before we go home to the mission house.'

I did as I was told. I didn't want to choke like that again and I could see the powdery dust still falling to earth, coating everything with a uniform grey blanket that looked deceptively soft and harmless.

Preacher had caused the eruption with his little crystal and a single shot of his pistol, after which the worm had caught and burned like an erupting volcano. How big was the creature? How many people had died to feed it over the years? Would there ever again be a cool, quiet place I could go to, to gather my scattered wits?

The sun was coming out and the dust was clearing. I unbent and looked around me. The Preacher had removed his long coat and was beating at it with the palm of his hand, his dark curls grey as Junjie's sparse locks. He was the centre of a cloud of pinkish grey dust and his eyes squinted almost shut against it.

Colin's cleaning routine, however, was a lot less mundane. He held his arms out from his sides, closed his eyes, and bowed his sooty head. There came a soundless concussion and an expanding sphere of dust exploded away from his body. He instantly gleamed cleanly once more. Now *that* was a useful talent and no mistake.

Then he stood and smiled at me with questioning eyes. I nodded and braced myself for what was to come. He brought his hands together, palms towards me. He bowed his head once more and shrugged his shoulders as if pushing something away.

What happened next nearly knocked me off my shoes, it was another unique sensation to add to my growing collection. The air wrapped itself around me and swept over my body with probing fingers. For a brief second, I couldn't breathe, then I felt as clean as a polished wineglass. Every inch of me tingled with pleasure too, it was a sensation it would be all too easy to get addicted to.

The Preacher watched everything with raised brows and held his arms up with his long coat in his right hand.

'I'd be mighty grateful for a touch of that magic if'n you'd be so kind as to oblige, please, Colin.'

Soon he was as clean as the pair of us and looking his capable self once more. He donned his coat.

'How can something so useful feel so damn good? Did you experience a pleasurable tingle when Colin did that to you, Nathan?'

Somewhat embarrassed to admit it I nodded. 'I can't quite describe how it felt, but yes. Pleasurable indeed.'

Colin grinned and nodded, looking a little abashed.

'I'm still learning my way around this stuff, but the cleaning charm was one of the first things Rowan taught me. It's one of the most basic childhood skills in Scytaer Faehl.'

I chipped in, 'Sorry, you lost me there, Colin. Please, who's Rowan? And what or where is whatever you said? Sounds like one of the Orkney islands.'

'Rowan's my beautiful wife and Scytaer Faehl is my home.' He glanced at the Preacher who nodded. Colin turned back to me and continued, 'We call it the "City between the worlds", and its home for people like me. Elementals, the fey folk.

'We can travel from there to anywhere on this planet in the same way you would open a door from one room to another. It's a mighty fine place and older than the hills, but it's always changing and becoming more beautiful. It's home for a people who can manipulate the elements of the Earth the way musicians play their instruments, however, the more we think of our differences from humans the more we learn our similarities.'

He grinned, 'For example, Earth children attract dirt like little magnets and so do young elementals. Nature made the cleaning charm pleasurable as an incentive for them to stay clean, and it works well, except for one small detail. Elemental children now deliberately get dirty for the pleasure of making themselves clean again afterwards. I guess that's why the experiment wasn't rolled out across all the species. We probably spoiled it for you guys.'

I resisted a strong temptation to roll in the dust and get Colin to clean me again. Chatting about Colin's city the three of us walked back towards Songun village. We could clearly see the devastation wrought by the dying worm as we drew closer. The snarling tiger cave was gone to be replaced by a narrow ravine. Water spurted from the end where the cave had once been, which must once have been a fast-flowing underground river.

The ravine snaked down into a pool where the ornamental zen garden at the centre of the Stone Lotus Temple had been, now completely open to the elements. The site was almost unrecognisable, and we saw shocked locals picking their way around it like sleepwalkers. Every once in a while, someone would stoop to pick something from the ground and place it in a wide basket at their side. Orange robed monks stood stunned and stared in disbelief at where their home had once been.

The Stone Lotus Temple had filled with water, which flooded out into the street through its open doors and then ran away into the culverted streams at the sides of the road. The temple was collapsing gently into the swift current, its walls sliding down like a tired fighter seeking rest. With the snarling cave destroyed the temple had lost its defensive purpose so its soft demolition seemed apt to me.

The worm would have done much more damage if Songun village had been as crowded as Lijiang itself, but almost everything around the temple remained undamaged. Even the flooding was contained by the temple building and the culverts. We asked whether anyone had been injured during the 'quake' and the Preacher tended to a few scrapes and bruises before we made our way back to the mission house. Songun had had a narrow escape.

Our own household had not been so lucky. An agitated Nuo ran towards us as soon as she saw us approaching, her pretty face a frantic mask of distress.

[17]

She rushed us to the study where we found Junjie unconscious and bleeding on the floor. He lay close by the window the bomb had demolished the previous day. A three-legged stool lay on its side by his feet. He had evidently been standing on it when the tremor jolted him to the ground. A hammer, some tacks, and a sheet of plywood were scattered around him. He must have been planning to carry out some spot repairs to the window.

The Preacher wasted no time. He hustled to the prone figure and, without moving him, carried out a hasty examination. He probed the man's head and neck then ran his hands down Junjie's spine before manipulating his joints. He nodded his head with satisfaction.

'Nothing broken or fractured. He'll have a headache when he comes around and his left eye will show some bruising – as will his left wrist and elbow. Can you gentlemen help me get him up to his bed? I think it would be better than this hard floor.'

The old man weighed even less than I had thought he would; he seemed shrunken in his unconscious state. All that humour and vitality contained in a birdlike parcel of ribs and stretched, parchment-like skin. He groaned a little when we lifted him, so Colin and I carried him as gently as a newborn child. We almost tiptoed up the stairs in complete silence so as not to rouse him.

We took him to his room where Preacher almost instantly re-joined us with his Gladstone bag.

'Thank-you,' he said. 'I'll take over now. I'll see you downstairs shortly. I think we'll all benefit from a drink, don't you?'

A lot had happened since the wine at the Portuguese bar, but a fair amount of it was still in my system. I opted for a beer rather than anything stronger. So much had happened since I met the Preacher that I thought it wise to keep what few wits I possessed in some sort of order. Colin accepted a tall glass from me and sipped at it thoughtfully.

Nuo bustled into the study where she found us poring over Gregory Pallant's notebooks. She offered us a little bow.

'Will the gentlemen be requiring dinner?'

I looked at Colin and he shrugged back at me. The Preacher and I had dined well at the compound and taken more at the bar. I for one was not hungry.

I said, 'Just some cold meats or small bites for me, please, Nuo. Nothing too elaborate, we had a big lunch. Colin here might prefer a little more.'

Nuo had accepted an extra mouth to feed and an extra body to care for without any hesitation, I felt guilty for not introducing him and promptly made amends.

She bowed in greeting and then smiled, 'The American Fathers would eat what they described as "three square meals a day". They were always hungry, so we have plenty in the kitchen. I will prepare a selection of things and then you can choose what you like. I will serve the food in here for convenience and easiness sake.'

I watched her tripping out of the room. She lifted her skirts for a moment to step over the door bar and with a shock I suddenly realised that Nuo's feet must have been bound when she was a little girl. Her shoes were tiny, and her tottering gait was little more than a controlled fall.

I had seen rich men's wives promenading just like that along Square Street, usually with an amah or maid at each elbow. The women were little more than useless sex objects. Walking on bound feet was believed to make a women's inner thigh and pelvic muscles much stronger than normal, which was claimed to enhance their husband's pleasure in bed.

Mothers in poorer families would cripple their daughters like that in the hope of attracting a wealthy marriage, which must have been the case for our housekeeper. I heard that terrible practice had been outlawed in recent years, unfortunately too late for Nuo. Every step she took must have been agony.

It was an unhealthy practice too. The bindings would cause suppurating sores that reeked. If a Chinese person insisted on talking about something unpleasant at great length, their discourse was described: 'as long and stinking as my grandmother's foot bindings'. I couldn't bear the thought of Nuo running around after us on crippled feet. It was too cruel.

Rather than become a rich man's plaything the girl had dedicated herself to caring for Christian Fathers in a mission house. And she showed no sign of the excruciating pain that must dog her every step. My admiration for her had already begun flowering; her refusal to accept her fate as a sex toy brought it to full bloom, and that was the first-time unselfish love had taken root in my dented and miserly heart.

I chided myself. Love for a crippled servant girl? What was I thinking? What kind of life could *I* offer her? Would she want to join me trying to sleep curled up on a mat in a flop house? Would she want to help me find guide work for a pittance? I was a poor catch and I put such romantic thoughts out of my mind.

I told the Preacher what I had noticed when he joined us a few minutes later. He had happily told us that Junjie was resting peacefully and had been given something to make him sleep and help speed his recovery. But then the smile was dashed from his face by my news. His expression darkened.

He said 'It never ceases to amaze me how much ingenuity mankind puts into inventing ever more wicked ways to torture their fellows. There must be an evil sinew that twists at their hearts and inspires such cruelty. I hadn't noticed, bless you for your clear eye, Nathan. How could I miss such a thing? I must be blind.'

I had to explain what foot binding was to Colin and his face took on a look of shocked nausea.

'A mother would do something like *that* to her own daughter? How? Why? Why in God's name would anyone do such a thing?'

I told him that the practice had been going on for a thousand years and had probably started with an emperor's wife. I began to feel inexpressibly tired while I explained. These people weren't even human, what must they think? I wanted to apologise for my race.

'When a wealthy man has a wife with bound feet it's proof that he can afford to feed a useless mouth. She can't work, and she can barely walk, but then she doesn't need to, does she? She's purely there for his pleasure, a pampered, soft creature, a bed mate. She's as much there to be used as the bed she sleeps in. Desirable when young. Not so desirable when they grow older. A foul practice.'

And that was when Nuo teetered back in carrying a tray filled with covered bowls. It looked heavy, so I rushed to take it from her. She was so surprised she almost dumped the whole affair down my front and I had to catch it in both hands before disaster struck. Empty-handed she stood, arms akimbo, and regarded me as if I was a naughty schoolboy.

'What you doing? Rushing at me and scaring me like that? I nearly drop dinner all over the floor! The floor is plenty clean, but you don't want to eat dinner there. What's wrong? You got itchy fingers? Why you do that?'

She was quivering, and I couldn't tell if it was from suppressed rage or contained laughter. Her cheeks were flushed a delicate pink and her finely shaped lips pouted while she waited for an answer. God she was lovely. My tongue stumbled in my mouth while I failed to form a reply.

Preacher offered, 'Nathan just remembered he's a gentleman is all, Nuo. A gentleman will not stand idle while a lady carries a burden.'

She folded her arms and gave him a steady stare, then she looked me over as if trying to work out if the dirty street boy she had banished to the bathroom on his arrival had ever been – or ever could be – a gentleman. Then she turned on her heel, or whatever part of her foot touched the floor, and pattered out of the room. I heard her sudden outburst of laughter when she was halfway back to the kitchen and decided she must have made her decision. I was no gentleman.

Colin looked numbly at the tray in my hands. He said, 'If that poor girl went to all that trouble of preparing good food and bringing it to us here on her poor broken feet, I say we at least show her the decency of looking to see what she's rustled up for us. What do you say, *gentlemen*?'

He said this last with an arch look in my direction that broke the strange enchantment Nuo had cast over me. Even so, I blushed remembering that laugh of hers. I put the tray on the only free table and we started lifting lids to discover a delicious looking selection of dishes. Soon our mouths were too busy to talk.

I had grown to appreciate Chinese cuisine. It was a wonderful blend of flavour, colour and texture, but now I was able to appreciate what that meant in the hands of a person who was an adept mistress in her kitchen. I hadn't thought I was hungry, but I attacked that stack of dishes as if in a trance. I do believe I groaned aloud with pleasure.

When Nuo returned to collect the tray, it was littered with empty dishes. All that remained of the meal was the dissipating and yet still tantalising aromas. When she bent to the tray, throwing me a warning glance to prevent more 'gentlemanly' interference, Preacher stayed her hand.

'Nuo, would you grant us a few minutes of your time? Please, take a seat.'

18

She looked frightened. She glanced at me for reassurance and then turned all her attention to the Preacher. She sat with her hands trapped between tightly pressed knees. She looked impossibly young and vulnerable. I supposed she thought she was in trouble for something she'd done. I fought an overwhelming urge to put my arms around her, and not in a brotherly way.

The Preacher pulled up a seat and sat facing her. Under his silent scrutiny Nuo began to squirm uncomfortably. It occurred to me that the girl was alone in the house with two men she barely knew and one complete stranger. The unconscious Junjie didn't come into the equation.

The Preacher's dark face held an expression I had never seen there before. It was hard to describe, a mixture of compassion, pity, and anger.

Nuo blurted out, 'Was the food bad? Do you want me to cook something better? I can go to the kitchen if you want, you tell me what you want me to do.'

Preacher shook his head, 'No, Nuo. This is not about the food, which was wonderful, by the way. You're a marvellous cook. No, it's not about that. I'd like you to allow me to examine your feet. I'd like to help you.'

I saw the shock jolt through her as if she had been struck by a fist. Her mouth opened but no sound came out and her arms wrapped around her body like a shield. Then her eyes flared open and her face grew white with rage. She almost spat the words at him.

'What do you think I am? What kind of Christian Father are you? You want to see my... you want me to... I!'

She sputtered to a stop, and then looked at me with venom in her glare.

'This your idea? You want dirty lookee, see good girl's most private places? Dirty street boy with dirty street mind, I thought you better than that. I *liked* you.'

She glanced at Colin, exhaled hard, then turned back to the Preacher.

'You try anything funny and I scream your house down. Plenty people come running, you see. They don't like Christians here. Busybody strangers think they're better than us. You see, yes, you see! They burn your house. You let me go *now*. I'm leaving! I see Junjie for my money you owe me, I can trust the old man to be decent. You let me go...'

Preacher held up his hand. 'Nuo, wait. I'm a Christian Father, that's true, but I'm also a doctor. Please listen. I know you're a good woman, an excellent housekeeper and a very fine cook, very fine. Dinner was superb.

I'm not going to ask you to do anything you're unhappy about – and I don't want you to leave. This is your home as well as your place of work, so, let's not hear any more about it.'

Nuo was still shrinking back into her seat, her mouth working, filled with words she wanted to spit at him, but at least she was listening.

Preacher continued, his voice low and calm. 'I'm a doctor, and I know how much it must hurt you to walk on bound feet.' She made to protest, and he shook his head at her. 'Please, Nuo, listen to me. The choice is yours. I believe I can reverse the terrible damage done to your feet when you were a child, but if you're happy to live the rest of your life with pain I can barely imagine, well then – so be it. The choice is yours.'

Nuo said nothing. She stood up, her face a glowering mask of confusion. She leaned towards the Preacher as if she was going to say something, then she raised her eyes to Colin. Finally, she turned to me. Her hand lashed out and she slapped me across the face so hard my ears rang. I was rocked back on my heels. With a right hook like that I believe she would have given Gentleman Jim Corbett a run for his money, while he was still in his prime. Damn, that hurt.

'How could you let me talk to the good Father like that? You should have told me he was a doctor. You let me scream at him like a screeching cat with its tail in the mangle. If he gives me notice it's your fault, he should let you go too, street boy!'

Then she reached out to touch my reddening cheek and tears sprang to her eyes. 'I'm so sorry, Nathan. My head is full of chicken feathers and I'm chasing after them like a snapping fox. I don't know what I do. I'm sorry.'

She crumpled back into the chair and buried her face in her hands. Her whole body shook, and my heart was broken by the wracking sounds of her weeping. I didn't think, I automatically crouched down to her and enveloped her in my arms. I kept repeating, 'It's all right, Nuo, it's all right,' with my lips buried in her hair.

After a while the storm subsided, and she pushed me away, but at least she smiled at me with her tear-stained cheeks.

She spoke to all of us. 'My grandmother bound my feet when I was very little. I can't remember what it feels like to have straight feet like a man. Every morning I bind my feet again the way I was taught, and every night I unbind them before I sleep. The pain is there every day, but it always has been. I never know anything different.'

She produced a handkerchief from her sleeve and blew her nose.

'My mother took me to Square Street to promenade. She spent as much on my embroidered shoes as she did on my dress. She thought a rich man would take me into his house. She taught me skills in the kitchen and showed me books about how to pleasure a man.'

She shuddered. 'There were pictures. Then one day a mission Father I met asked me if I was happy with my life and we got to talking. He brought me here for some tea. The smell from the kitchen was terrible, like stink made by a sick dog with a sour belly, and the house was a terrible mess, like boys make when left alone too long.'

She laughed, the sun reappeared from behind the clouds.

'Grown men, and they couldn't even make tea properly. I chased the Father out of the kitchen and got everything the way it should be. I threw away the stew he was burning and made dinner for the house. Now it is three years later, and I am still here, but the Fathers have gone. And then you arrive. And you tell me you can make my feet better? Father, sorry, but that is not possible. I know. I have money and I visit doctors. They tell me no, it can't be done.'

She sighed, 'Sometimes I forget the pain, just for a moment. But it is always there waiting for me. You know something? The pain is the only thing I have that I can truly call my own, but I wish I could drown it in a well. Ha, instead it drowns me. I talk enough. I am sorry.'

Nuo stood up and stumbled towards the door like an arthritic old woman, placing each foot as if stepping barefoot on broken glass. All the swaying grace she had shown before had vanished under the impossible weight of her relentless pain. I felt the lump in my throat grow big enough to choke me.

'Nuo, wait.' Preacher was on his feet. 'The doctors you spoke to couldn't help you. They told you the truth. But I am also speaking the truth when I tell you I can. Colin, could the expertise of Scytaer Faehl repair so much damage?'

The tall blonde man nodded thoughtfully. 'Nuo would need to be rendered unconscious during the procedure or the pain would be too terrible. But we could certainly bring her to our surgeons as soon as she was ready. What do you say, Nuo? Are you willing to trust us? I promise no harm will come to you, I give you my personal guarantee that no-one will hurt you except to make you better once more. I promise.'

Preacher took Colin's shoulder. 'My friend is a prince in his own land. His promise is like gold. Please, let us do this for you. We can start tonight.'

I watched doubt chase hope and then resignation across Nuo's face. Her shoulders slumped under the weight of her decision.

'If you can't do it I don't want to wake up from the operation. I would rather not wake up than be promised release and then find I'm still chained to these, these...'

I strode to her side and lifted her into my arms. She weighed more than Junjie but not by much, and she relaxed after the briefest struggle.

'Where shall I take her,' I asked.

'To my room,' answered the Preacher. 'I have everything we need there. Colin will you join us?'

We made a solemn party while we mounted the stairs to the upper floor, the Preacher leading us. When we entered his room, I placed Nuo on the Preacher's bed and stood back to watch what might happen next. If I understood it right Nuo was going to be the subject for some kind of surgical procedure, but I couldn't see how it would be carried out without a proper medical hospital.

Preacher removed her shoes and her short stockings to disclose her tiny bound feet. He began to unwind the bindings on her left foot. I think they had forgotten I was there, so absorbed were they in their task. I gasped aloud when I saw what Nuo's grandmother had done to her own flesh and blood.

Nuo looked at me and shook her head, she said something to the Preacher.

He nodded and turned to me. 'Our patient deserves a little privacy while we get her ready. Please, Nathan, would you wait downstairs?'

I did as I was told, my horrified mind filled with the image of that distorted hoof of a foot. I was halfway down the stairs when I heard a report from the room, as if a massive gust of wind had slammed against the closed door. I ran back and threw the door open in alarm.

The room was empty.

19

I spent long minutes looking around that room in disbelief. There was not much to see. The bed still held the impress of Nuo's body, there were two chairs, a chest of drawers with a mirror mounted on it, and a wardrobe. On the wall above the bed was a crucifix, the golden figure of Christ stretched out was glittering in the warm light from the single window.

For God's sake, I thought, *this is a bedroom not a magician's cabinet! It's a place for sleep and contemplation, not mystery! What happened here?*

And yet three people had vanished from there in the time it took me to descend halfway down the staircase to the ground floor. I was compelled to move to the window and gaze out across the village's flaring, blue tiled roofs, and the snow-capped mountains beyond skirted by forest, all stretching away under a flawless blue sky.

I would not have been surprised to see Preacher, Colin and Nuo scrambling across the roofs away from me, but there was no sign of life other than a spiral of distant birds circling something beyond the Old Town.

So, I wondered, what now? Junjie was still asleep in his room but otherwise I was alone in the mission house. Is this what had happened to the four American Fathers? Had they simply dropped out of the world as if through a trapdoor?

Preacher had filled my head with the Sha-aneer: a creature, a monster, the worm that would devour mankind and wipe us from the face of the Earth. But what if there was something else at work here? What if this room was the focus for an energy that could steal people away in the blink of an eye?

That thought saw me make it to the other side of the bedroom's firmly closed door at a speed that would have shown any blink of an eye the dust of my coward's heels. And what of my room? Was that safe? What of Junjie?

Junjie! I hurried to the old man's crib and was glad to see him still sleeping like a babe in a manger. I returned downstairs to the study. I had yet to spend a second night in this house, yet every waking hour I had lived through since meeting Preacher Spindrift and his hound on Square Street had been salted with life threatening danger. Should I listen to my pounding heart and escape back to my old street life?

For half a year the worst that had happened to me was waking up to find one of the lotus eaters fruitlessly searching my pockets for enough cash to buy himself another pipe of dreams and escape reality for a few precious minutes. Since meeting the Preacher I had been blown up, threatened with a gun, confronted by nightmare, and had a bloodthirsty gang attack me with knives and cleavers. The reverend doctor offered a sterling cure for boredom.

I was at a loss as to what to do for the best. I returned to that quiet study and contemplated the tray of empty dishes that had so recently held our delicious meal. The savoury aromas still tempted my nose with the ghosts of rich promises. A solitary fly meandered around them. It spurred me to collect the tray and take it back to Nuo's kitchen.

The mission men may not have been able to make a pot of tea, but Nathaniel Whittaker knew his way around a washing-up tub. A day spent boiling my hands in hot suds while making kitchen utensils and dishes spotless had earned me more than one meal of pork, vegetables, and rice in a thick gravy. And what Nuo had prepared was worth the work and plenty more.

I slowly filled the drying rack with clean bowls and pans. The mission men had brought the twentieth century to the house with them, I had found pan scourers and Peet Bros' Crystal White soap to use. Nuo had already filled a pan with water and left it on the range to heat. I hoped it was for dishwashing but just in case refilled the pan and put it back on the range. It would be there for her if she ever returned to use it. The hot work gave me something to do. It diverted my buzzing mind from the mysteries of the day.

It also took my mind away from the sight of her poor crippled foot. Her foot had been folded like a fist; with its heel jutting down like a stump and her toes folded under and around the out*side* of her sole. I couldn't imagine how such a thing could be done, let alone how it felt to walk on such an insult to nature.

Never had I felt compassion for those pampered creatures promenading on Square Street, hobbling along supported by their amahs as an open display of wealth, but I did at that moment. With my reddened arms deep in that tub of soapy water I found myself pitying the wealthy wives of Lijiang.

'You look very much at home there.'

I turned like a magnet attracted by the sound of her sweet voice. I dripped suds and water onto my clothes and the floor. It was Nuo. But she looked different somehow, more upright. She was dressed differently, and her hair had taken on an added lustre. I instantly dropped my gaze to her feet and my heart sank. The work must have failed. They were still thrust into those small embroidered bootees she had been wearing.

I remembered what she had said about not letting her wake up if the procedure miscarried and wondered how disappointed and distraught the poor girl must be. And then chided myself as an idiot when I realised that

71

there hadn't been time to start any such complex medical operation, let alone complete it.

And then she grinned at me and without a word she stepped lightly out of the bootees, graceful as a dancer, and she twirled for me on her perfect, fully restored feet. She had been standing on tip-toe, just her natural looking, beautiful toes thrust into those tiny shoes.

She spun again and laughed at the expression on my face. I've spent a lot of my life in the company of fools and know when to laugh well enough, but I supposed the look I gave that sweet girl in that kitchen would have earned a hoot in a *Harry Randall* music hall production. I would have brought the house down in one of those gurning, slapstick single-reelers that broke up the stage acts and gave the performers time to change costume.

I felt dizzy and confused and happy all at the same time. How could that tortured little hoof have been transformed into a dainty, natural foot in the time it took me to wash a tub of dishes? Where had the three of them gone. Why wasn't I running screaming from the house and searching for a wise old Chinese head doctor? Because it was plain I was caught up in a madhouse – or an adventure written by a lunatic. Whichever it was only time would tell.

I was so happy to see her I dried my hands and I ran to Nuo, holding my arms out towards her. She stepped back with a look of alarm. I stumbled and dropped my arms back to my side.

'I'm sorry,' I said. 'I thought we, that is... I'm sorry. I don't know what I thought.'

'No silly,' she giggled, 'but you're all wet and sweaty like a washer-woman. Get yourself clean and then we'll see what "we" are. I'll put the dishes away where they belong. You've put them everywhere, all the wrong places. Go on now. Go get yourself clean like nice boy.'

I wondered at her new self-assurance, and my head was so full of questions that they got all jammed together before reaching my mouth. I once got talking with a self-proclaimed journalist who, like me, was working his voyage as a deckhand on an oiler on the Indian Ocean. He told me that any news story is based on five basic principles: 'Who? What? Where? When? and How?'. Get those, he said, and you've got your tale by the tail. Okay.

I believed I had the 'Who' but the rest escaped me. And then I discovered that I didn't even have that much. I was walking away from the kitchen on my way to the bathroom with Nuo's delighted chuckles still ringing in my ears. I was unbuttoning my shirt as I went – and thinking about what she and I might *mean* to each other – when the door to the study opened at the other end of the hall. I paused, expecting the Preacher or Colin to step out and hail me.

What met my startled gaze was the tall figure of possibly the most strikingly beautiful woman I had ever seen, except Nuo. And she was a complete stranger to me. I froze.

20

I had barely remembered to drag some air back into my startled lungs when Colin followed the woman out into the hallway and grinned at me while he placed a proprietary arm around her slim waist. The slimness of her waist accentuated the fullness of her curves, and her hair shone in auburn curls above a mischievous face that dimpled in a smile and held two large, long lashed and adorable hazel eyes.

Those eyes glittered with gold sparks. She was the pure distillation of everything I thought wonderful about women. And yet, somehow, I also saw a slender shadow standing between her and me, and my fickle heart was shredded with shame. How could I compare this paragon of her sex with Nuo? How dare I even think the thoughts that cascaded hotly through my imagination? But I did.

'Nathan, there you are. Please, meet my wife, Rowan. She's heard all about you and insisted on making a visit to say hello.'

This wonderful creature was Colin's *wife*? I wish I could claim that fact threw cold water on the images burning in my brain, but it didn't. I was hot as a dog on a street corner and all but panting after her with my tongue hanging loose. And then sanity came crashing to my rescue – they made a striking couple and made me even more aware of my shabby condition.

I was wet and sweaty as a coolie and in no fit state for polite company, to the point that even our lovely housekeeper had just thrown me out of her kitchen. I pulled my shirt closed over my naked torso.

'I'll be back,' I stammered. 'Ah, right, yes. I'll be back, I've got to wash up first.' I hustled away, then remembering my poor manners scuttled back. 'Nice to meet you, ma'am. I'll be back. I have to...' I scurried away.

When I had spare coppers burning a rare hole in my pocket I had sometimes taken trips on the fun rides, trains, and river rides of the travelling carnivals and funfairs in London. I had immensely enjoyed the thrills I experienced when things popped up from holes and out of cupboards, some even fell from the ceiling!

Every twist and turn of the rides brought something new into view. It was exciting and, sometimes, a little scary, but in my heart, I always knew that it was just a ride. At some point it would end, and I would find myself back in the real world, breathless, exhilarated, and a few farthings poorer.

Even when working my way across the fat belly of old Earth the days had thrown up few real surprises, not like those rides. They had a glamour to them that never palled. Drifting the seven seas brought new horizons and cultures, people with different languages and customs, but also grimy, back-breaking work and squalid, insanitary lodgings. Reality had a solid, grey predictability about it that had never really altered – until now.

Somehow fate had thrown me onto one of those rides for real, and I had no way of knowing when things might return to normal, if they ever did. My head was in a whirl while I rinsed myself under the shower and lathered with the same brand of Peet Bros soap I had used to clean the dishes.

The clean smelling block of white soap was big and hard in my hand and I scoured my body with it. I started with my hair and finished with my feet, making sure I had thoroughly washed every inch in between. Preacher had said that Colin was a prince amongst his people, surely that meant Rowan was a princess? I had to look my best for royalty.

Especially when royalty looked that good. My body reacted to the thought of her with shameless inevitability; I was also haunted by visions of Nuo's lithe form outlined under her simple dress. I slapped my imagination across the chops and finished my shower with a blast of cold water that did nothing to cool my burning flesh. I gave up and climbed out of the stall in a state of excitement.

I wrapped myself in a towel and bundled my soiled clothes under my arm, then scampered barefoot towards my room. Luckily, I didn't meet a soul in the hallway or on the stairs. I heard voices in the study and hastened my step, in case the door opened once more to disclose Colin's princess bride. Even swathed in a towel I was in no condition to meet her, or Nuo.

When I reached my room, I fumbled at the latch and dropped my clothes. While picking them up my towel loosened and dropped to the floor. I was naked when I finally got my door open and practically fell into my room, where I was greeted by a gasp of surprise.

Nuo was in there, laying out fresh robes and pyjamas for me. She turned her face away from my exposed hide and covered her eyes while I scrabbled to cover my most private parts with anything I could grab. I have no false illusions about my body. A fair appraisal of my physique might say that I am lean to the point of being slender, honed and without an ounce of surplus fat. A less generous description would have me as scrawny as a skinned cat. Either way, a naked man is the last thing one should inflict on a young woman without fair warning, even if she was unexpectedly encountered in said man's room.

Especially when that same man had been harbouring erotic thoughts about that young woman while showering, and his body gave more than ample evidence to that fact. I make no excuses for my state of tumescence, I was a young man with a young man's urges, and I had not expected anyone to witness my aroused condition while I was in a state of nature.

I wrapped my towel around me once more and willed my errant flesh to return to a more dignified shape, or at the very least to point a little further south. But to see Nuo by my bed and to be very aware of the closeness of her slender curves, while we were alone together, was not helping my cause. Keeping her back to me Nuo edged around my room until she was almost at my side. She bent to gather up my clothes and I moved away to give her the room.

Once she had collected my bundle of damp, sweaty laundry she stood and turned her face to mine. We were so close I could feel her breath on my face. Her lips parted slightly. Like a butterfly alighting on a bloom she leaned forward and kissed me on the mouth. It was the merest ghost of a kiss, barely a touch, but I felt it from my hair to my toes. I closed my eyes and my knees buckled under that delicate impact. I groaned with the pleasure of it.

And then it was over and when I opened my eyes once more she was gone, and the door was closing behind her. From that moment on I knew one thing for sure. Rowan might be the female of the species at her most vibrant, with colour and charisma that fell somewhere between a flaming autumn tree and a tigress stalking her prey. I would readily admit she was magnificent.

But in the eyes of Nathanial Whittaker she lit not one candle that outshone the quiet light of my sweet Nuo. Nuo had melted my defences and captured my heart in a cage so sweet and delicate that it still felt like freedom, and, even though I did not yet know how I was going to achieve it, I was going to build the strongest foundations for our lives together.

When she kissed me, her lips were cool and sweet as mountain air, but I could feel the heat of her body so much it hurt. I dropped my towel and glanced down at the thick stiffness at my groin, it seemed to sniff at the air like a hunting dog scenting a fox.

'You can just wait your turn,' I said. 'Don't get presumptuous ideas about that sweet girl until you've been properly invited.'

And with that I got dressed in my fresh robes and padded back down to the study. Nuo had driven a lot of my questions from my mind with the unexpected gift of her lips, but as I approached that panelled door they crowded back and began clamouring for attention. I hoped I would be able to get answers to at least two of them without stumbling over my foolish tongue.

How had Nuo been healed so quickly? And where had they taken her for treatment?

21

I knocked at the door and waited rather than barging in. I believed I would be made welcome, but I preferred to be invited. Anyway, it had proved another long day and I hadn't had time for much sleep the night before. That, combined with the alcohol I'd consumed, was manifesting itself as a thudding headache over my left eye. I hoped the Preacher might have an effective remedy.

Colin opened the door. He had another glass of beer in his hand and it was half empty. He grinned at me, catching my glance at his drink.

'If they were to introduce prohibition in China I think I'd have to move back home the same day. Can I fetch you a refreshment, Nathan?'

'No, thanks, Colin. In fact, I was going to ask Preacher Spindrift if he had a powder for a headache.' I rubbed my forehead. 'I enjoy a drink, you know, but I think I reached my limit and went way past it since lunchtime.'

Colin ushered me into the room, a hand between my shoulder blades. I saw the Preacher sitting with his legs straddled across one of the wooden seats and his arms folded across the backrest. Rowan was curled up on the two-seater sofa, her feet tucked under her bottom. She had been leafing through Pallant's notebook but raised her glorious eyes to me when I entered.

She smiled and got to her feet, which I noticed were bare. The way her body moved reminded me of a cat stretching in the hot sun, elegant, beautiful, effortless, and lazy all at once. She suited her skin very well, and her smile impacted the poor wits of a London boy like I was bathing in warm cream.

'Nathan, lovely to meet you properly at last. You were looking a little flustered the last time I saw you.'

I was momentarily lost for words, but then the sweet memory of Nuo's kiss brought me back from the brink and I regained some of my composure. Unfortunately, my tongue didn't, and I gabbled like an idiot goose. I think I said 'Any wife of Colin's is a wife of mine' before Colin stepped into the breach and saved me from myself.

He rested a hand on my shoulder and said, 'You'll have to excuse Nathan he's not at his best just now. He just told me that he's suffering from an excess of the good stuff, and he's got a splitting head. Satan, have we something that might help our young friend?'

Preacher came over to me and examined my eyes, then he nodded. He strode from the room and I heard his feet on the stairs. Rowan gave me a brief sympathetic hug and told me Satan would look after me. Even though I knew it to be the Preacher's true name, I still couldn't get used to these people using it in such a familiar fashion. Even so I truly enjoyed the hug. Rowan felt firm and yielding at the same time.

The Preacher re-entered the study and handed me two tablets which he told me to swallow and wash down with a draught from one of his steel cylinders. Almost instantly a sense of wellbeing washed through me. I still felt as if I was floating around in a cloud of silky haze, but at least I had regained some control of my faculties. My tongue was my own once more.

'Please,' I said. 'May I fire a few questions?'

Preacher answered, 'It's getting late and we have an early start tomorrow. Can't it wait until morning?'

'No, please. My head's buzzing, I need to know. Just five minutes.'

'Okay, fire away, Nathan.'

I blurted out everything that was buzzing around my mind. How had I found the room empty seconds after I'd seen them in it? How had Nuo been healed in the time it took me to wash a tub of dishes? And where was the city between the worlds? What was Colin? And how could he fly? And what was the Preacher really? I even wanted to know where we were going in the morning after our early start.

Finally, I wound down like a clockwork clown and fell silent. Rowan looked from Preacher to her husband and then back at me.

'I can answer some of those for you, Nathan, if you'll trust a stranger to speak the truth?'

I bade her to please continue. She took a deep breath before beginning, which proved a very enjoyable and distracting sight indeed. I forced my eyes up to her face.

She explained, 'The room was empty because Colin and Satan had brought Nuo to our home, Scytaer Faehl. It is the city of elementals, Colin is a prince of the air there. I am of the earth. We say the city is between the worlds because it is between here and the First Realm of Light, the place where humans travel when they leave this life and move on to the next stage of existence.

'You might call the Realm the afterlife but that isn't strictly accurate. It's not heaven as such, but it has been manifested and is ruled by an intelligent being of pure light who is the voice and hand of God. We call her the Conduit. To us she is female, and she sometimes judges errant elementals. She also shapes the souls in the realm to reflect the lives they've led.'

She shifted on her seat and leaned forward, her face intent.

'We can move between our city and here in the way you can move from one room to another through a doorway. Except we can manipulate time when we do so. When Colin and Satan brought poor Nuo to us our healers were horrified by what they found. The poor girl's feet...'

'I know,' I said, my voice tight. 'I know, I saw.'

Rowan nodded, 'Then you understand that it was going to take time to correct the dreadful torture the poor girl had suffered for so many cruel years. I can't imagine...' She faltered. 'I have some sympathy for humanity. I've met many fine people, noble people, but I fail to understand how someone could do that to another human being, torture them like that, just for the selfish pleasures of men?

'Nuo was resigned to her fate, she believed there was nothing to be done. She had accepted a lifetime of crippling agony and service, and yet she told me there was one unexpected good thing that had come into her world. A thing she had never thought possible. She met a good man she believed she could love.'

I was shocked to realise how upset I was at this news. I should be happy. If Nuo had found someone to take care of her, someone she could love, then I should be happy for her. But there was no escaping the pang of disappointed misery that had rocked me to my core.

'So, then,' I asked, my voice tight. 'So, who is this man? Is he one of the merchants in town?'

Rowan grinned, but I failed to see the funny side of any of it. Cold water had been dashed over my wits. Rowan leaned across to me and touched my hand

'But no, Nathan, surely you must already know? She was talking about you.'

[22]

An early start saw me hunched sleepily over a coffee while sitting at table with the Preacher in the pale light of dawn. Nuo had already been busy with breakfast things when I came down from my room and wished her good morning. Her perfunctory, 'He's waiting for you in the refectory,' was balanced by her next observation, 'You look nice with clothes *on* too!' The smile she gave me warmed my shrivelled, morning soul.

I have never been an early riser. I prefer to join the day after it has washed its face and pulled its boots on. They call the light of dawn cold for a reason, and in my opinion, it is best seen from under a warm blanket. But if the boss wanted to get a wriggle on then Nathaniel Whittaker would just have to sacrifice his sleep to the call of duty.

Nuo brought two warm plates into the refectory. They were piled with strips of fried pork, eggs, tomatoes and mushrooms. She bustled away on happy feet, almost dancing. The transformation was incredible. I thought over some of the things I had learned the night before.

It had taken more than four months for elemental doctors to manipulate the bones in her feet back to where they should be. In the process she had been more crippled for a while, rendered completely incapable of walking. She couldn't put any weight on her broken feet, not even *her* slight frame. The elementals put her in a rig they called a 'cradle' which catered for her every need.

The night before Colin had said he knew what she was going through. He had spent longs months in one of those contraptions after his adventures in France.

He had told me he was just waiting for his hair to grow, but Rowan objected saying he also had to recoup a good proportion of his skin that had been burned away – and the precious body fluids that had been boiled out of him. He had also broken several bones. He was barely alive. When I asked what had happened to him the Preacher answered.

'We destroyed a Sha-aneer. There was quite an eruption. Almost wiped out a small town. Colin got caught up in it after we got separated. It was bad.'

I asked, 'Was it like that one at the snarling tiger cave?'

'Bigger, much bigger. That one at the cave was a calf, albeit a mature one. The worm in France was ancient and full grown.'

I quailed in my seat. 'And the one we're after, the one you call the mother, is that as big as the French one?'

The Preacher had sipped at his wine before he answered, which didn't bode well. He gazed at me with bleak eyes and chewed at his answer before he spoke.

'Before we came to Earth and seeded the Eden born, the Sha-aneer was the top dog on this planet. It is an acute example of a separate evolutionary strand, it could almost be described as a super-evolved amoeba. It can divide and calf, we know that, and it is close enough to the common evolutionary stock to be capable of absorbing human and animal tissue.

'However, the worm also absorbs the human soul, devours it. It robs its victims of their God-given birthright to redemption and eternal grace. When we destroy the worm, we release its victims to peace and oblivion, and that's the very best we can do. And we know no more about it than that. Whenever we get close enough to examine the worm we must destroy it before it destroys us.

'All our research to date has been defensive or destructive. It fires paralysing quills, we know that. They immobilise its victims long enough for it to envelope them. The quill poison isn't lethal, the worm prefers living meat to dead. It won't touch a corpse, no nourishment.'

He sipped at his wine again. I was very aware that he hadn't answered my question. I decided to prompt him, I wanted an idea of what we were up against. If the French worm had burned the hide off a man like Colin Cahoon it must have been something awesome to see. The man could *fly* for Pete's sake. I had seen him do it.

'So,' I said, 'the worm *we're* hunting is as big as the one in France?'

'No,' said the Preacher. 'The one we're hunting is the last of its kind. And it's the first, it's the mother. The one we're hunting, Nathan, was the first Sha-aneer on Earth, it is the oldest and the largest. It's also the deepest of the deep wise worms. Two of my companions died discovering its hiding place. And you know something? Just as *it* is the last of its kind *I* am now the last of mine here on Earth. I must finish this. Then perhaps I too can rest in peace.'

And now the pale light of dawn shone greyly onto our dining table and we chewed the fat without saying a word. We ate in silence. I had not gone hungry since meeting the Preacher, but I suspected we might have lean days ahead of us. Colin had promised to join us if we needed him, but last night he had gone home to his city between the worlds with his extraordinary wife.

That morning the Preacher and I were embarking on a worm hunt, and not just any worm. We were seeking to destroy the creature who had established the nightmare breed before God made the fishes and planted the first tree in the garden for Adam and Eve. Was this the original model for the great

Behemoth in the Book of Job? Was it the Leviathan? Or was it something else altogether? Something so secret that the ancients remained unaware of the terrible creature lurking far beneath their feet?

Nuo had found me some tack in the Fathers' wardrobes to replace my accustomed clothes but I wondered what I could wear on my feet during our trek? I knew my feet were too small for any of the Fathers' shoes without a ludicrously thick padding of socks, but I needn't have worried.

She had been out before the sun peeked over the mountains and had woken up an outfitter she knew. She presented me with a fine pair of sturdy boots that fit me just fine. She looked pleased as Punch when I told her so.

The outfitter had also been good for a pair of knapsacks, a compass, and some bedrolls. Preacher had asked Nuo to rustle up some travelling grub which she packed in greaseproof paper and placed in our sacks. Alongside them were linen bags containing a few changes of socks and fresh underwear. I noticed Nuo became increasingly subdued as the time for our departure grew closer. Once, when we were briefly alone, I asked her what was wrong.

She shook her head, then said, 'You are going where the fathers went – and they're dead.'

I replied, 'We don't know that, Nuo.'

'We know they didn't come back.'

She had me there. I didn't know what had happened to her mission men and I didn't know what would happen to me. I was putting my trust in God and a man called Satan. I told myself I'd never call another man a fool for as long as I lived. Then I saw tears begin to build in Nuo's eyes. They pearled like jewels in her long eyelashes. Damn if my own eyes didn't start to sting a little. You could have used the lump in my throat to priest a whale.

'Look,' I said. 'When we get back, you and I need to talk. There's a lot I want to say about us and what the future might hold. What I mean is, Nuo...'

She put a finger to my lips to shut me up before I made a complete ass of myself, and then she kissed me as if she meant it, pressing her warm body against mine. I shut my eyes and took her in my arms. At a sudden sound we leapt apart. My eyes flew open to find the Preacher standing in the doorway with a knapsack in either hand. He looked a touch apologetic, but that half-moon grin was plain on his face.

'You young people say the word and I'd be right proud to perform the rites, but just now we've got places we need to be. Nathan, if you're ready to take the first step on the stony path.'

Nuo stepped towards him, her voice tight with misery, as if her throat was being squeezed by a fist.

'You bring Nathan back or I'll never forgive you!'

'Nuo, trust me, I'd never forgive myself.'

I took my knapsack from his hand and we walked to the street door, but I couldn't just walk away, not like that. I put the sack on the floor and quickly strode back to her, taking her in my arms once more.

'I love you,' I said. 'I love you and I'll come back to you.'

She kissed me, another of those brief electric touches of the lips.

'You'd better, Mr Nathan Whittaker! You better, or I'll marry Junjie instead!'

The battered old man was out of his bed and had been standing in the hallway ready to see us off and wish us good luck. He laughed aloud at what Nuo had said, laughed until he was interrupted by a spasm of hacking coughs. He wiped tears from his eyes. 'Can I have that in writing?' He grinned, 'I'll keep her to that.'

[23]

The trail from Shuhe and Songun Village to the Upper reaches of the Tiger Leaping Gorge, where our hunt would start, would take us some fifty miles to the north. I estimated our journey would take between six to eight days of hard marching. It would be a long journey before we could even start our worm hunt.

Junjie had told us it took at least another three days to follow the gorge along the Jinsha River from the cliff-sided heights of the upper gorge to the lower levels and a place called Walnut Grove.

The weather was favourable, clean, fresh water was plentiful, and the landscape was beautiful in the morning sunshine. Early mists made everything look like a silk painting drawn by a master; trees and mountains stood subtle as ink stains against the pearl light. I would have walked in rapture if I hadn't believed in my heart that I was marching to an appointment with certain death. And if I hadn't just left the woman I loved back at the mission house, convinced I would never see her again.

Less than an hour later we had left even the meanest footpath behind us and were reduced to following the faint traces of animal trails across the densely forested, steep and rocky terrain. Below us we could see terraced fields following the line of meandering streams and climbing the slops into the highlands. In China every place food could be harvested was used, even if the farmers had to climb like goats to get to their crops.

The sunlight strengthened as the shadows shortened and we maintained a steady pace. The air was still and warm. All was silent except the stridulating chirrup of insects, fluting birdsong, and the scrabbling sounds of small creatures disturbed by our approach. I noticed that the Preacher kept looking back over his shoulder as if searching for something. I shielded my eyes and gazed south. Then I turned to him.

'Are we expecting company?'

'No, Nathan. But we *are* known to be Christians and we're out in the open, and that makes us prime targets. I wouldn't be at all surprised if the mission house had been kept under surveillance and we picked up a tail before we left the village.'

'Then what should we do?'

'Be aware and be vigilant. Our mission is essential, and we can't afford for anyone to get in our way. We must get to Tiger Leaping Gorge and I'll allow no-one to stop us, no matter what it takes.'

He opened his coat and pulled out the assassin's Navy Colt revolver. He handed it to me butt first.

'I know you know how to use this. It's fully loaded.' He pulled out a heavy pouch and put it in my fist. 'There are your spare shells. Don't shoot yourself and don't shoot me, but if anyone runs at us with a knife put him down quick as you can. Don't aim to injure, we don't have the time. Stop them, put them down. Finish it as quickly as possible. Understood?'

I nodded. Preacher had developed a desperate air I hadn't noticed before, as if he had become deeply frustrated with the petty dealings of men and had much bigger fish to fry. If the gangs were on our trail I felt sorry for them. The fight would be loaded against them, or so I thought. Knives and cleavers provide little defence when up against one of Samuel Colt's finest in the hands of a capable man. We had proved that down by the river.

Even so I placed the pistol in one pocket and the shells in the other with a sense of foreboding. If the Preacher thought I should carry a gun he must be confident I'd need to use it. Some men are happy around guns, they thrive on a diet of weapons and warfare, but I believe most are like me – we'd rather not need them.

My soldier boy father told me I have a natural talent with the things. Rifle or pistol I can shoot fast and straight. He said it must be something I inherited from him. I don't know about that, he put a gun in my hand as soon as I could stand straight and squint down a sight. I learned to squeeze the trigger not pull it or jerk at it, and to aim a little low to allow for the buck of the barrel. I'd put that assassin's gun to good use if I had to – but I'd rather not if I had the choice.

Preacher looked down and smiled. 'Hello, old friend.'

I swear that midnight hound of his must step clean out of mid-air. One second, we were alone just above the tree-line on the outskirts of northern Shuhe and the next that powerful beast was gliding between us. Preacher ran his fingers through the silky pelt between its ears and it responded with a low huffing growl that I felt in my gut. Preacher looked back towards the treeline and stood tall.

He shouted, 'Nathan, get ready.'

They came at us in a flat run. Six of them; five armed with wicked looking curved swords and the last with a rifle that he started firing from the hip as soon as he was clear of the trees. Preacher shot him before I could get my pistol clear of my pocket, the hammer had caught in the fabric of my coat, so I had to use both hands to drag it out into the open.

Our attackers only had to cover just under one hundred yards of open ground once they made their move. They would be on us in seconds. I cocked my pistol, aimed, and fired three times in a single sweep. The third man was thrown backwards to the ground when he was hit by two bullets simultaneously, mine and the Preacher's. His chest spurted blood and he must have been dead before he landed.

We reloaded before we approached the bodies. Five of them had been clean shots, instantly fatal, but one of the Preacher's targets was still breathing. He was on his knees, frozen in fear, and gazing in mute dread at Preacher's dog which had his wrist clamped in its massive jaws.

He inched his other hand towards his sword and the hound growled a warning, curling back its lips to show its wicked array of creamy teeth. The Preacher reached the pair with me at his heel. He leaned down and took the sword by the hilt then studied it with care before throwing it into the shrub. He cocked his pistol and thrust it into the unarmed man's face.

The attacker was bleeding from a gut wound. Blood soaked his tunic and he held his free hand against his belly, but all his attention was on the barrel of the Preacher's gun held rock steady just inches from his nose. His eyes crossed trying to see if Preacher's finger would tighten on the trigger. Then the Preacher began to talk, his voice low, flat and dangerous. I didn't recognise the dialect but whatever it was it shook the injured man to the core.

He had already been pale due to shock and loss of blood but when he heard what the Preacher had to say he turned white as a ghost and his mouth twisted into a rictus grin that held no humour in it. I almost felt sorry for the poor wretch, but then he had come running at us with that sword, so I guess he only had himself to blame for his sorry position.

Preacher continued his inquisition. His dog had released the man's arm and moved away behind us. The man placed his left hand on the ground and leaned against it. I remained entirely focused on the deadly tableau before me. Preacher kept talking and slowly cocked his weapon. His captive looked around wildly at his companions. Their corpses were already attracting flies, Nature never could resist a free feast and we had provided an ample bounty.

The report of Preacher's pistol shattered the peace and I jumped. His captive's little finger vanished from the hand on the ground and only the bloody knuckle remained. The action had been so fast that the gun seemed to merely flicker for a heartbeat and then return to the shrieking man's face. Preacher pressed the hot barrel against his captive's forehead and pulled back the hammer once more.

The man was whimpering, nursing his injured hand in his other fist, clutching it against his bleeding stomach wound. All colour had drained from his face. I thought he must faint from shock. Preacher growled another question at him in that odd dialect and prodded his head hard with the barrel of his gun.

The man began talking. A torrent of words spewed out of him, some of which sounded like pleading, some curses, and while Preacher listened his eyes glared.

I found this cold, cruel aspect of my employer's personality shockingly disturbing. More than once I had seen him kill in self-defence and I knew him to be a capable fighter. But this harrowing torture of an unarmed, injured captive seemed at odds with the kind-hearted soul who had been so angry over Nuo's crippled feet, and so concerned about Junjie's injuries.

Perhaps this inhuman facet of him was where the more traditional concepts of a brutal, wicked Satan had originated. I saw him in a new light and could not be sure what had been disclosed; or who. The captive had finished his confession with a coughing fit and a gurgling spatter of blood. His eyes were glazed, and his face became dull and slack. All humanity was draining from him, his clothes sodden with gore.

Satan Spindrift, the Preacher, holstered his pistol and reached into his long coat. He extracted a slender metal cylinder and unscrewed the top before handing it to the man. He said something in a gentle tone and the man answered gratefully, grabbing the cylinder and taking its contents down in one gulp. It fell from his nerveless fingers when he slumped bonelessly to the ground, dead.

Satan picked up the cylinder, carefully screwed the top back on, and then replaced it in his coat. He stood and looked down at the fresh corpse and then across at me, his eyes bleak as midwinter. And then he cast his gaze over my shoulder and grinned as if Christmas had come early and all his wishes had been granted at once. I turned to see what he was looking at.

The black hound was nowhere to be seen, but in its place, I saw a big bay mare that was one of the most beautiful examples of horseflesh I had ever clapped eyes on. She was magnificent. She was also fully saddled and already had our sacks and bedrolls across her back. I looked around in confusion.

Where had she come from? I hadn't heard her canter up, but then, what with everything going on between Satan and his captive an entire brigade of cavalry blowing trumpets could have galloped up behind our backs and I wouldn't have known.

Satan approached her with his arms open in greeting. "My beautiful friend, you are a blessed sight for sore eyes this day.'

He stroked and patted her muscular neck, and then turned to me with joy on his face. 'Nathan, we shall ride to the gorge in style.' He regarded our victims. 'And the sooner we put this sorry place behind us, the happier I shall be.'

[24]

The horse was strong, sure-footed, and carried both of us easily. We set off at a good lick. Satan, for – after witnessing his cruel treatment of his captive – that was the way I now thought of him, favoured a big western saddle. At least that was how this mystery horse was equipped.

I had to straddle the mare the best I could. I was tucked behind Satan, lodged between the horse's back and her croup. To stop myself bouncing off I was pressed up against the saddle's cantle with my hands gripped tight to its Cheyenne roll and my back firm against our bedrolls.

I was not much of a rider and had little technique. I just pressed my thighs and knees to the horse's sides as firmly as I could and hung on. My muscles were unused to such work and soon began to ache from the strain. I began to think it would likely prove a long, and very arduous, fifty miles, but at least on horseback we would reach our destination that much sooner.

We rode in silence. To my shame I bit back my concerns about the way Satan had casually shot away the injured man's finger. He had done so in the same callous way a child would snap a twig from a tree. I had been deeply disturbed and felt my world view tilt away to a much darker place. I thought I had come to know the man, damn it! I'd respected him and come to like him. I couldn't imagine the Preacher would do something like that. But Satan could. Satan had.

It was around midday when we finally stopped to stretch our legs and grab a bite from our supplies. I could taste the fresh tang of snowmelt on my tongue when I took a long draught from my freshly filled water bottle, but it did little to alleviate the tightness in my belly and throat. I had found Satan's actions too tough to swallow and was in danger of choking on them.

I felt his eyes on me and turned to face him. He looked relaxed, seated in the shade on a flat rock by the side of a tall hill. I was only too pleased to stand. The ride had put a severe strain on most of my more delicate nether regions, to the point where I was seriously considering forgetting the horse and walking a few miles to loosen up.

Truth to tell my posture as a rider and the back and forth rocking motion of the horse's gait had gone a long way towards forcing my genitals into my back pockets. I was worried that just a few more miles on horseback might put a big question mark against my ability to father a child in the future, if the opportunity ever arose.

Satan's face was expressionless. He cocked his head as if expecting me to ask him a question, but he remained silent. His mute invitation rang loudly in the still air and, in the end, I filled the pregnant moment with hot words.

'How could you shoot that man's finger off like that? What kind of barbarian are you? I thought you were a good man, but now I don't now *what* to make of you. Maybe I'm not the right man for this job, maybe I'm not bloodthirsty enough. If that's the case I can walk back to the village from here and leave you to it. What do you say?'

'Nathan,' he said, coolly, 'your bluntness and honesty does you credit. I truly appreciate your candour. Most men would rather bite their tongue than flap it at their boss like that. No matter, I guess we've put enough distance between ourselves and our attackers that I can risk a few minutes to offer you the explanation you deserve. May I start with what happened to that killer's finger?'

He lifted his own left hand, his gun hand, and looked at it grimly. He took the tip of the little finger between the thumb and forefinger of his right hand and waggled it thoughtfully.

'Fact is, I didn't shoot it off, it was already gone. That fellow would have cut it off himself to demonstrate his loyalty to his gang bosses; all men of his kind are missing that finger as a mark of honour. I thought you might have noticed when we studied the bodies.

'The men by the river were the same. I've had my suspicions ever since we were attacked yesterday and that man this morning confirmed everything I suspected. By the way we're not dealing with Chinese Triads or Boxers, this gang is Japanese. They are the gokudo, and they're as lethal a band as ever walked the Earth.'

'Wait,' I said, too stubborn to accept everything without question. 'Wait, that man's knuckle, it was bleeding where you'd shot it, why was that if his finger was already gone?'

He smiled and shrugged. 'It must've been scraped by rock fragments thrown out by my shell. I deliberately fired at his hand to let him know that *I* knew who, and what, he was. And I had to act tough to make him believe that I meant my threats otherwise he would have happily died without telling me anything.

'The gokudo are more afraid of losing face than they're afraid of death; and providing me with answers would have meant a major loss of face. They're also known as yakuza, and they call themselves ninkyo dantai, which means the "fearless organisation" and they have spread like a cancer all over the globe.'

He picked up a stone and threw it, hard. 'If it's criminal and there's money to be made the gokudo want a share of it, and woe betide anyone who gets in their way. This particular gang were running pubescent girls in Lijiang, what they call "comfort women". A vile mixture of slavery and prostitution.

'The innocent mission Fathers blindly set up an initiative to save the fallen women and set them back on the path to righteousness, and it was proving effective. The problem is the Fathers didn't know what they were dealing with and the girls weren't talking. They wanted to be saved and didn't want to scare their saviours away.'

He chuckled, a strange light in his eyes. 'The Fathers could not be allowed to continue their good work, the gokudo had to stop them – using brute force if they needed to – or lose their precious face. They moved to wipe them out, but the mission Fathers had already disappeared, as we know. The poor devils had met the Sha-aneer, a fate much worse than anything the cruellest gokudo could have imagined.

'But the gangsters still wanted their revenge against the western church and its interfering clerics. Someone must pay, and I became the prime target as soon as I arrived. I'm afraid, Nathan, that you also became a target as soon as I met you on Square Street, and the pair of us have been drawing hostile fire ever since.'

I was trying to imagine what it would take to make me slice my own finger off. My imagination supplied me with a ghost sensation of sharp agony that made me shudder. I had once slashed a fingertip on a sheet of paper and that stung like the devil. And I had cut my thumb while slicing a lime, that brought tears to my eyes in front of a bunch of hard as nails merchant seamen. Not one of them mocked me, they knew what it was like.

'I'm sorry,' I said. 'I should never have doubted you. Please, forgive me. I'll still go back if you like. I've been a fool.'

'No, you've been an honest witness. I would rather hear an honest opinion than suffer a two-faced liar who says one thing but thinks another. Thomas doubted the Lord, but he was still a saint last time I looked. You'll do for me, Nathaniel Whittaker. You'll do fine. Come on, mount up, we've a distance to travel before we settle for the evening.'

By the time we camped that night we were nearly halfway to the gorge and I was a long way towards becoming a eunuch. I was limping tender as a cat on hot coals and I couldn't bring my thighs together when I walked. I was a sorry specimen. The Preacher couldn't ignore my discomfiture for long.

'You suffering a little there, Nathan?'

What could I say without sounding like a whining baby? 'I'm fine thanks, Preacher. Just a little raw after the ride. I've never had much practice on a horse and I couldn't find a comfortable seat. I'll be fine.'

All the while I was talking I was hobbling around like an old woman with bound feet and a severe case of haemorrhoids. Trying to pull the wool over the eyes of a medical man like the Preacher is a thankless task. I saw that half-moon grin of his glinting in the gathering gloom and he shook his dark head at me.

'Okay. I want you to do something for me.' He reached into his coat and pulled out one of those silver cylinders while he spoke. 'I want you to drink this...' he unscrewed the cap, '...and then strip off your pants and shoes. Heck, take a towel with you and get naked.

'There's a stream over there screened by those bushes. Get what pains you down into that cold water and it will help reduce the swelling. It should be right refreshing too. I'll get supper started and we'll eat when you feel more comfortable. How does that sound?'

I was ready to try anything. The thought of facing a night on the hard ground in my delicate state was daunting, and he would want me up on that steed again in the morning. I dug a towel from my sack and held my hand out for the cylinder. Then I hesitated before bringing it to my lips. In my mind's eye I saw the injured man that morning. He had sipped from a cylinder just like this before instantly crashing to the ground as a corpse.

Preacher raised a quizzical brow. He chuckled, 'I can read you like a map, Nathan. I like a doubting man, but you suit me all too well. Yes, that is the same brew I gave that injured assassin this morning, and yes, he died. He was already dying. I gave him something to ease his pain, helped him pass peacefully. That's an analgesic tonic that should help make you feel a mite more comfortable, but the choice is yours.'

He reached out for the cylinder, but I was already draining its contents. I handed it back to him empty. He screwed the cap on and I hobbled down to the stream. I was already feeling better when I rounded the shrub and started to strip away my clothes. A cool breeze coming up from the fast-moving water made the hair on my body stand on end, but it couldn't mask the sense of well-being spreading through me.

I quickly lowered myself into the stream and instantly began panting as its freezing shock took the air from my lungs. That water was pure snowmelt and we were near its source. I juddered like a newborn in a basin while my body tried to compensate for the arctic drop in temperature.

And then something wonderful happened. Warmth bloomed through me, and while the surface of my skin tingled with cold the rest of me was bathed in bliss.

When I finally emerged from the stream I was ready for anything. I had never felt so well. I think I literally glowed with health and my injuries from the ride had subsided to a slight heat in my privates. I towelled myself dry and dressed quickly. I was famished and looking forward to my meal.

I rounded the shrub and saw the Preacher had got a fire going. By it's light I could see he was talking with two figures. Even from that distance I could see they weren't human. I checked my pistol was still in my pocket and walked slowly towards them.

[25]

I was reminded of the clockwork figures I'd seen at funfairs and carnivals; automatons they were called. They could perform like living creatures and I had seem some wonders, including a band of frogs playing ragtime, Alice at the Mad Hatter's tea party complete with a dormouse in the teapot, and a huge fat man eating a table full of pies – and I mean the whole table. In one bite. The table would reappear through a door to one side and he would gobble the whole thing down once more.

Those creatures with Preacher were just as fantastic, but they moved smooth as silk. The automatons had a jerkiness to them that told you they were just clever animated puppets filled with cogs and strings; these things were real, no matter how improbable. They were tall and wore robes made from a material like finely woven precious metals. Their faces looked like beautiful masks cast from liquid mercury and their heads glowed with a multi-coloured nimbus of light.

One of them was holding something out to the Preacher. Whatever it was he wanted none of it. It looked like a cap of shimmering lace and seemed harmless enough to me, but Preacher wouldn't touch it. When he spotted me approaching with my fist in my gun pocket he put a hand up to me. The tall creatures turned, and when they saw me they reacted as if a wolf had turned up in church on a Sunday. They fired out a stream of musical sounding gibberish and waved their arms as if trying to shoo me away.

I said, 'Do you need a hand with these strangers, Preacher?'

He smiled and shook his head. 'Stay away from them, Nathan. They're nothing to do with you and they're just leaving. Wait there a moment.'

He spoke to them in their own language, a liquid stream of birdsong. The one with the thing in his hand held it out again. I swear it looked like he was offering Preacher his handkerchief. That it was much more than that was proven when Preacher drew his gun and threatened to blow the creature's hand off. It slumped away from him, its back and shoulders bowed as if under a terrible weight. It was a picture of despair.

The other robed figure said something brief. Despite its musical nature I could tell it wasn't too complimentary. It swivelled in my direction, looked hard at me, and shook its head. Its eyes glowed hot with anger. I was getting the blame for something and I didn't know what it was. I shrugged, it wasn't the first time, and I knew it wouldn't be the last.

I believe the second creature was attempting to stomp away in a fury, but at best it achieved a piqued looking, elegant glide. It was a fine apparition and I wondered if it was a side-effect of the Preacher's tonic. I knew about drug induced phantoms. I had never taken opium, but I have woken at night in a heavily drug fogged room and seen strange things in the darkness, things I couldn't clearly recall come the morning.

'Preacher, what did I just see? Were those things really here? What were they?'

He took a deep breath and shut his eyes. For a terrible moment all the fire drained from his body and he slumped. His knees buckled slightly, and his pistol hung from his hand as if it was too heavy for his nerveless fingers. His face crumpled, and he looked inexpressibly tired and old. I thought he would collapse with exhaustion. I didn't give myself time to think, I ran to his side and reached up to put my arms around his shoulders.

I hugged him as hard as I could; it was the first time I had ever done so to a man. But if ever a man looked like he needed a hug from me it was the Preacher at that moment. He sighed, and it was a sound of profound grief, then he excused himself and pulled away slightly, so he could draw his handkerchief from his pocket. He blew his nose and dabbed at his eyes, then he smiled at me.

'You are as subtle a vessel as I have ever met and filled with surprises, Nathan. You're a true gift from God. I'm proud to know you, mighty proud. Now, please, forgive me that demonstration of weakness, my spine has been drawn thin over too many years and I'm tired. Let's forget it and eat before supper's ruined and I'll tell you what just happened.'

While we ate he told me how those creatures of light were his people, angels from Heaven. They were two of the crew of the Eden ship called the General Organism Development System or GODS which had been despatched to Earth millions of years ago and was now parked somewhere out beyond the orbit of Mars, a globe of anonymous black rock tumbling amongst the asteroids.

And at the ship's heart was a beautiful garden that was a perfect example of all that remained of the planet called Eden. It had been Preacher's home and they called it Heaven.

He said he had closely resembled the crewmen before his fall from grace. He had been one of them until he was brought down by pride. He explained how he had foolishly allowed himself to be worshipped as a god by the very people he had been put on this Earth to serve – us.

We are the Eden born, he said, and to nurture and guide our development was the only reason for his existence, but that evening he had discovered how completely things had changed.

'I am the last of us here on Earth, my fellows have been destroyed by the worm. They were called Baphomet and Asmodeus and they too were Preachers amongst the Eden born. The angels you saw were Michael and Barachiel. It was Michael who diminished me into this form and set me on my path as a humble guide and servant to mankind.

'We didn't know about the Sha-aneer back then. The worm first attacked when humankind had proliferated across the face of the planet, but it quickly developed a taste for your flesh – and your souls.

'You humans are unique on this world. You alone have the same immortal souls that blessed the people of Eden and brought them closer to God. That was before they, their world, and even their sun was destroyed by an unstoppable force of nature they called a black hole.

'We received their last messages of farewell and hope for our success, but the airwaves have been silent for long millennia. A noble race has been lost to the universe, and the stars themselves should weep.'

While he spoke, I felt a strange sensation building inside me, as if something immense was standing nearby and pulling me towards it. If I had been standing I would surely have tumbled to the ground. I felt faint and my eyesight blurred, I had forgotten to breathe. My bowl of stew slipped out of my grip and fell to one side. I began to choke.

It was the Preacher's turn to support me. I felt his hands on my shoulders and he held me close against his chest. His words were little more than a mumble to my ears, a gentle clatter of nonsense sounds. I was away from him for a minute or two, I think I was out of my body and hovering above us like a bird. I could see me bowed by the fireside. I was crumpled in the embrace of something I didn't recognise. It was huge! I looked like a child in its arms.

The figure holding me was man-shaped but dark as a storm cloud and shot through with ruby light. Its eyes burned like pools of liquid fire and its head was crowned with a nimbus of purple light. It was the pure embodiment of power, and it was charged with a stark energy that made me seem puny and shrivelled in its grip. I looked like a drowned kitten in its hands, and yet for all its strength I pitied it.

My spirit tumbled back into my flesh and with a shudder I opened my eyes once more. The Preacher's dark face was close to mine and I saw fear written there, fear of losing me to something beyond his powers to cure.

'I saw you,' I gasped. 'I saw you; I saw who you really are, what you are. My God, I can understand why you were worshipped, you are like a god. Why do you hide your light behind that human mask?'

That sense of an immense presence threatened to overwhelm me once more as the Preacher's burning eyes came close to mine. I saw the fires banked in their dark depths and a great weight of sadness that no mortal heart could withstand.

I felt Preacher's immense strength, felt his power, but also the loneliness of too many years not only spent watching and fighting a mortal enemy like the Sha-aneer, but also knowing, loving, and losing the short-lived creatures he had vowed to defend. How many of us had been his companions over the years? Did he think of us as friends or pets he had come to care deeply about?

I pressed my hand to his cheek. 'You poor, damned soul,' I said, my voice choked. 'What has been done to you? You've lost so much; will you never get it back? Are you condemned to rot here with us forever?'

My sense of where I was tilted once more when the Preacher stood, rose to his full height, and gazed up towards the stars. I experienced a powerful feeling of vertigo and clutched at the ground to stop myself sliding into the abyss. And then it was over, and my world returned to what I call normal.

'You saw them, Nathan, they let you see them. They no longer cared about remaining hidden from human eyes. My fellow crewmen came here this evening to offer me transport home, at a price. If I had said yes, we would have been gone by the time you returned from the stream and you would never have seen me again. You, the Eden born, would have been left alone to face the wise worm of the deep earth, you would have been abandoned to the Sha-aneer.'

[26]

The GODS craft was leaving our solar system for good. The angels of heaven had surrendered us to our fate and were travelling to another, more promising star, and a population that had evolved beyond bloodshed and hate. War, wickedness, and the worm, were the three things that had made our creators abandon us in shame. We had driven them away.

His crew had come to Satan Spindrift one last time to offer him a place on the last transport to his spaceship home before it departed, but only if he agreed to have his personality wiped. That silver lace he had been offered was a device called a neuro-net – and it was the dreadful price he would have to pay the ferryman to take him home.

'I have been amongst men for more than eight million years,' he explained, 'and my fellows believed I had become contaminated by the cruelty of humanity. I suffer, they said, from an "excess of personality". They reminded me that the last time I had met with my kind I had shot one of them, which is true.

'If I had placed that neuro-net on my head it would have cleansed me of everything that makes me Satan and I would have become Lucifer, the shining star, once more. Everything I have become since arriving here so long ago, the memories of a long lifetime, would have been erased. What remained would have been an eager servant of the GODS, and happy to abandon humankind to its just desserts.'

Sitting on our bedrolls we ate the stew he had cooked, our camp high in the Chinese mountains, our faces warmed by his fire. The landscape of rock, trees and snow-covered peaks was lost to the night, as was the world I knew. I had become completely immersed in his story.

The star born creatures he called his fellow crewmembers had been created for one purpose, to impregnate the most promising species on their chosen planets and nurture the results while they evolved into the chosen race. The Eden born.

But, we had failed them. Even without the Sha-aneer to contend with we had spent the last several thousand years of thinking up bigger and better ways to enslave, torture, maim and kill each other. The interminable war in Europe had festered its way across the world and taken the flower of youth with it. For GODS' angels it proved the last straw.

Elsewhere the spirit of Eden had been reclaimed and burgeoned into great civilisations inhabited by wise people who understood the importance of love and compassion. They had worked together to match the heights of Eden itself, and then outstripped them in the sciences and the arts. GODS' angels walked among the populace and worked with them to create wonders.

Not one of those planets had developed cannon, bombs, machine guns, or rifles. They were not divided by ideas but united by them, and they used the riches of their worlds to build great craft in which they could explore their star systems and learn more about the secrets that defined our universe.

Preacher's eyes sparkled with starlight while he spoke. His voice was filled with awe. 'They have invested their energy in combatting disease, famine, and ignorance instead of each other. Imagine what great things humankind could have achieved if you had done the same.

'But no, right now the resources of great countries are being squandered while hundreds of thousands of brave young men are lining up to kill hundreds of thousands of other brave young men. Old men study maps to decide where their troops must go, and scientists invent bigger and better ways for the young men to blast each other to smithereens. Earth is seen as the diseased relative among the Eden born, deranged and dangerous, a psychopathic world.'

Not for the first time I had to ask him to explain a word. What was psychopathic? When he told me, I explained that the word had been around for a while, but we called it 'evil'. He shook his dark head at that.

'To call something evil you have to accept that it knows what it's doing is wrong and enjoys inflicting pain and misery. Humanity isn't aware that war is wrong, if it was it might stop fighting long enough to talk it through and find a better way. Both sides in any conflict believe they're fighting for the common good and that the price is worth paying; they believe winning is worth dying for; and to justify it they paint the enemy as sub-human monsters. They even believe in a 'Just' war.

'Civilisations come and go on this planet like waves on a beach, they ebb and flow, rise and fall. But war sets barriers in the sand and one day the tide will go out and never return. Then, when the dust of conflict finally clears, there will just be an empty beach under a careless sky, and the sun shining down on the vanishing footprints of a long and best forgotten people.'

Then he pointed at me with his spoon. 'But then there are people like you, and Nuo, and Junjie, and Caleb Sawyer. Fine people who reflect everything that mattered most about Eden. *You* are worth fighting the worm for, *you* are worth standing shoulder to shoulder with and making the effort. You are worth forfeiting heaven for and remaining on this crazed lunatic of a world long enough to give you good people a chance to make a difference.

'Who knows, perhaps you madmen on this ball of insane rock are even worth dying for. Ha, listen to me. Who knows? Perhaps my people are right, and I have gone native after all! Here's to an excess of personality and all the shit that goes with it.'

We toasted each other with some strong clear spirit he kept in a flask and then settled down for the night. Before sleeping I thought about everything he had told me, and finally I drifted off to dream about brave new worlds where people lived in harmony with each other and the sun shone down on a heaven on Earth.

Then I dreamed of an empty beach under the Preacher's careless sky, and I watched while an errant breeze erased the last traces of life on a dead world. It was a bleak scene and I awoke shivering in my warm bedroll. What kind of legacy were we leaving for our children?

I awoke with the dawn to find my face dripping with icy dew and the rich smell of brewing coffee on the air. I scrambled behind a nearby tree and relieved myself of a heavy belly and a straining bladder, cleaning myself with some conveniently large and soft leaves. Preacher had put out a bowl of fresh warm water and white soap for our ablutions and I blessed him for bringing civilisation into the wilderness. He was a good man to share the miles with.

He welcomed me to the new day with an enamel mug of good coffee and a steak sandwich. I asked where the food was coming from and he told me his horse was a good provider with deep saddlebags. I made a point of thanking the horse for her generosity. What a wonderful creature.

The Preacher had fully recovered his spirits after our dour conversation of the night before, and once more he displayed all the energy and resolve I had come to expect from him. His half-moon grin shone frequently, and he seemed excited to be on our way once more. He showed me how to make my seat on his horse a little less arduous. I climbed onto the patient bay's back and practiced the gentle bobbing motion he recommended while he broke camp and cleared away the evidence of our fire.

The sun quickly burned away the mist and we set off towards the gorge, riding through another fine morning and a glorious landscape. I asked Preacher if he had ever been to London and he admitted he had, but not for a long while. I asked him what that meant in his terms, were there people there then or monkeys?

He laughed easily and said, 'Romans. They were a complex people. Very structured order at the beginning, but the people in charge had lost any sense of decency and order by the time they got to Londinium. Nathan, it took me years to get the stink of what they called fish sauce out of my nostrils. They were addicted to the stuff!

'They put it on everything savoury. You have no idea what fish sauce did to the taste of a fresh fried egg. It took a strong stomach to try it, but it was alright once you got past the smell of fermented fish guts. Garum they called it, and they cooked with it and used it as a relish. I can still remember it now.'

He shuddered, and his horse turned its head to look at him. 'Say what you like, you weren't there. The Britons were good with boiled pork but if you wanted something different you had to go Roman or starve, and that meant fish sauce. Nathan, have you ever drunk heather beer?'

'No, is it good?'

'I think it's gone out of fashion and I'm not surprised. Terrible stuff. Roman wine was like sharp vinegar, but British beer was worse. I do hope things have improved in old Albion.'

We continued in this vein, bantering like madmen on a jamboree, the horse sometimes nickering as if it understood the joke and was joining in with our laughter. In this fashion we made our way to the uplands of Tiger Leaping Gorge. That evening we camped with the sound of the Jinsha River in our ears.

Preacher's humour turned dark. 'We'd best get as much rest as we can tonight,' he told me. 'Tomorrow we hunt a dragon and a worm. I think if we find one we'll find the other.' He sniffed the air. 'No trace of it here, but then it's deep. It's very deep. And it's waiting for us.'

[27]

The next morning, we awoke to the sound of the river surging through the rock-littered gorge far below us, but we couldn't see it. We couldn't see anything. The mist was so thick it was as if we had been enveloped in a cocoon of wet cotton. We couldn't start our search until the mist lifted so we drank coffee and breakfasted after performing our toilet and washing – thoroughly.

Preacher had what he described as a 'burr under his saddle' for cleanliness, especially around food. I was grateful for his advice on the subject. I had experienced a few sour stomachs during my travels and wanted no more of them.

'Pears or Peets it makes no never mind, soap is your very good friend. Keep your hands properly clean and your bowels will thank you for it every day of your life. Contagion hides on every surface, on raw meat, and in your own bodily functions. Keep that in mind, Nathan. Stay clean and it may save your life one day.'

That's if the worm doesn't eat me first, I thought. I'd warrant that it had never washed any part of its anatomy, but then, why should it? It swallows men whole, bone, brain, belly and all. I willed the mist to stay put and allow me a little more time to live. The ancient worm could go hungry for a while longer.

Preacher had been studying one of Pallant's notebooks while I was lost in my morbid muse, then he looked across at me with an intense expression on his dark face. He remained silent as if absorbed in thought, and then he nodded with satisfaction. He had evidently come to some important conclusion.

'Nathan, the picture is becoming clearer. Pallant and his fellows could not have met their fate here, it's impossible. They were still recognisably human and in the early mobile stages of the infection when the unfortunate Sikhs apprehended them. This place is much too far from Lijiang to be the site of their infection, it would have taken them too long to get back to the town from here.

'I had begun to believe that their researches brought them to the snarling tiger cave near the Stone Lotus Temple, which is where the host took them – and this notebook says I'm right.'

He held up the slender, leather-bound volume with a look of triumph on his face.

'Pallant the pedant would argue the sun out of the sky in summer; and he has a way of pounding the life out of a phrase until it lies on its back, spent and exhausted. It's enough to make a literate man weep, and even brings a tear to the eyes of a fool like me. But stick with him and you'll find the information you seek buried somewhere on the page, much like a rock covered in bird guano under a nesting colony. You just need to be ready to spot it when it rises up out of the crap.'

He had saved me the task of reading the notebook for myself and wouldn't even quote from the pages 'thanks to the risk of putting our friendship in jeopardy by boring me to tears'.

'It's enough that just one of us need suffer the leaden slings and arrows of this man's English. I'll just cut to the chase.'

In short, Preacher told me that the general was not alone when he died in that cave. He had troops who had formed an honour guard of four men and they had carried the general and the dragon as far back into that cave as they could. They described his final resting place as the secret bowel of the Earth, a deep sinus of sweating rock, lichen, and white, eyeless lizards.

The survivor said it was 'hot as a dragon's mouth and just yards from a stinking midden'. He also said he could hear the voices of the dead in the courts of Diyu, or Hell, the subterranean maze to which they believed souls are taken after death and where they would be tortured to atone for their earthly sins.

Preacher explained that Pallant had gleefully squeezed every ounce of juice out of the subject; describing the exact number of levels in Diyu and how each had its own deity. He had gone into interminable detail regarding the differences between Buddhist and Taoist versions, and how some describe the maze as having three to four Courts while others list the Ten Courts of Hell, each of which is ruled by a judge collectively known as the Ten Yama Kings.

'None of which helps us,' said Preacher, his eyes looking haunted. 'Pallant scrapes together every legend and theory he can find and just dumps them onto his pages like a child collecting every shell on the beach. Legend and speculation is no good to someone looking for clues. I've read more than is healthy about things the ancient Chinese believed should be inflicted on dead souls trapped in the Eighteen Levels of Hell.

'I think the good Father quite enjoyed the idea of the wicked soul being tortured to death and then revived so the nightmare can start all over again. I can almost hear him smacking his lips while he details the gruesome flaying, evisceration, bone breaking torment, and crushing under great weights the hapless soul was forced to undergo. As if any soul is corporeal enough to be tortured like that. It's pure fantasy.'

His eyes blazed, 'But if you shuck away the crap what's left is pure gold. We have a deep cave that stinks like a midden and is filled with voices. Does that remind you of anything? We also have a survivor, just one from four men, who says that his fellows were cut down by arrows fired by demons and that they almost got him too. He was lucky enough to be out of the direct line of fire and ran away in a panic.

'Okay, we know the worm fires quills to paralyse its victims, they could easily be described as arrows. We know it stinks, and we know it speaks in the voices of the host. What we have here is nothing less than the verbatim report of an encounter with the Sha-aneer, and it states that the survivor even left a map showing where the entrance to the cave could be found.'

I gasped, excited to know more. 'Is the map in the book?'

'No, that's just it, it isn't. Says here that the map is carved into the wall of the snarling tiger cave near the Stone Lotus Temple. Pallant and his team had gone there to find it and copy it when they became infected by the host.'

'Wait, are you saying we have to go back after coming all this way? And surely the cave has been wrecked. It was smashed when the other worm died. It blew up!'

'No, we don't have to return. There are other ways.'

At this he flicked a glance at his horse which returned him a guarded stare.

'Nathan, I have an eidetic memory, I remember everything I see down to the finest detail. Right now, I'm remembering what happened to that cave. The ceiling has gone, and the floor blasted out. The rear wall collapsed, and that stream of water spurted out to flood the temple, so you would be justified in thinking the cave is destroyed, but it isn't. The side walls are still there, and that is where people left their carvings and inscriptions.

'I can still clearly see them in my mind's eye. The survivor's map may well still be there amidst all the other carvings and drawings. We just need a better look at those walls, and we need to see them with a very special eye. A very special eye indeed.'

Preacher squinted into the dense mist. 'We're going nowhere in this, too dangerous.' He put the notebook down and stood up. He walked to his horse's shoulder and said something quietly into it's ear. It offered him a rueful glance and nickered appealingly. He shook his head and spoke again. It nodded and settled onto its knees as if preparing to sleep. Preacher strode to me and thrust out his hand, taking mine in a firm shake.

105

'Nathan, while you're with me you'll see things that are best kept quiet. I'm trusting you as a friend and as an honest man. You'll not talk about any of them. Have I your word?'

What passed between us at that moment is hard to describe. At first it was not a sensation so much as an emotion, a feeling of complete trust and wellbeing. I could no more break my word to that man than I would lie to myself. I couldn't put into words what I felt when I nodded and said, 'You have my word, Preacher, on my life.' However, that feeling of vertigo returned and I felt myself poised on the brink of something immense. I shut my eyes.

Light washed through me and burned away petty thoughts and doubts. A sense of calm certainty and rightness took hold of me. It was as if I was Saul of Tarsus on the road to Damascus, blind to the world but seeing truth in the darkness.

I forgot to breathe. Circles and cycles of light cleansed and restored me. I saw them do to my soul what Preacher insisted I do to my hands before touching food, but that light was stronger than any good white soap. When I opened my eyes once more I felt truly blessed. I felt worthy. And then my world spun on its axis like a giant wheel and everything I thought I knew was turned on its head.

The scales had dropped from my eyes and I saw the truth. The man standing before me was still Preacher, I knew that, but with my new eyes he was so much more. For a heart-stopping second, I saw his true nature. I saw Lucifer, light bringer, son of the morning. He shone so brightly in all his glory and my heart pounded in adoration. I was touched by his grace. His skin was like bronze beaten smooth and alloyed with gold, his eyes like windows open to the infinite.

If I had not been seated I swear I would have fallen to my knees before him. I blinked and rubbed my eyes to see him better and it was over. My friend the Preacher called Satan Spindrift was there once more, and his half-moon smile warmed me. His eyes shone with mischief.

'Enough of that, Nathan, enough of that. I need a friend and companion not a worshipper. That's what got me into trouble in the first place. On your feet, man, on your feet. What you saw was nothing, just an echo of Eden. It was merely a shadow of what humankind might one day become if you put down your swords, guns, and hatred, and take up the true adventure, science, exploration, and love.

'And remember my friend, I am a servant of the GODS and a humble gardener here on Earth. You are the seed that flowers and it's you I must protect and nurture until the glorious fruits are ripe and ready for picking. Now, shall we go looking for that map?'

I was still stunned by what I had seen, and my mind whirled for a moment. Why was he talking about maps at this moment of divine revelation? And then I recovered my wits and the mundane mantle of the here and now fell back around my shoulders.

'So, then,' I said. 'How are we going to see the map from here?'

He moved to his horse's side and ran a hand down her sleek neck.

'With the special help of an old friend.'

[28]

The horse glared at him the way a prim woman might glare at a loud, drunken sailor in a church on Sunday. It looked extremely offended. Preacher grinned, patted her, and then sat cross-legged beside her and closed his eyes; his hands lay loose and open in his lap, palms upwards. She too closed her eyes and lowered her long head. They looked as if they were meditating together.

They became utterly still, a frozen tableau against the cool pearl blankness of the mist. The world held its breath. Birdsong and the rustling sounds of small animals ceased. Even the ceaseless roar of the river became muted. It whispered rather than bellowed.

I watched Preacher and his horse in rapt fascination. If they had both floated into the sky like kites on strings I would not have been surprised. They had become the axle around which the world turned, immovable and strong as the rock on which they sat.

The horse's left eye opened. And then it continued opening until the eyeball was fully exposed. It swivelled in its socket to regard me. The muscle holding it in place opened like a dark red flower and the eyeball fell out. The operation was bloodless but still turned my stomach. I saw that the empty eye socket sparkled as if filled with stars before its eyelids closed over the wound once more.

The eyeball hovered in mid-air as if taking its bearings. It drifted purposefully towards me and with a feeling of horror I watched it float closer and closer until it stopped, poised and still, just inches from the flinching flesh of my face. And then, faster than thought, it was gone.

It darted into the mist in the direction of the Old Town. I watched the eddy in the mist that marked its passage until everything was still once more. I swallowed a lump in my throat the size of a baby's head and breathed out explosively.

Preacher and his horse remained unmoving. Both looked relaxed, although the unnatural concavity of the flesh over the horse's eye socket ruined the splendid symmetry of her elegant features. In that mist shrouded place, they looked like creatures of legend, the dark man and his one-eyed horse praying together before setting off on their epic odyssey. And here was I the faithful companion, waiting for instructions.

I waited silently, not knowing what was happening or what I was supposed to do, so I did nothing. I sat and watched events in a detached, dreamlike state. The morning meandered towards midday and the mist began to clear. Soon I could discern details of my surroundings, and slowly the sheer beauty of the Tiger Leaping Gorge became apparent. Preacher had been right, it would have been much too dangerous to go stumbling blindly about.

Literally scant yards behind me was the cliff edge. A careless step over that sheer drop would have sent us plummeting dozens of feet down to the unforgiving, jagged rocks of the Jinsha River. The gorge was not a tame place carved by a placid river, but a sinewy artery riven through living stone. It demanded respect and would punish those who failed to bend the knee.

It was a fitting grave site for a general and his stolen dragon.

Somewhere below us brooded the great worm. The last of its kind – and the first. We must kill it, or it will devour us, the story comes down to that, it is that simple. Tigers once stalked this land and men's fear had seen them all but eradicated. Tigers would never have taken every human from the face of the world. The worm will. We must kill the predator worm, or we will all die.

There was nothing primitive about the Preacher, but his function had become honed and polished over the years until all that remained was the most primitive function of all, he must kill, or we will *all* be killed.

His journey on this planet had been shaped by the worm in the way the stone of the gorge had been shaped by the violence of the river. He had arrived as a gentle husband working towards the future of mankind, he had even described himself as a 'gardener', and yet circumstances had forced him into the role of a cold and efficient killer.

I had seen his true nature. I had seen his light, his brilliance. What had his long quest done to his mind? Which was the truth? The beauty of Lucifer, the wise councillor? Or the exhausted warrior beaten by time until he had been driven beyond his ability to react with mercy? He was a cold killer because that had become his only mission, and nothing could be allowed to stop him.

But what then? I wondered. What happens if he succeeded? We would survive to flourish or destroy ourselves in endless warfare. And Preacher would be trapped here, trapped with our insane breed as an eternal witness to our madness.

Perhaps he would be the last coherent creature standing when the last bomb falls and the last lunatic dies. Would he walk the derelict world and mourn us? Or would he wonder why he had destroyed the worm, just to give us the time we needed to commit suicide.

Thoughts tumbled around in my skull like bees in a hive. The questions were too big for me, the canvas too grand for my art. I was born a simple London boy, but now I found myself an actor on a stage too large for me.

My life had never been about life or death, it was about finding my way to my next meal or the next new landscape. I was never the hero, and I had never met one before. I had only ever met people like me, stumbling through life as if we were lost in a permanent fog.

I raised my eyes to the Preacher and his horse. What brought you to me? I wondered. What strange ray showed you the path to me? And what shackles bind me to your side? How can a creature like you care so deeply for a wasted scrap of flesh like me? And the feelings that welled up in me were so complex that I almost wept. Pity, sorrow, fear, and love confused the few wits I had left. I felt my pulse pound.

And then I remembered his true face and my heart calmed in my chest. I was gripped with an iron resolve not to let him down. I might die but I would never fail him. It was not for me to be great, but for me to support *his* greatness. Like the last pieces of a puzzle my little role in the drama fell into place. I was ready; at least, I hoped I was ready. I gazed across the gorge immersed in thought.

Preacher's voice rang out again and this time I heard it, 'Nathan, can you bring me the notebook and something to write with, please?'

I jolted to my feet. Preacher was still seated motionless on the ground next to his mount. His eyes were tight shut, and his head bowed, but his left hand was held out towards me. I scrambled for the notebook and pressed it into his hand then fetched a pencil from my sack. He thanked me then leafed through the book until he reached blank pages. Without opening his eyes, he began to draw.

The precision of his work was astonishing. I believed I had a passable talent for drawing, but his blind sketching left me cold in the dust. What he was doing and how he was doing it was beyond me; it was like a conjurer's trick. Even as I watched he rapidly filled a page with lines, tone, and shadow that created the facsimile of a stone wall with photographic accuracy.

At first the work seemed much like a brass rubbing, as if every detail had been reproduced with equal importance, but then certain elements became highlighted and stood out from their surroundings.

Carved ridges and lines seemed engraved into the paper and I could see how their contours were time worn and weathered despite spending two thousand years protected in a cave. It was a breathtaking rendering, but I could make neither head not tail of it.

He held the pencil up and I saw that he had worn the point down to the wood. I took my knife and sharpened it for him then handed it back. He continued his draughtsmanship for a few more minutes and then he opened his eyes. He handed me back my pencil with a word of thanks and then we both studied his artwork.

'The map is two thousand years old,' he said. 'But the gorge shouldn't be so very different from when the general was here. Trees have come and gone and maybe landslides and water flow have altered the terrain a little, but the general outline should be the same.

'I think I can see where we are now and hopefully that should help us find the entrance to the cave and lead us to the dragon, the general, and the mother worm. Luckily this place is in a state of nature, if it was a town or a village it could have changed beyond recognition.'

'Where are we on that?' I couldn't see the map he was talking about in the maze of lines and shading he had created. I could see faint Chinese characters, what might have been a lion or a tiger, but nothing like the charts we had used to navigate the oceans. If anything, it looked most like a mass of broken veins on a drunk's nose, some with hatching on them.

The Preacher pointed to a thicker artery on the nose. 'That's the river,' he said. 'The hatching indicates trees. Cartographers in the Han Dynasty were the first to produce maps in the classical style and their work was quite sophisticated, but remember, this was carved from memory by a soldier.

'What's more he was a soldier who had barely escaped with his life and had run away from this area in terror. We have to make allowances, but the broad picture should remain the same.'

He traced the thicker line with his fingertip. 'We need an aerial view that we can compare with this. We can wait a few minutes longer until my good friend's eye returns to her here, or we can call upon her services and send her other eye up straight away. I say the latter, can I rely on you once more, old friend?'

The horse made a sound of utter disgust, but its other eye was soon lost to sight above us and the Preacher was once again deep in blind study. I don't know how he could see through his horse's incredible flying eyes; what talent linked them? And I wondered how he could differentiate between one eye and the other? Surely the information from both would mash together in a confusion of colours and shapes.

The horse looked sick and made a low whimpering noise. Maybe it couldn't sort out the information flooding into its poor mind and was suffering as a result. The Preacher, however, gave a shout of triumph.

'I've got it, I can overlay the map with the true landscape and I can see where the cave is, that's marvellous. The soldier must have had a natural talent for mapmaking, he was astonishingly accurate.'

111

Then his eyes flew open and he leapt to his feet.

'Nathan, get ready. It's a good job we've got our eyes out there. We're about to have visitors and they don't look friendly.'

I was astonished, 'How could they find us? How could they catch us? This is ridiculous! What are those bastards, bloodhounds?'

'They're on ponies – and you're right, they've got hounds with them. While we've been waiting for the mist to clear they've been following our trail and now they've caught up with us.' He closed his eyes and concentrated. 'There's five of them and all of these bastards have rifles,'

I had never heard him so angry. There was no fear in his voice, just fierce irritation.

I said, 'So, what do we do?'

'Do? Those men are like flies around fresh meat. They need to be swatted away before they spoil everything. Something final needs to happen to them, and that right soon.'

'Yes, but what?'

'Me. With your help, we stop it here. We have much more important work to do than waste time swatting flies. Are you with me?'

'What do you need me to do?'

He told me. We didn't have much time. His horse had recovered its eyes and had been sent to hide in the shade of a copse away from the campsite. She was too valuable to risk in a gun battle. I, however, was to be the bait in the trap. I placed my life completely in his hands and sat with my back facing our enemy's direction of approach.

My spine tingled with anticipation. Any moment five bullets could drill into me from five different rifles and I could do nothing except wait and pray the Preacher was as good as I believed him to be.

I had the assassin's pistol ready, cradled in my hands and tucked between my legs, but for all the good it could do me it might as well have been a bottle of beer. In fact, beer might have brought me more comfort. My throat was as dry as the stone I was sitting on.

I tried to distract my unease by watching a spiral of mist rising from the river far below. The sun was bright in the sky once more and when its rays caught the mist they created an elusive rainbow that danced enchantingly in mid-air. Such a pretty thing in a world fraught with danger. A butterfly of light and water.

I remembered that the gorge was named after a tiger that was said to have leapt across it to escape a hunter. A tiger, another thing of great natural beauty. I had never seen a tiger in the wild, but I had seen them in a zoo. The poor creatures looked so wrong prowling in a cramped cage, back and forth, back and forth. They belonged in Blake's 'Forests of the night'; brightly burning examples of God's fearful symmetry.

My grandfather loved William Blake. He had collected books of his work and encouraged me to explore them in his library. He had an illuminated copy of Blake's *The Tyger* framed under glass where he could see it from his desk. The artist had created a beast of legend using line and colour, but I was never too sure about its face. To me it looked much like a striped mastiff.

Even as I pondered T*he Tyger* my ears tried to swivel backwards to better hear the men's stealthy approach. *Then,* I chided myself, *how did I know they would be stealthy?* They might fly at me whooping like banshees. After all there was five of them and just one of me, and to all intents and purposes I was innocent of their approach. And they all had rifles.

Did they need to approach at all? They could ride to the crest and shoot me from several yards away. I wondered how the impact of the bullets would feel. Would I have time to experience pain before they ripped the life from my broken corpse? I shivered at the thought.

If I died now would I travel to the afterlife as the Preacher had promised? I tried to sense the soul that permeated my flesh. Was it shaped like me? Or was it more like the dancing rainbow, a formless spirit thing. Would I still be me? Would I even know my name? Too many questions.

The muscles of my back were corded like wood and ached, but at least the pain told me I was still alive. Would they think me too stiff, sitting so upright on my rock? Would they suspect a trap? Did they know there were two of us and scout around looking for the other man? Would they think he might have gone on, taking his horse with him? Would they just shoot me and leave me to rot in the dust while they continued their search?

It was the Preacher they wanted, not me. But I was all they had, so they might as well make the most of it. 'A single bite of a shared apple is better than no fruit,' my grandfather used to say. He also said, 'A sound education is the best investment any parent can make for a child.'

He made sure I had my letters and paid for me to practice the piano. He indulged my love of art and allowed me the freedom to draw and paint. He would have been horrified to find me seated on a rock like a tethered goat waiting to trap the tiger. What a waste.

Grandfather was a good man and he supported mother and me to the best of his ability. Grandmother had died before I was born, and mother was her only child. Mother had grown up to become the living image of grandmother, and grandfather doted on her, and me when I came along.

There were no recriminations about a child born out of wedlock. A wedding was planned, but the soldier boy was called away to Somaliland and never came back.

Mother died a year later leaving grandfather and me alone. We rubbed along for another two years like shipwrecked survivors clinging together on a raft, and then grandfather discovered that he had squandered his small fortune on sham gold futures. We ended up with nothing but the clothes on our backs and the change in our pockets.

It broke the old man's heart and despair scattered his wits. He died rambling in the poor single room we had been reduced to, paid for with his beloved Blake – which he sold for a pittance.

It was a terrible reversal of fortunes for a good and trusting soul. I hoped the afterlife was treating him better than London had. At least he hadn't lived long enough to see his grandchild used as a tethered goat. I heard a sound behind me and stiffened. Was that the clop of pony's hooves and the clink of a bridle?

My eyes tried to swivel around to see the truth. I wished I had thought to fetch my shaving mirror from my sack. Then I heard it again. Yes, there was a sound. The clash of stones rattling together. I knew I must remain still and look relaxed, but I had begun to shiver and couldn't stop myself. My breath became laboured.

Every instinct I possessed screamed at me to drop to the ground behind my rock and start firing before the bastards could bring their guns to bear. I could hear my pulse pounding so loudly in my ears I was almost deafened by it. *Come on, Preacher,* I howled silently, *why are you waiting? Take them for God's sake.*

Laughter, and the distinct sound of voices. They were no longer trying for stealth. There was only one unsuspecting tethered goat against the five of them, what reason was there for stealth? I could feel their gunsights on me. Easy prey, they would think, easy meat.

For some reason I thought of Nuo. Would she have to marry Junjie if I didn't return from our trek? At least she would be looked after. I liked the old man, but would my lovely girl want to share a bed with him? I thought not.

Was I meant to be deaf or just stupid? Must I ignore the sounds of five men clattering around behind me? Must I act as if I was a block of wood waiting submissively for the axe, or a docile chicken offering its neck to be wrung. Laughter again, triumphant and unpleasant. *Get on with it will you?*

Mother always said I was a patient boy, she told me I had the patience of a saint. On my birthday I would never touch any of my presents until we had enjoyed my cake, and I would carefully unwrap them to save the paper.

Grandfather wrapped them in brown paper and tied them with string. I think everybody got the same paper and the same string on their birthdays. Mother and I would wrap grandfather's presents. *What was I thinking about?*

Patience, patience is a virtue. Wait and be patient, the time will come soon enough. I heard that low snigger again. I hated that laugh, it sounded too self-satisfied and confident about its success. I could imagine the sneer on the men's faces. Look at the stupid goat on his rock just waiting to die. He couldn't even hear them as they almost got close enough to touch him.

Why waste a valuable bullet? They could club me to death, kick me to death, throw me down the cliff into the river and smash me on the rocks. Why waste a bullet? And then I heard the sharp sound of a gun being cocked and I couldn't take any more. I leapt to my feet and turned, my pistol in my shaking fist.

[30]

Shropshire and four of his Sikh troopers put their hands up. The gun I had heard cocked was in the hands of the Preacher who was crouched behind them. Two hounds sat at Shropshire's feet, panting furiously with their long tongues drooping from their open mouths.

The lieutenant waggled his fingers, 'May we put our hands down without getting shot at?' he said. 'It's just that this feels a little ridiculous. All right?'

Preacher holstered his pistol and nodded at me to do the same. I put the assassin's gun into my pocket. My head was light with excitement and my hands were still trembling.

I had come within a hair's breadth of shooting a British officer. I felt my face turn scarlet with embarrassment. What a fool I was, scaring myself witless with an excess of imagination. My palms were sweating and slippery

'Your dogs badly need a drink,' observed Preacher, 'and your ponies need water and a rub down. You've been riding them hard. What's so urgent? I didn't take you as a man to mistreat animals like that.'

Shropshire fired orders at his men who instantly dispersed to attend to their animals' needs. The lieutenant took long strides to Preacher and shook his hand, then turned to me and gave me a thumbs-up. I was regaining my composure by the yard and had managed to tone my shivering down to a mild tingle that was more acceptable to polite company.

I felt able to walk and joined the two men in time to hear Shropshire explaining that a group of men had been murdered just outside Shuhe and that he and his troop had been following the trail of the killers.

'Bit embarrassing, but it brought us straight to your door,' he admitted. 'Expecting black hat desperadoes and find a Christian Father and his ward. Not quite the article, you know what I mean?'

The dogs had been watered by then and sauntered over to me. They sniffed at my trousers and started barking, wagging their tails furiously. Shropshire looked from the dogs to me with raised brows.

'Bugger,' he said. 'They only do that when they've found their prey. Means I have to make this official and ask you both to come back to Lijiang with me. Sorry about that, bloody nuisance I know.'

Preacher gazed at the dogs. 'Animals like Nathan, he attracts them. He has a natural gift for it. A special kind of charisma. I think your animals have fallen under his spell and been diverted from their path. I can see why you might think we're the culprits, but if they had found their "prey" as you put it, wouldn't they be barking at me too?'

'Now you say it, I suppose...'

At that precise moment the Preacher's great black hound flowed towards us. The other dogs stopped barking and turned to face the newcomer. As it grew near they yapped at it and rolled onto their backs, wriggling in the dust like puppies. It was the most blatant display of canine subservience I had ever seen. Preacher's hound rumbled deep from its throat. It ambled to each prone dog and gently licked at its muzzle.

The dogs leapt to their feet and circled the black hound excitedly, with their tails beating like furious pennants and tongues lolling. And then they both stopped, scented the air, and sent up an odd ululation. They scampered away back to the track and the trees that Shropshire and his men had ridden through so recently, and waited there, howling.

Shropshire stood like a stunned bull, his jaw hanging loose and his eyes bulging from his head. His troops had unsaddled the ponies and had been currying them with stiff, short-haired brushes, but they too stood wide-eyed, amazed by the dogs' antics. They turned to their lieutenant.

'Well, by all that's... Well I never.' He pointed at the black hound. 'What did your pet just do to my hunters? Never seen anything like it. Bugger me! What just happened?'

Preacher squinted at the howling dogs. 'Looks to me as if they've picked up their quarry's scent again. Became accustomed to Nathan's magic and got straight back on the job. Good pair of hunters you've got there, Shropshire, fine animals. You must be very proud.'

The Sikhs were already saddling the ponies which had mostly recovered their wind. They were sturdy little creatures but looked as if they would have preferred a bit more pampering rather than a return to the chase. They accepted their saddles with an air of resignation and regarded the animated hunters with an expression of loathing.

Preacher's hound sat quietly, its head tilted to one side. It was a picture of calm innocence. I almost laughed aloud and fought the grin that threatened to smear itself across my features.

Shropshire looked from us to his men to Preacher's hound to his hunters. It was evident he thought something suspicious had just happened, but he didn't know what. He was way out of his depth and couldn't touch bottom. Preacher gave him no time to untangle his skein of thought.

'How far do you think the culprit will have gone while we've been chatting? Must have put a few more miles between you by now. When did the killings take place? The mist here was like a blanket this morning, couldn't see the nose in front of your face. We didn't dare continue our journey or you would have found us gone too.'

It was plain that the lieutenant had questions he wanted answered, but that he also wanted to get back to the chase without delay. He took a few steps towards his men and the ponies, gesturing for them to mount up, then he hesitated and turned back to us.

'I presume we'll be seeing you in Lijiang again before too long?'

Preacher nodded, 'As soon as we've completed our little jaunt.'

'Excellent, then we'll look forward to your company at the compound as soon as you're free. Perhaps then you'll explain how you got this far so quickly on foot. You chaps must run like horses. Good luck with your... jaunt.'

He smiled and shook his head. 'Every time we get together, Preacher, I walk away thinking there's much more to this world than meets the eye; a great deal more in Heaven and Earth, Horatio, than I've dreamt of in my philosophy.

'Except I dread to think of the marvels I'd hear about if we started talking philosophy in earnest. See you soon, father, and you too, Nathan. Safe journey and sweet destinations.'

He climbed easily into his saddle and took the reins, then trotted back to us.

'Funny thing, our killer was on horseback and we only found traces of the one horse. Have you seen or heard anything of a rider during your travels?'

Preacher and I shook our heads. The hound made a strange sound that was something between a growl and a muted chuckle. Shropshire gazed at it.

'Damnedest thing I ever saw.' He raised his voice, 'Right! Come on lads, we've got a horseman to catch.' And then, almost to himself, 'Must have ridden right through here. Hoofprints all over the place and then they stop. Clever bugger, yes, very clever.'

The hunters bounded away with Shropshire and his men in close pursuit. They didn't look back and soon vanished amongst the trees. Preacher stroked his dog with a gentle hand. It closed its eyes and raised its head to his touch.

'Thank you, old friend. You created the perfect distraction.' He turned to me, his half-moon grin in evidence. 'We can't take the horse where we're going, so we can only take what we can carry. I know where the cave is but after that we're working blind.

119

'Let's grab our sacks and get going. I think we want to be elsewhere when Shropshire's hunters run out of a scent and come looking for you again. Let's go kill ourselves a monster.'

[31]

If I had thought our trip to the cave mouth was going to quick and simple I was soon disabused. Preacher explained that, as the crow flies, the cave was quite near, but that one would need to *be* a crow to reach it both quickly and safely. The choice was fast and dangerous or slow but sure; he had opted for slow.

'But wait,' I cavilled, 'you can fly. Why don't you just swoop us straight to it? Surely that's better than humping all this gear for miles?'

He shouldered his heavy sack and helped me adjust mine for greater comfort. While he did so he explained the situation.

'What I do is not so much flying as powered ascent and descent, it lacks nuance. The cave is in a vertical section of cliff about a mile from here and its entrance is both narrow, awkward, and under an overhang. My method of "flying" is too risky for us under those circumstances.

'I'm fine in the open air with a direct line of sight, but I'm likely to smash us into the rocks if I try to navigate our way into the cave from the air. Colin could do it, but not me. We would be better trekking past the cave's position and then making our way back to it along the cliff-face on foot. Safer and surer for both of us, if a little more arduous.'

He patted my shoulder, 'Buck up my young friend, you're as sturdy as a pit pony and just as sure of foot. I have every faith that we'll reach the cave safely, and I'll be with you every step of the way.'

I pointed at the nearby copse. 'Yes, but what about the horse? Are we just going to leave it here?'

Preacher studied the trees then looked at his hound as if expecting to find an answer in its face. If a dog could shrug I believe that one would have done so.

'The horse has gone back where it belongs. When and if we need it, we'll find it again soon enough. It's never very far away.' He took a deep breath. 'You ready for this, Nathan?'

I didn't like the sound of that 'when and if' statement. Just 'when' would have been better. I squinted along the trail. 'Not really, but it's why we're here. Lead on, Preacher.'

With that we started along the safest and surest path to almost certain death; and if it hadn't been for that fact the trek would likely have been immensely enjoyable. The afternoon was pleasantly warm and views from the cliff paths that lined the upper gorge were both beautiful and spectacular.

Our route was wide enough for two men to stand shoulder to shoulder and we conversed as we walked.

'I wonder,' I said, 'that you don't get frustrated and bored with the ideas and opinions of men. You've seen so much and done so much, you must think we're mental pygmies by comparison. But no, you listen to me chatter on as if I'm worth listening to. Surely, I must seem like little more than a smart monkey to you? Come on, Preacher, if you're honest, admit it. We're mental pygmies and you know it.'

'I've met pygmies, very smart people. They thrive in an environment that would kill most people, and they do so in a way that doesn't damage their home forests. Humans are a pleasure or an agony to be with. I try to avoid the agony and I relish the pleasure – but it's not always easy, you're right about that.

'All too often the people in charge are the worst. Humans are bright enough, but many of you are so severely mentally or emotionally damaged that no-one notices any more. Sanity has become the exception instead of the rule. Have you ever read a story called *The Country of the Blind* by Mr H. G. Wells?'

I admitted I hadn't. He pulled a rueful face.

'The tale itself is old, it pre-dates Christ by centuries. The gist of it is that in the country of the blind the one-eyed man would be king. In Wells' story a sighted man stumbles into the country of the blind and tries to put this idea into practice; he plans to become king thanks to his superior vision, but his plan soon backfires.

'Wells has a subtle mind, he sees clearly enough, and so did his protagonist, but the race of blind people had no use for sight – they had grown up without it. They think our hero's talk about this strange sense called "vision" is a form of mania which they attribute to the strange, squishy, orbs he has either side of his nose.'

'His eyes?'

'Precisely. And to save his sanity they propose to remove his eyes, to blind him, and cure him of this crazy illusion called sight. He barely escapes with his life and his vision intact. I see humanity as being much like that blind nation.

'Sometimes – all too rarely – a person can see clearly. They see the truth, and they try to share their vision with those around them. Instead of listening and learning from the visionary their blind fellows turn on them, and, well, history records what happens next.'

I thought back to the gold crucifix around Preacher's neck, and on the wall in his bedroom.

'You're talking about Jesus Christ?'

He nodded, 'Jesus, yes, and John the Baptist, Buddha, Mohammed, Confucius, Abraham , Moses, and many more over the long centuries. And, of course, hopefully, those yet to come. The list is long and has some great names on it. Not all were martyred, of course, some died safely in their beds, but too many were considered enemies of the ruling class and were silenced; sometimes brutally.'

'Were any of them your people?'

'We're hard to kill, and if we made ourselves too noticeable people might wonder why the great teacher never seems to age or die. Methuselah and Noah lived long enough to become noticed. The flood happened in the Mediterranean basin, you know. The great curtain wall that joined Spain and Portugal to Morocco collapsed and let the Atlantic in.

'The early States of Sumer, Mesopotamia, Egypt and Crete had been mentored by the Mediterranean people, they were fabulously advanced for their time. It took civilisation thousands of years to recover what was lost under the waves. I sometimes wonder what might have been achieved by now if that curtain wall had held?'

I chewed this over for a few moments while working to keep up with his long, loping stride. He was inexhaustible, I was not.

'So, you're telling me that Noah and his ark happened? All those animals two by two, the big boat, everything?'

'He wasn't called Noah, his name was Utnapishtim, and the ark was round. But the craft *was* big enough to hold his family and friends plus his flocks. He was an architect and a geologist, and he had an idea of what was going to happen to the great curtain wall.

'It happened over the course of years. The wall was chalk, you see, and the pounding of the waves had been wearing away at it for millions of years. Its fabric was continuously crumbling, like your white cliffs in Dover. Then a seismic shift caused a massive ramp of water several miles wide to pour from the Atlantic into the Mediterranean basin. It wasn't God who warned Utnapishtim of the forthcoming disaster, it was his own clear vision and his sharp mind. He was ready.

'He built the ark round because that was how they built their homes back then – and his idea was to build a safe, seaworthy house with stables where his people could survive the disaster. It was not the best design. His boat spun in the deluge like a top, but it didn't sink. There was a lot of terrible seasickness during the first few days. The boat soon stank of animal dung and vomit.'

'How do you know?'

He grinned at me, 'I've been a shepherd in my time, as well as a king, a preacher and a teacher. I know because I was there. I helped watch the flocks, keep them calm in the storm, and I mentored the little family when we landed on what was the high shoulder of a mountain but had briefly become the coast of a new land. It took a while for the ark to be driven to its place of rest. Do you know what a tsunami is?'

'No, but I guess you're going to tell me.'

He chuckled, 'You'd be right. In Japanese it describes a great wave, or "nami" breaking upon a harbour, "tsu". When the curtain wall was breached it created a tsunami of literally biblical proportions. Countless people were killed in a disaster that entered folk memory and has been recorded in the legends of Gilgamesh in Sumer and Genesis in the Hebrew Bible, the Tanakh.

'It describes an event that changed the geography of the world and had repercussions on every continent. But that was a long time ago and we need to concentrate on the here and now. What we do here is like that ancient tsunami and will affect humanity in a similar way. We must win, Nathan, or *everyone* loses.'

While Preacher explained how the great flood had happened more than five million years ago, I sensed the immense and impossible weight of antiquity that must press down on his shoulders. How had he not buckled under the impossible weight of all those years? I became dizzy, the numbers were too immense. The Preacher was older than mountains and much more than the man I had come to know.

I had caught just a brief glimpse of his true nature. He was a titan born under a distant star, and here I was, a poor man walking at his side in a possibly – probably – hopeless venture to save the most unworthy species on our little planet. Us, humankind.

A thought occurred to me. 'Was Jesus one of you?'

He stopped and regarded me for a long moment.

'Yeshua ben Yosef? No, Nathan, Christ described himself as a child of God, he told his followers that they too might find God in their hearts. We don't say that, we've never said that.'

'Well, then, what are you?'

'Me?' he paused, 'Label me a servant of humankind first, and GODS' warrior second. But no, now my GODS has deserted me I am just the last guard on the wall. The last guard...' I heard leaden weariness in his voice.

'But then, Nathan, *quo custodiet ipsos custodes*? Who guards the guardians? If I fall who takes up the sword to defend you? We must be careful, my friend, but we have no choice but to try. Still, we know these are the final chapters in the gospel. My job will be over soon, one way or another.'

'I've got your back, Satan. You'll never be alone while I'm with you.'

I jumped at the sudden and unexpected sound of his voice. Colin had joined us like a phantom appearing through a crack in a wall or a jack leaping out of his box. One moment Preacher and I had been alone, conversing and walking along the cliff path, and the next we cast three long shadows instead of two.

I could never understand how Colin found us so readily. Perhaps, I thought, he was like a magical magnetic compass and the Preacher was his north pole.

Preacher held up his hand, palm outwards as if warding away the idea.

'Thank-you, Colin, but you've already been through more than enough. You're very welcome to walk with us, but Nathan and I must enter that cave alone. It's the way it must be done, I'm sure you understand.'

'No, frankly, no, I don't. Three can die as easily as two, and three can survive as easily as one. An extra pair of hands and a steady eye with a gun is surely welcome on any such enterprise? And anyway, I'm an unpaid volunteer. How can you say no? Where would Arthur be without his Parsifal?'

Preacher shook his head, 'Where would your Rowan be without her Pelosen? She nearly lost you in France, my friend. I would not do that to her again. Do me this favour, please, just be ready if we call you. We might need pulling out in a fierce hurry, and you have the only tools for the job.'

Preacher took a curiously intricate slab of metal from his pocket and held it up where Colin could see it. 'I keep this with me always; which means I've also always got you with me. Promise you'll be ready if we call you, and you'll be the best ally and friend we could have. Can we depend on you for that?

'We only want the fewest possible number to risk entering the lair of the worm, but there must be two and one must be human. Nathan is with me here, and you were my human by proxy in France. Remember, you wondered why I rescued those terrible nuns. It was my destiny to do so, I had to, they had become my humans in peril.

'There are forces at work here that have rippled through the centuries, Colin, powerful forces I can't ignore. And there are set rules by which I must abide, or my purpose will fail. Nathan and I must enter the cave. We must destroy the thing we find there or be taken up by it.

'Meanwhile you must be ready with the rest of the elementals to decide what to do if we fail. You're the rearguard, we're the advance party, and you know what that means, captain?'

'I do, captain.'

Colin snapped off a spiffy salute that looked odd from a bloke in a robe. I have to say that if I was honest I resented that man's easy relationship with the Preacher. He was too familiar, too demonstrative, too much the back-slapping buddy.

Why I resented him so much I didn't know. They were friends who had been to war together, they had fought together. Colin had nearly died, what was I thinking? Of course, they were close. Who wouldn't be?

I badly wanted to take my stupid, unwarranted jealousy by the scruff of its neck and beat some sense into it. And I desperately wanted to like Colin – he was a likeable man for God's sake – but back then I couldn't. I'm afraid I saw him as like one of those privileged classes of Londoner that used to look down their noses at a poor fellow like me and see what they expected to see, a pathetic thing to be pitied or ignored.

A 'scruffian' on the streets, we called ourselves. A mongrel cross between a scruff and a ruffian. It didn't matter what was on the inside, they couldn't see past the dirty clothes and the grubby faces. If they walked over us to reach the heights they'd need to wipe their feet on a coir mat to scrape off the dirt.

I know I was being unfair to Colin, but just standing next to the man made me feel diminished somehow, as if he was a looking glass that only reflected my least attractive traits. What was I doing in his company?

And why was I with the Preacher if not to die by his side? I was resigned to my fate. Nuo would be better without me. Nuo...

At that moment something squeezed at my heart like a fist and hot tears stung my eyes. I left the friends to their chatter and stumbled away to be alone with my misery. What did I have? Colin had Rowan, Preacher had his mission, Junjie had his house with its view of that gnarled bridge, I had Nuo in my heart, but could she really become part of my life?

What woman would readily accept the gift of life with a grafting pauper, a threadbare 'prince' of the streets? What could I give her but the mean life her mother was ashamed might happen. She had had her poor feet broken and bound to help her escape from poverty. I considered myself the way others might see me, and my spirit shrank inside me.

What a weak and lost soul I was at that moment, just another cork adrift in an ocean of lost souls all feeling sorry for themselves in the face of a life too big to understand.

Something pushed at my hand. I looked down. Preacher's hound was licking at it and making a quiet huffing noise. She gazed up at me with all the wisdom of a gentle animal recognising a fellow creature in pain and offering solace. I pushed my fingers through the silken ruff of midnight fur along the back of her neck and stroked her. I smiled and sniffed away my tears.

'Thank-you,' I told her. 'It means a lot.'

I felt a hand on my shoulder and turned to find the Preacher standing next to me, concern writ plainly on his lean features.

'Nathan, are you alright?'

'I'm fine, I was just feeling a bit sorry for myself, you know what it's like. Where's Colin?'

'He's gone home to Scytaer Faehl. He feels he must warn his people and prepare them for war against the Sha-aneer. It's just us again, Nathan. And it's getting too late in the day to reach the worm's nest before sunset. We should start thinking about making camp.'

I looked around, 'This is no good, too narrow. If we turned over in our sleep we'd be straight down the gorge. Let's look for a better place around that bend.'

What we found was a two-storey house. It boasted a vertical sign on a pole and a large stable. Preacher regarded the sign.

'It says this is the Jade Tiger Guest House. Looks neat and clean enough. What do you say, Nathan? Shall we each spend the night in a good bed after a tasty meal?'

'I love the sound of both. Let's see if they have any vacancies.'

As we approached the door it opened, and a smiling, elderly woman stepped out to greet us. She bowed and ushered us in, chattering and grinning. I paused on the threshold, there was a strong hint of something unpleasant on the air, like a midden laced with vinegar. I hoped it wasn't the kitchen. I glanced at the Preacher. His eyes were hooded, and his lips tightened into a thin line.

[33]

The Jade Tiger proved to be one of the popular rest stops on the Silk Road leading from Southern China to Tibet and India, a thoroughfare which passed by just a few hundred yards down a gentle slope behind the guest house stables. It was a pleasant, roomy place, and busy. Preacher and I had to share a room, but not a bed. Our airy room had a view across the gorge and two single cots that looked comfortable enough for weary travellers.

Whatever that smell was that I'd noticed, it wasn't from the kitchens. Our dinner was excellent and very welcome after we'd freshened up in the surprisingly modern bathroom facilities on the ground floor. We drew a lot of attention from our fellow diners, especially after our hostess, Mrs Zhou, introduced us to the room as wealthy businessmen from America looking for sound investments.

She might as well have introduced a pack of starving wolves to a platter of raw meat. The diners exchanged arch glances that spoke volumes. We might not be on the dinner menu, but our new friends would be vying with each other to be feasting on our wealth that evening; fresh blood was always good for business.

In a low voice I asked the Preacher what he had told Mrs Zhou. I was treated to that half-moon grin.

'What I said and what she heard seem to have become a little unhitched. I told her we were in China looking for opportunities and excitement. I guess something got lost in the translation.'

'Or added to spice the soup. The sharks are beginning to circle. Here comes a great white.'

Not all Chinamen are small and slender like Junjie. The burley fellow bellying up to our table would have looked at home in a Sumo ring, and the wide stripes on his suit made it look not so much tailored to fit as wallpapered to his paunch. His face was dish shaped with a knob of a nose in its centre that thrust out like a thumb poking from a clenched fist.

The light glinted from his slick, pomaded hair. He exuded a strong scent of body odour and lilies that flavoured my meal when he was still feet away. His eyes were small black berries buried in folds of sweating flesh that drooped from his skull like porcine meat. His mouth was wide and mobile. No doubt he believed his smile was welcoming and full of charm. He was wrong.

However, his voice was a surprise. It was light and musical, and he spoke English with a middle European accent. All the while he spoke he tapped the ends of his pudgy fingers together, like a fat boy in the school playground waiting in vain for someone to throw him the ball.

'My, friends,' he said, 'I am Wang, *the* Wang, of Wang International Enterprises. Welcome to China, may your visit be profitable and rewarding.'

He bowed as deeply as his belly allowed, which wasn't far, and then eyed us greedily down the yellow slopes of his bloated cheeks. Taking my eyes from Wang, *the* Wang, to the lean muscular features of the Preacher, was like looking from a tethered and flaccid balloon to a dark blade. I was tempted to warn *the* Wang not to come too close in case he was punctured. I wondered whether he would fly around the room making the ripe raspberry sound of a burst balloon.

Preacher eyed him coldly, 'Mr Wang, as you can see we are at dinner. We do not conduct business at dinner, it is not proper, and it insults the cook. Thank-you for your welcome and now we wish you good evening.'

The man visibly deflated. He bowed again before he wobbled away back to his table. I had caught the faint raspberry sound he made as the lance of Preacher's disdain pierced him to the marrow, and the air thickened with something other than lilies and body odour. Some of the diners laughed nastily. The atmosphere in the room took on a complex nuance. All eyes were on us.

Preacher addressed himself to his meal. He said, without looking at me, 'The poor man must have had the pork. He is evidently martyr to the same malady as the good Dr Fisher. A promenade of the gardens might help clear his wits and ease his bowels, do you think, Nathan?'

I failed to stifle my involuntary shout of laughter, and when I looked around the room there was no mistaking the murderous resentment stamped onto the features of the unfortunately flatulent Mr Wang. His face was quite literally livid with rage. The group of men sharing his table were also marking us with unfriendly glares.

Preacher stood up and straightened his shoulders. When he did so two things happened, the crucifix around his neck glinted in the light and his long coat fell open to expose the pistol on his hip. He held his pose for a dramatic second and then grinned at me, his dark face split by the white half-moon.

'Well then, shall we take my advice and enjoy a walk around the guest house grounds before retiring? It should help settle that excellent meal.'

I wiped my mouth on my napkin and joined him. We both bowed to Mrs Zhou as we left the room. Preacher complimented her on the quality of the food and she twittered back at him. Her voice was light and charming, but all the while her eyes anxiously scanned the tables of diners over our shoulders.

I checked reflections in the windows and saw Wang and his cohorts pushing themselves to their feet. My scalp crawled under the hostile intensity their gaze.

'I think we've made ourselves some enemies, Preacher.'

'They're flattering themselves if they think they're the biggest problem we're going to face in the next few hours, Nathan. I plan an early night and an early start in the morning. Best to get any nonsense out of the way first, you agree?'

I agreed readily, but my mouth was dry enough to be used as sandpaper. Preacher may consider himself as God's warrior, I mused, but I preferred to think of myself as one of God's quiet men who sat in the corner and didn't get involved. I was surely in the wrong company for that. I took a deep breath and joined him in the cool evening.

It was quiet. Birdsong and the high-pitched chirruping of insects blended together to create a background that seemed to enhance the silence. Even the turbulent Jinsha River was muted under a clear sky ablaze with stars. Fine cool mist tingled on my cheeks. I had never felt more alive, nor more aware that I walked on the skin of a ball of rock spinning through raw space.

Preacher handed me one of his metal cylinders. 'Time for a toast I think.'

I downed the liquid in one long swallow. It instantly bloomed in my mouth as if evaporating at the touch of my body's heat. I felt it insinuate itself behind my nose like fresh horseradish or strong English mustard, then flow up into my brain on millions of pointed feet. Its affect was astonishing.

It was a Damascene experience and I could see, truly *see*, for the first time in my life. The sky brightened overhead and the stars I already thought to be ablaze, burned anew with a light and beauty beyond imagination. What a great gift was this, to offer a poor human the riches of the universe laid out for his inspection. The night looked polished to its full glory.

'Oh,' I breathed. 'It's too beautiful.'

Preacher said nothing, and I looked at him, looked *through* him to the titan of a creature he truly was. Like Blake's Tyger he burned brightly, surrounded by a halo of brilliant stars. His flesh was a fabric of precious metals gleaming with internal light, his eyes lamps of silver and gold. A nimbus of purple radiance surrounded him and cloaked him in splendour.

'So then, friend American,' growled a fat voice. 'Are you ready to talk business now?' It was Wang.

[34]

All pretence of conviviality had evaporated. Wang's face was thickly smeared with petulance and contempt. His bloated body provided a lot of space for his fury to boil to fever pitch, and he had become a quivering cathedral devoted to the celebration of rage. Preacher had verbally slapped the man down in front of his peers, and he had followed us outside to take his revenge.

By the look of them, the brutes he had brought with him had not been chosen for their sparkling wit and after dinner conversation. They rolled the muscles of their shoulders like boulders under an elastic tarpaulin and slapped their fists into their palms. They hulked like bulls in a barn, and if their hands were dangerous their sour breath was worse. My eyes watered at the reek.

Preacher spoke, flat and calm. 'We have nothing you need, Mr Wang. We are but travellers who have crossed your path.' He held out his hand. 'Come now, let us be friends and continue on our way. As a businessman, you must surely know not to waste your time and effort where there is no profit?'

The came a crashing noise from the house behind Wang. He turned to look at it, then brought his serpent's smile back to the Preacher.

'Nothing I need? We shall see, my friend the American. A business associate of mine is examining your room even as we speak. Purely in the spirit of enterprise, as I'm sure you understand. I would like to know more about the man who rejected the hand of friendship in front of valued colleagues, but now offers it in the dark where none shall see. What have you to hide, Mr American?'

Preacher had quickly dropped his hand, and like me he gazed silently up at the window of our room. Despite the open threat offered by Wang and his brutes I still felt calm. I was a detached and curious observer in the eye of the storm, watching the dramatic little scene unfolding around me. I watched and waited to see what would happen next.

I felt sorry for Wang. He would have been better playing with fire – with his pockets full of gunpowder. There followed a scream of pure terror, and then another. Then the window of our room shattered, and a bulky figure leapt to the ground. It landed heavily, still shrieking and jabbering in horror. A sleek, black shadow followed him down, emitting a sound straight from the primeval forest.

Even in my artificially calm state I felt the savage power of that snarling demon. It raised itself high on its hind legs, paused, and then thrust down hard with its fore paws. It repeated the action again and again. The associate stopped screaming, his only movement a floppy judder each time the hound struck home. Wang's ruffians writhed in confusion, waiting for an order.

'You shouldn't have done that, Mr Wang,' said the Preacher, smiling like a wolf about to strike. 'I do believe your associate has discovered more than he bargained for. You should be careful where you poke your fingers, Mr Wang, or you might find them bitten off.'

Wang made a strangled sound, then hissed, 'Take them, break them! Teach the gwailou bastards the meaning of respect.'

I braced myself, resigned to a beating, Preacher, however, was not. And he didn't touch his pistol. The brutes weren't armed, so he wasn't; I suppose he lived by his own strict codes. The fact that there were four of them and they towered over us as if we were children didn't matter, the Preacher *moved* – and the men fell.

There followed a few seconds of fluid motion punctuated by several meaty impacts. I swear Preacher walked across the face of one of the thug's. When it was over he stood in a ready but relaxed pose, bouncing gently on his toes. The grin was still there, and he was breathing steadily with no sign of exertion.

His dog finally finished worrying at the supine mound of Mr Wang's associate and it pattered over to stand at the Preacher's side. It regarded Wang's nether regions and licked hungrily at its strong creamy teeth. A faint raspberry squeak punctured the night and Wang whimpered.

He was frozen to the spot like an actor caught in the limelight who has just discovered himself to be in the wrong play – and hasn't learned his next line. He was quivering like a jelly in a gale. He had been supremely confident that his tame thugs would administer a short and brutal lesson to the gwailou barbarians; it was evident that he had done it before.

Business by violence was a rare but accepted model for international commerce along the Silk Road. The militia disapproved, but this far away from the Ink Slab people had to rub along as best they could. Gangsters like Wang prospered, and his victims were too intimidated to report the beatings.

Such attacks would not be frequent enough to alert the authorities, and they would be very carefully targeted. However, that evening Wang had chosen the wrong targets.

Four of his business associates were scattered around him like battered sacks of shit, the fifth was slumped under our window. Not a peep escaped any of them and not a drop of blood had been spilled. The brutes neither groaned nor rolled about in mute agony. They were still and silent as dead men. For all I knew they were. I was wrong.

'Murderer!' wheezed Wang at last. 'Murderer! You murdered my employees. You will hang for this I promise you.'

He fished in one of the pockets of his dreadful suit and almost drew out a little twenty-two pistol that looked tiny in his fat fist. Before he could bring it to bear he felt the barrel of Preacher's forty-five pressed hard into his plump cheek.

'I think I'll take that, Mr Wang,' growled Preacher. 'You might hurt yourself. Toys like that can accidently go off. I'll leave it where you can find it again, don't worry. By the way, your employees aren't dead. They'll wake up with headaches and a few bruises, but they're not dead – at least – not yet.'

He handed the little gun to me and I checked the safety was off before trousering it. I wondered why such a big man should bother with such a small weapon, then I fetched the pistol back out. I examined the trigger guard and then glanced at the gangster's chubby fingers. How could he even fire the thing? Those sausage-like digits would barely reach the trigger.

Preacher spoke, his voice low and sounding like stone grinding on stone.

'Unlike you I don't make idle threats, Mr Wang, I make promises. I promise you that if my colleague or I are bothered by your employees or you for the remainder of our stay in the guest house, I will give you a personal demonstration of everything I did to your henchmen.

'I also promise I won't kill you, Mr Wang, but I will hurt you. Bear that in mind. And now, good evening to you. Unless you wish us to wait with you until your associates come around? There may wild animals up here and I should hate for any of these men to be hurt.'

The quivering Wang looked helplessly down at the inert piles of muscle that had once been his most effective weapons, and then with shuddering chins he forced himself to gaze at the Preacher. He visibly shrank in horror at the thought of that steel hard man inflicting pain on his blubbery body. Every ounce of courage drained from his excessively larded frame.

He whimpered, 'Who are you?'

Preacher holstered his pistol then reached down and ran his fingers through the silky fur at his hound's neck. It looked up at him with a steady gaze and then back at Wang. Preacher straightened.

'I'm here to do something important, Mr Wang. It will probably be done tomorrow and then we will be on our way. Don't worry, you can get back to your vile little trade without fear of interference from me.'

Wang pulled his tattered courage around his corpulent frame once more.

'It's not me who should be afraid. You mess with me and you mess with the ninkyo dantai from the Ink Slab. They will eat you *and* your dog, and they will use this boy's bloody bones for chopsticks. You'll see; you don't know it, but you're already dead, American.'

'So, you're working with the gokudo, ha!' What Preacher said next was said fast and in dialect. I missed all of it, but I saw it's effect on Wang. I heard it too. His bowels would always offer clues to the man's state of mind.

We walked away from the fat man and his associates. Preacher seemed lost in thought, but I had to know.

'What did you say to him?'

He snorted, 'I'm afraid I was a little rude, Nathan, but he annoyed me. I told him that the next time he pulled the gokudo hand out of his ass long enough to kiss its three fingers he shouldn't be surprised if there's nobody attached to the wrist.'

[35]

Mrs Zhou accepted that we had had a burglar who had broken our window but told us she had no spare rooms for us to move to. She sent a boy up with us who tacked a sheet of ply into the frame and cut the cool breeze from the gorge. Mrs Zhou had seemed surprised to see us return intact from our postprandial exercise and I noticed she had wandered inquisitively to the doorway as if to see what had happened to Wang and his cronies.

It had been another long day, and I was dropping from exhaustion, but as soon as we reached our room I asked Preacher if he wanted me to stand guard while he slept. He shook his head but took me by the shoulder with a smile.

'Thanks, Nathan, my God but you're a game fellow. You get your head down while you can. But a word of advice; boots off but make sure they're handy and keep your clothes on. We may have to move in one hell of a hurry and a naked man's much too vulnerable to fight or run. Good night.'

I know I slept because I dreamed. I dreamt I was alone in the dark and hunting for a lamp to make light and find my way out. There were dozens of lamps around me, but they were all empty. In increasing panic, I felt around and lifted one lamp after another, and shook it by my ear, desperate to hear the heavy glug of oil, but they were all empty. And then I lifted something that glowed in my hands, but it wasn't a lamp. It was a wickedly grinning skull.

The jaw swung open and it breathed on me with the foul stench of Wang's associates, and with dream logic I knew the fat man and his henchmen had followed us into the darkness and died there. Whatever had killed them was now waiting for me. I wondered if I could somehow use Wang's blubber to light one of the lamps. It was then that something grabbed me by the shoulder.

I squeaked in shock. Preacher whispered in my ear, 'Nathan, Nathan, wake up. Nathan, wake up, lad, come on. Quickly now.'

I gathered my scattered senses; the room was as dark as my dream. For a moment I hovered, caught somewhere between the realms of sleep and wakefulness.

I whispered back, 'What is it, Preacher?'

'There's someone in the room with us. Quickly, get under your bed and wait until I call you. Make no sound.'

Barely daring to breathe I slid to the floor and tucked myself into the narrow space under my bed. I strained my ears to hear what was happening.

My nose and throat itched and burned and my eyes watered. The floor was very dusty, and I had to fight hard to stop myself from sneezing, but it was hopeless. I lost the battle and sneezed explosively, twice, scaring up a cloud of dust around my head.

Something thumped into my mattress and then a white flare of light illuminated my cramped hideout. To one side of me I saw a pair of very sensible woman's shoes. I heard the urgent click of a well-oiled pistol being cocked.

Preacher's voice barked, 'Put it down, Mrs Zhou. Do it now and do it very carefully. NOW!'

Mrs Zhou? What was going on in that room? I sneezed again and caught my head against one of the harsh rope slings supporting the mattress. Next to me the woman fell to her knees. Her hand reached under the bed and made to lash at me with an odd-looking dagger. I rolled beyond her reach and out into the open.

I pulled myself upright and sprang to my stockinged feet just in time to see the Preacher wrestling with our hostess. He was trying to prise a long and wicked looking thorn from her right hand, the beam from his torch flashing around the room. And then Mrs Zhou said 'Oh', a quiet, small sound, and she collapsed in a boneless heap to the floor.

Preacher glanced at me, 'She didn't get you? No, of course she didn't, you're still conscious. Are you all right, Nathan?'

I shook my head trying to rattle some sense into my dazed wits. I had been too recently woken to gather the meaning of events over the last few minutes.

'Preacher, please; Mrs Zhou? What's going on here?'

'She came through there,' he pointed behind me. 'Can't you smell it?'

I turned and saw a neat little hatch open low down in the wall. Too small to be obvious but big enough for a person to crawl through on all fours. Preacher was right, a strangely familiar stench rolled into the room from the hatchway. The air it emitted was dank and cold.

I pointed at the woman, 'What happened to her?'

'Caught on her own stinger,' he replied. 'See it sticking out of her arm? That is a Sha-aneer quill. She'll be unconscious until morning, longer if I leave it where it is. It's like a bee sting, there's a little muscle at the end that will keep pumping the poison into her until it runs out. Nasty little thing to use as a weapon and just as effective against it's user as against its proposed victims. In this case, us.'

'But why us?'

'Wait a moment, be quiet. You'll see.'

He used a handkerchief to extract the quill, then extinguished his torch. We didn't have to wait very long. There came a light tap at the door, and then it swung silently open. Two of Wang's brutes loomed in the darkness, one of them uttered a curt question.

Preacher answered by turning his torch on and flashing it directly into their eyes. Both men reared back with a bellowing roar. Preacher jabbed at them with the quill like a fencing master. They fell, and we both had to skip away to avoid being caught under their collapsing bulk. The floor bounced under their weight. Jets of dust shot up from between the floorboards, I sneezed again.

Preacher shut the door, kicking one of the brute's feet out of the way to do so. He crouched down, shone his light into one of the men's eyes, and I saw the half-moon grin white in the sharp shadows. He touched his fingers to the body's thick neck and pressed in, hard. He waited a while, then straightened up.

'Not much life in the brain to begin with, but the body's hale and hearty enough. So, Wang's working with Zhou to feed the worm, is he? I wonder if his gokudo friends know about this little arrangement?

'No doubt Mrs Zhou thinks that feeding strangers to the worm will keep her regulars safe, and I bet Wang's end of the bargain is to keep the victim's tack. His confrontation with us this evening was Wang coming off script. We must have really put his nose out of joint in the dining room, wouldn't you say?'

I silently questioned the word 'we' but nodded my agreement anyway.

'So, what do we do now?' I asked.

Preacher bent to the hatchway and inhaled deeply. 'So many people have worked so hard to get us into there, it seems a shame to disappoint them. Fetch your pistol, Nathan, let's go visit an old friend.'

'Wait,' I said. 'Are you telling me we can go straight to the mother worm from here without climbing down to the cave?'

'No, I don't think so. The mother's deep, really deep; we couldn't smell her from up here. This is probably another calf, like the one in the temple, but it might be older and more powerful. Let's go see, shall we?'

He reached into his coat and fetched out one of those cylinders, opened it and handed it to me.

'We can't use the torch down there,' he said. 'You'll need the dark sight once more. Drink this, all of it.'

I had such a cocktail of the Preacher's potions boiling through my veins by then I'm surprised *I* didn't glow in the dark. Whatever they were they weren't natural, but I trusted him not to poison me – at least, not *too* much. I handed back the empty cylinder and it instantly vanished back into his coat. He extinguished his torch and we waited until the room swam before my eyes in that strange phosphorescent monochrome I had experienced before.

I saw Mrs Zhou and the bull-like men glowing on the floor like corpses, which was an unfortunate image to take with me through the hatchway.

'Okay,' I lied, 'I'm ready.'

[36]

We bent double and shouldered our way onto a wooden landing at the top of a staircase. It was evident to me that Wang's over-muscled thugs could only have climbed down that narrow staircase sideways, dragging their unconscious burdens behind them.

Had it not been for the Preacher one of those burdens would have been me – but then again – had it not been for the Preacher I would never have found myself in such a position.

The stairs brought us to a panelled corridor that would have been pitch dark without the strange tincture that provided sight without light. I told myself I must ask Preacher how it worked once we had completed our job, but my heart was hammering so powerfully in my head that it had knocked the thought deeply into the rough before we'd gone ten yards.

To our right the corridor ended in a plain wooden door that no doubt led into the house kitchens. The smell of food was very strong there. There was no knob on this side of the door, just a keyhole. I wondered if on the other side it might be disguised as part of a wall or the back of a cabinet.

Preacher touched my arm to draw my attention, tapped his nose, and pointed down the corridor leading away from the door. I nodded, he was right, the worm stink was coming from along there. With my pulse pounding I followed at his heel. I noticed that his dog hadn't joined us, and I was struck by the sudden, sour realisation that the beast had a lot more sense than me.

I had expected the corridor to be interminable, but it only stretched a few dozens of yards. The panelling ended abruptly in a tunnel of living rock.
The plain door was lost in the shadows behind us, but I could still pick up the savoury tang of the kitchen underlying the midden reek of the worm. Of course, I realised, the corridor couldn't be too long. Wang's brutes were strong, but they weren't built for distance.

Preacher put his mouth right by my ear. 'Listen,' he breathed. I strained, and then, at the very edge of hearing, I discerned voices. I couldn't make out what they were saying but that oily susurration brought the hair on the back of my neck to attention, and my gut knotted in dread. It was unmistakeable, the Sha-aneer was nesting there. We headed towards it.

Soon the sound was loud enough to make out some of the words. I heard English, Mandarin, German and God alone knows what else. The thing was telling itself how very clever it was, how beautiful, and what it longed to do to the Eden born – to me – once it had me. I felt sick. The words hissed and

140

bubbled like water on hot rocks, as if a snake was trying to talk like a man – but through its arse.

The stink was a real nose twister. It reached the point that my eyes were stinging, and I was breathing through my mouth trying to lessen its impact. That's when I realised that the tone of the voices had altered. They changed from boastful booming to sly whispering. They knew we were there.

With luck they thought we were Wang's goons come to deliver an early breakfast, or a late dinner. It was hard to know what time it was in that tunnel. Day and night had ceased to exist, and everything was outlined in the silver tracery of Preacher's dark sight. Even though I could feel the hard rock underfoot I cast no shadow. We seemed to be floating through a dream, the rock just an illusion.

I pressed my palm against the wall to reassure my errant senses. I felt the moist warmness of the stone. It had an unpleasant, spongy, fleshy quality and I made an involuntary sound of disgust. The worm heard me.

They are here, they are here with our new guests, more flesh for the Host. Sweet meat, sweeeeet meeeeat, so tender. The soul and the meat of the Eden beasts shall melt and become part of us; we shall take them, welcome and enrich them, and make them part of us, the beautiful Host.

The words skidded and coiled against each other and insinuated themselves like leeches into my mind, battening fast to my senses and sucking everything good and clean from my memory. I felt soiled by the very air around the worm, I had to destroy it. I could not live knowing that vile creation was breathing the same air as me. I drew the assassin's gun and cocked it. The sound rang out like the chime of a bell.

The worm hissed, *What, was that? Is it bringing guns to the feast? Guns are forbidden, guns are not allowed at all. Who is this who brings a gun to the Host of the Sha-aneer? Who? Who is this?*

And from nowhere a sinewy curtain of silver flesh exploded into the tunnel. We were literally yards away from its pit and the thing reared up ready to fall on us like a wave of thick flesh. Preacher flung three of his globes into the air and I instantly shot one towards the filthy creature. It exploded with an actinic glare that instantly blinded me. I staggered back, tripped, and sprawled headlong.

I experienced an intense stabbing pain in my calf and made to reach down and check whatever had caught me, but my arm wouldn't move. My entire body was paralysed, totally drained of energy. Even my eyes were fixed into an unblinking upward gaze. I was still breathing, and my heart was beating but the rest of me was completely frozen. I could feel nothing, do nothing.

141

My ears and nose still worked. The sound of the worm's fury was a perfect storm of chaotic screeching, the hiss of spitting fat and twang of wrenching tendons. I was being jolted around like a doll in a Moses basket. I think I would have wept in shame if tears would come. I had given the game away with my ill-timed pistol cocking and now I had killed myself and the Preacher. If he died the world would soon follow.

Then I felt myself lifted by a wave of burning worm flesh and knew I must be consumed with the monster. Somewhere in the maelstrom of sound I heard Preacher scream 'Colin! Now!' I prayed with everything left of my shattered mind that he would escape the terrible fate I had brought upon us both. The glare of the hissing worm grew brighter and then brighter still. I thanked God that the thing would kill me but not take my soul, and that I could feel no pain.

[37]

I'm dead, the race is run. So, what happens next? I thought. Where am I? Where do we go when we die? More people have answered that question than are alive on Earth today, but they're not talking. Not unless you believe the table turners and spirit botherers. Why don't they just let them rest in peace? I've heard about such things but never believed them. Sounds like foolishness to me.

But, never mind, I was dead, it's over. Now it was my turn to find out for true what lies beyond the veil. Where *do* we go when we die? All I had to do was open my eyes and I would know.

So, I wondered, *when* I open my eyes who or what would I see first? Would I have my own body, my own arms and legs, or would I be a wraith? What *does* the human soul look like? There was so much I wanted to know.

And how would I be spending eternity? What about redemption and damnation? Had I escaped the soul-eating worm just to spend an eternity of torment in a pit of hellfire? Would it help if I told the demons I was a personal friend of Satan? I had to find out. I opened my eyes.

The Preacher gazed down at me with a full-blown silver halo around his dark head. Damn, I thought, the bastard got him too. Well, looking on the bright side at least I knew one person I could talk to. At least the halo looked promising, I doubted they saw too many of those down in the pits of Hell. I tried to smile but my face hurt too much. I groaned. Colin's face came into view.

'Try not to move too much, you're still saturated with quill venom. Satan protected you from the worm's fire, but you were stuck full of the quills. Nathan, my friend, when you got here you looked like a porcupine's ass. Took Rowan nearly an hour to get them out of you and your blood was running like corn syrup the whole time. Damndest thing I ever saw, and I've seen some things. How you feeling? Can you talk? Can you see okay?'

And I thought *I* was full of questions. I waited until he ran out of steam or paused for breath, whichever happened first, and then I asked, in a voice that sounded like a creaky door, 'I hate to sound like a cliché, but, where am I?'

Preacher answered, 'We're in Colin's home. He came for us and pulled us out of the tunnel before it was too late. We owe him our lives.'

I looked at Colin and attempted that smile again. My face still hurt too much. I settled for a nod of gratitude. I would have stuck my hand out for a shake, but it felt like it weighed a thousand tons. I was in too poor a state for gratitude.

Then Rowan joined her husband and the world became a brighter, lovelier place. She was followed by a sweet, slight figure, who instantly became the sole focus for my attention. Nuo.

She frowned at me. 'You go for a walk with the Father and the next thing I hear you're stabbed full of holes and poisoned. What you think you're doing? You want me to marry old man Junjie? He's a nice fellow, I like him lots, but really!'

I lay like a toppled tree stump and gazed helplessly at her. 'I didn't do it on purpose,' I croaked. 'We were in a tunnel...'

'I heard all about it.' She spat some words in Naxi dialect. Judging by the storm warnings in her eyes it was probably for the best that I didn't understand any of them. My companions evidently did. Rowan turned away to disguise a blushing grin, Colin's ears turned dark pink, and even the Preacher raised a quizzical eyebrow. I had won myself a true firebrand and no mistake.

'Look, look, Nuo, I'm sorry,' I stuttered. 'But what happened to the worm? It was burning when I blacked out. Did we kill it?'

Colin brightened up, 'Did you? I'll say so. You can kiss the Jade Dragon Guest House au revoir and a good piece of the cliff face with it. Most of the inhabitants escaped with their lives, but from what Satan tells me the good Mrs Zhou and Wang's bully boys got their just desserts. I'm afraid all that's left of your tack is what you were standing up in when I fetched you. Your room's gone with all the rest.'

'Nothing in my luggage was as precious to me as my hide and my life. Thanks to you I still have both. The rest I can work for, I can't say...'

Nuo eyed me, 'You think I let my husband walk around in a towel for the rest of his life? You can think again. Anyway, you keep dropping towel all over the place, and frightening servants with private partings that are best kept private. Anyway, that's what I'm thinking. Mrs Rowan helped me get you some fresh gear in Lijiang. Try not to get too many holes in this outfit. Next time you get your own, mister!'

My future as her husband seemed to be settled in her mind. In my mind I turned over the idea of taking Nuo as my wife and I couldn't see a flaw in the plan.

'Nuo,' I said. 'If we had a Pastor and a ring I'd marry you here and now, if you'd have me.'

The girl shrieked and grabbed me up off my sick bed to plant a full-blooded smacker on my lips. It didn't hurt as much as I thought it would, but I still winced with pain. She lowered me gently and pressed her full lips against mine.

'I have you,' she whispered. 'I have you before someone else spoils you for life with a good woman, good woman who knows how to cook.'

Preacher coughed politely. 'Excuse me for interrupting this tender moment, but I *am* ordained to perform weddings. And I'm sure Prince Pelosen would gift us a suitable ring if we asked nicely?'

Colin laughed with delight. 'I'm still getting used to that name, Satan; still getting used to my new life, truth be told. Wedding rings coming right up. Gold still the favourite currency? And if you're looking for a best man, Nathan, well, I'd proudly put my name in that hat, if it's not too bold of me to say so on such short acquaintance?'

My head was spinning. I was still too poorly to sit up straight, and these people were planning my nuptials around me while I lay flat and helpless as a beached fish. Images of my future with Nuo streamed through me and my guts knotted like a fist.

'Wait,' I cried out. 'Wait...'

Nuo stepped towards me, her brow furrowed, 'Why should we wait? You think you need mother's permission? We don't. And father's dead too many years to worry. You have my permission to marry me, okay?'

I finally produced that smile I'd wanted earlier, and I did it without breaking my face too badly. I was improving fast. I also managed to lever myself up on my elbows. I looked my girl straight in the eye and she gazed back at me with the spirit of a wildcat in her eyes. God, I loved her. And now I was going to hurt her feelings.

'Nuo, listen, please. Since I met you I've done nothing but think about you. I didn't know I could care this much for another person. To take you for my wife would make me the proudest, happiest... I love you, but what kind of life could I offer you?

'We would be church mouse poor, street people. I was living in a flophouse when I met the Preacher. An opium house, a sewer. I love you, Nuo, but I can't ask you to suffer that life with me. Please understand, I love you too much to marry you!'

At the look on her face I felt my heart pull free of its moorings and crash down into my knotted guts. I tried to bite back the tears, but to see her so hurt was more than I could bear. With all my broken heart I wished I was dead.

[38]

'You listen to me, Mr Whittaker, and you listen good. I don't know how poor a church mouse is and I don't care. If I with you I the proudest church mouse under God's sky.' Nuo's teeth were clenched, her mouth was ugly, and her words had been squeezed until they squeaked, but the sound of her raw misery still pounded in my ears like cannon fire.

I must have made a pretty picture too. My mouth hung open and I had strings of snot dripping onto my chin. All the things I wanted to say had crowded up into my mouth at the same time and got caught there, and the lump in my throat felt as big as my whole head. I couldn't breathe properly.

The dry, sensible voice that had whispered I was right, and that what I was saying was true and it was all for her own good, had been silenced under an onslaught of hot emotion. I was watching the pivot on which my world now spun crumple thanks to the pain *I* had caused – and it was too much. I couldn't let her suffer like that. Every wrack of her sobs tore through me like knives.

How I did it I don't know. One second, I was weak and helpless on my back, and the next I was standing with Nuo pressed into my arms and holding her so tight she groaned from it. The logjam of words finally broke and they spilled out of me like a torrent. I was sorry, I told her, we would find a way. Fortune had brought her to me for a reason, we belonged together. Could she ever forgive me? I was a fool, I said, forgive me.

For a delirious moment we were the only two people in the room, and we kissed as if we had been welded bone to bone. Nuo looked frail as a bird but there in my arms, she felt strong and vital. Electricity poured between us at every point we touched, and we touched at every point. I had never felt more alive, never felt so complete.

Incoherent sound roared in my ears and I was truly happy. For the first time since my mother died I had discovered a foundation on which I wanted to build a future. I was investing a lot in this woman, but I knew she was worth every ounce of the trust and hope I had piled onto her slender shoulders. I just knew. Sounds like we both did.

The storm finally calmed enough that we remembered the other three people in the room and we separated. I felt alternately hot and cold and I could feel Nuo shivering. The feelings we had just released had been held tight behind locked doors for a lifetime and the irresistible surge had smashed our defences to splinters.

We had no choice now, we were no longer just two people in love. We had become us, at that moment we were a single entity. Nuo wiped my nose with her handkerchief, the light in her eyes burning so bright I felt it scorching my skin. I borrowed the handkerchief and, using the dry corners, I mopped at her cheeks. Eventually we turned to our friends.

'I think we must get married as soon as possible,' I said. 'It's not fair to the free men of this world to let this beautiful woman roam around without a ring on her finger. Best if we're tied together for their safety, don't you think? Be for the best all around, yes?'

I think Colin and Rowan were nearly as pleased as we were, he pumped at my hand boisterously and she hugged me like a long-lost sister. And, you know, for all her astonishing beauty I felt no trace of the charge that had sparked between Nuo and me, albeit Rowan was a fine armful of grade 'A' prime womanhood and I was very aware of her charms.

And then Preacher caught my eye. I walked to his side as if reeled in on a line, leaving my wife-to-be to the congratulations of our friends. He turned his back to the room and put his head down. He spoke quietly.

'Nathan, I can't ask you to join me in the cave of the worm. You have your whole future ahead of you with Nuo. It wouldn't be fair to you and it wouldn't be fair to her. I've rarely seen such alchemy between two people. Colin and Rowan, have it, Caleb Sawyer and Alice had it. In all my long years on this Earth I can count such events on the fingers of my two hands. You deserve your happiness, and the world deserves to learn from your example.'

'No, Preacher. I tell you, no. You can't do this. Yes, Nuo and I have a future together, but if we don't destroy the worm first then the future's bleak. What if we have children? And what if they have children? When will the Sha-aneer come out of its nest and spread again? When will it take away our children's future. No, this must end now, and I'm going with you. I have the best, most special reason in the world to be with you, and you can't argue with me. Understood?'

'Nathan, I...'

'You listen to my man, Father. You listen to what he says.' Nuo was right behind us. She was beautiful as a storm cloud – and just as dangerous. Preacher topped her by more than a foot, and he was her boss, but she spoke to him as an equal.

'What kind of life will we have if every day we know that monster is still out there and wants to eat us all up like drinking hot soup? It's no good, he must go with you. We need you to kill it, Father, and Nathan will be right there with you to make sure you do it properly. He's proved that already, look, the monster can't kill him. It tried and he's still here, see, see!'

'Nuo, I...'

She shook her head, 'You don't try those clever words on me, Father. I know you're a clever man, you're like Confucius, you can talk up a big barrel of clever stuff, but you know I'm right. Nathan must go with you or he's not the man I want to marry, and he is, so there you are. Okay!'

'Nuo, look, I...'

She held up a hand, 'What? You think Nathan not good enough? You think he's a street boy and not good enough to fight with you? You think he's a snotty-nosed street boy who eats with dogs and sleeps with cats in a sewer? I tell you, Father, you're thinking again or you're not the man I think you are? And you are, let me tell you. So, good, all done, is decided.'

She grinned at me. 'You scared off yet? Or shall we get married now?' She was more persuasive in English than any woman I'd ever met, and it was her second language. What chance did I have?

I smiled. 'You know, you're beautiful when you're angry.'

She grinned, 'Tell me that when I really angry, like busting belly angry! You want to see me angry? You'd better come back from that cave alive or I come looking for you, wherever you are, and then you see me angry like a python on a skewer! You'd better look out that day, even gods will be hiding.'

She turned to Preacher, 'Okay, Father, when do I say "I do" so everyone get to kiss the bride? I'm in the mood to kiss a good man and make a sinner out of him, best if we're married first I say, or angels weep.'

Preacher Satan Spindrift gazed down at her in silence for a long moment. I could see expressions flickering across his face like clouds in a hurricane. He shut his eyes and took a deep breath. And then he began to laugh, he laughed so hard that tears rolled down his lean cheeks. He bent and slapped at his knees.

Everyone was so startled that we all joined in, his joy was as infectious as a yawn on a long hot afternoon. I was crying with laughter myself. I found myself shocked to the marrow by love and happiness.

And then Preacher made the day complete. He took Nuo's waist and elbows in his big hands and he lifted her clean off her feet as if she weighed no more than an idle thought. He held her, so their eyes were level. 'May I?' he said. She nodded, looking a little nervous. He gently kissed her on both cheeks, and then he put her down.

'Thank you, blessed lady, thank you. Thank you for reminding me why I'm here, and for reminding me of everything I ever loved about the Eden born.'

And he bowed low to her, and then looked around the room with mischief dancing in his eyes. 'Time for a wedding,' he said.

[39]

I was a bemused and happily married man by the time Preacher and I returned to the Tiger Leaping Gorge a day later. I was a wearing an ornate gold ring on the third finger of my left hand, Nuo wore a more delicate version of the same ring on her finger. They had been our wedding gifts from the royalty of Scytaer Faehl. We had exchanged vows and signed a book and danced until we could no longer put off the inevitable. Then we retired to bed together.

I was nervous as a tender-footed cat on a bed of nails. Nuo was my wife. I wanted to please her. Nuo told my some of the things she remembered from the pillow book her mother had made her read, especially some of the illustrations. We explored each other's bodies as if seeking treasure in our most secret places. When we finally succumbed to sleep we were exhausted and thrilled at the great potential we had found for future pleasures.

I had kissed Nuo goodbye when Preacher and I were set to leave. I promised to see her soon at the mission house in Shuhe. She told me I'd better, or else. I'd had just one day as Nuo's husband, I couldn't believe I'd be lucky enough to share a lifetime with someone so wonderful. Just one more day would have been a bonus.

But instead I was a soldier going to war, with my wife's kiss still warm on my lips, her scent in my nostrils, and the thrill of her body impressed upon mine. We had tried to cram a lifetime of loving into a single day; but had found that well to be bottomless. The more we gave to each other the more we found to give. The servant girl and the street boy, richer in love than any King and Queen in their fancy palaces.

And yet, and yet... and yet there was a worm to kill. No matter how full it is the heart must wait until the war was won. I put sweetness behind me and masked my joy with bitter resolve. I checked my pistol was loaded and the safety was on. I noticed Preacher doing the same.

I had lost the assassin's pistol while paralysed in that foul tunnel and so had borrowed a gun from Colin's personal arsenal. I was told that Elementals didn't employ such things; that they could fashion weapons from any materials at hand. A gun was a crude device and not worthy of their interest. Colin had been a soldier before he became a prince, he knew the value of a gun, and collected them.

The pistol he had provided was a hammerless Colt 1908 semi-automatic that could sit snugly without snagging in a pocket and was instantly ready to fire once the slide was pulled back and the hammer engaged. It had seven .25 ACP cartridges in its magazine, one more than I had become used to in a revolver. I hoped one would be a good plenty to get the job done, but a few more are always welcome.

Preacher and I holstered our weapons simultaneously. The next time we drew them would be in the face of the enemy. Colin had opened our portal back into China near the exploded cliff where the Jade Tiger Guest House had been. He explained that to bring us closer to the cave would have been too dangerous, the cliff path being too narrow for the elemental portal to be positioned safely.

We said our farewells and stepped out onto a landscape that had changed almost completely since we had last seen it. The causeway of the Silk Road was still there at the bottom of the hill and was relatively untouched, but the house and stables were gone as was a good chunk of the cliff face, along with Mrs Zhou and Wang's muscle boys. A jagged, sheer rift had been blown from the side of the gorge.

Far below us the Jinsha river had found its turbulent way around the choke of debris. In the morning sun it glittered and splashed whitely against the raw stone. The fractured, jagged edges would be worn smooth once more over centuries to come, but that morning they still looked like the teeth and ribs of some great prehistoric beast, or the shattered remains of a dragon. We turned our backs to the devastation and followed the remaining cliff path once more.

Preacher pointed along the cliff to a point where, he said, a steep ledge angled back towards us. 'That's where we're going,' he explained. 'You can't see the cave mouth from here because of the overhang, it shields it from sight, but can you see the way that ledge seems to disappear into the cliff?'

I told him I could, but in truth I wasn't sure. The cliff was as seamed as an elephant's hide. I could see ridges and tracery all over it and one ledge looked much like any other to me. But I trusted that he knew where we were going and would deliver me safely to the cave – and our fate. At that thought I fought an impulse to pull out my new gun and practice by loosing a few shots into the trees.

Preacher told me that we had to be extremely careful. The ledge had worn a lot since the soldiers had carried their general and the dragon to their final resting place. Once the cave might have been a sacred place, like the snarling tiger's mouth by the Stone Lotus Temple, both of which we had destroyed. Hopefully we would be doing the same again.

There were twenty-eight bends to the Tiger Leaping Gorge. I wondered how many there would be when we had finished our work that day. How big was this mother worm anyway? Big enough to devour humankind, Preacher said. But was it big enough to split the fabric of the Earth itself, like a knife slicing the rind of an orange? Did we really know what we were doing? I voiced my concerns.

Preacher answered my question with another question. 'If you were told you had a cancer that was certain to kill you, but the doctor told you she *could* save your life, but she would have to cut off your arm to do so, what would you say?'

I held out my arm, 'I'd say, take it. Waking up to another new morning is worth the loss of a diseased wing. Take it, doctor, and arm be damned.'

'I agree, Nathan. We must do what we can for the best in such dire circumstances. In that cave is a cancer that will kill us if we don't cut it out. We might lose an arm, a leg, or in this case a large chunk of Southern China, but that cancer must be cut out or the whole body dies. Whatever it takes, my friend, we must take our scalpel to the worm and slice it away for once and for all. We have no more choices.

'This mother worm has been seeding the planet for tens of thousands of millennia and I have been cutting out her plantings wherever I could find them. Always I've been looking for the mother, following the trail until I found her. Today is the day we excise the arm and save the patient, Nathan. Pray we don't die with the diseased arm, but if we do, it must surely be worth it.'

I prayed he was right. The climb down to the ledge was just around the next two bends, and then we would begin our tricky traverse to the cave.

'Lord,' I said, 'give us the courage to do what must be done, and the sure feet of a mountain goat to get us where we need to be.'

'Amen to that,' said Preacher. 'Amen to that.'

[40]

We saw the change in the weather rolling towards us from a long way off. The peaks of the mountains quickly disappeared into heavy mist that swallowed all sense of distance. Within minutes we were blind and walking cautiously through a sodden, pearl grey fog. I could see the Preacher and a few yards of our path and that was it. He turned to me.

'Are you okay to go on in this?'

'So long as I can see where I'm putting my feet I'll be okay, sure.'

'We must be careful; the ledge might become slippery in this mist, and we could lose our footing. If you want to start thinking like a mountain goat this would be the perfect time.'

'So long as I don't have to chew the cud. I prefer to eat my meals just the once, if it's all the same to you.'

'Please yourself. Goats seem happy enough with the arrangement.'

We both moved further away from the riverside edge of our cliff path. Now that we could no longer see the river below us the gorge seemed infinitely steep, I could feel the fall sucking at my will. It was daring me to step out into the greyness, urging me out into space...

'Nathan, come away from the edge. This rock might crumble, and I might not be able to catch you in time. I think a little less mountain goat and a lot more caution is called for here, my friend.'

It was as if his words had broken a spell. I reared away from the abyss and fought a sudden urge to lie full-length on the ground. Our path seemed little more than an island of stone in an infinite expanse of featureless grey. It started from nothing and ended in nothing. I needed to feel the firmness of the stone under me, I needed to see the horizon.

Preacher took my shoulder. 'Bide here a moment, we've got time. Whiteout fog like this can be disorienting for the most experienced climber. Take a moment to catch up with your wits. You'll need them when we climb down to the ledge.'

'How much further?'

'Just around the next bend. There's a notch we can wriggle down to reach the ledge. It was carved by a stream of water, so you might get your boots a little wet, but it seems the best option.'

'I'll live. This miserable fog has already covered me in drizzle. I'll need wringing through a mangle before I'll be dry enough to worry about getting wet again. Let's go, I'm ready as I'll ever be.'

I had to keep telling myself that I was only there because I'd insisted on it. Preacher had offered me a valid escape clause and I'd turned him down flat. A married man should be away on honeymoon, not groping about halfway up a cliff in the Chinese version of a pea-souper. Except this fog was very different.

The London murk had a different, much more odious character. It would sidle along the cobblestones of the city like an unwashed and over-familiar ragamuffin who insisted on draping himself across your shoulders and breathing foully in your face.

The fog in the Smoke stank of burnt coal, stale oil, and too many unwashed people. It irritated the eyes, nose and throat of anyone who had to breathe it, and it turned a white collar black and greasy where it touched the skin of your neck.

They call it smog, an apt word. It was dark and dirty enough to turn day into night – and night into something from the inner circles of Hell. The only sounds to pierce the noxious vapours were people coughing and sneezing; or retching and hawking great gobs of dark phlegm into the gutter.

This bright cloud was clean and tasted of salt, it was dense but also luminous. I had the sense that we were inside a great glowing globe. And it was unnaturally still and peaceful. The birds had stopped singing, and even the roar of the river seemed distant, as if everything we knew was happening in an adjacent room behind thick walls.

We were lost in our own, very private world. I felt myself to be not so much walking through the fog as enfolded in it, possessed in its chill embrace. I licked salt water from my lips and pushed damp hair from my eyes.

'There's the notch, Nathan. See there?'

I saw it, and with a sinking sensation realised he was right about the waterfall. It sprayed from the stones like a lively silver snake and vanished down into the mist in a bright arc of glittering diamonds.

The smoothly polished stone was black, wet and slippery looking. It was green with a thick coating of slimy algae. Climbing down that shallow groove in the cliff side looked to me like a recipe for suicide, but Preacher said it was the best option. Was there really no other route that was safer and drier?

When Preacher got to the waterfall he reached into its stream and pulled out a gleaming length of rope that had been lying flat against the wall where it was almost entirely hidden from view. It was blackened by time and greased with the same algae that crawled down the stones into the mists. He held it up and grinned.

'Here we are. We didn't want to climb down there without something to hold on to. I'll bet this rope has been the lifeline down to the ledge for decades, and it's still strong as the day they drove the pitons into the rock face.'

He leaned backwards and hauled on the rope as if trying to unhitch it from its moorings. He grunted with the effort, and then – still leaning on the rope at an acute angle – he stepped through the stream of the waterfall and down into the notch. He spread his legs wide to avoid the worst of the green slime and the slippery stream of water. Without any hesitation he began to ease himself down the cliff face.

He looked across the cliff edge at me. 'Wait until I'm a few feet down then follow my lead. Take it easy, we don't need to rush. Take all the time you need. It's safe enough if you're careful. Okay? So, give a me a few moments, then it's your turn.'

And with that he was gone, and I was left alone watching a rope twitching in a spray of icy water. I cautiously made my way to the edge and looked down. The rope descended straight as a lance into the luminous mist. There was already no sign of the Preacher. I decided I had given him time enough and leaned into the waterfall to take a grip on the rope.

The shock of the water pounded the breath from my body and forced a gasp of surprise from my lips. I had soaked naked in meltwater in a stream just a few nights before, but that had been nothing like this. The water could be described as pure liquid ice. It hit me hard and I felt my knees buckle under me. I grabbed at the rope and angled my body away from the frigid stream.

My right foot slid on the algae and I spun helplessly around *into* the freezing spray. My fingers were numb, and I couldn't get a proper grip on the sodden rope. I fell to my my knees with a jarring crunch and with the last of my energy threw myself sideways onto the dry path and away from that deadly waterfall. I was deafened by the sound of my heart thumping like a beating fist in my chest.

'Nathan, Nathan, are you okay? I'm on the ledge. You can come down now. Are you okay?'

I'd be fine once I stopped shivering, I thought, and hauled myself back onto my knees. I nearly shrieked in agony. My knees were badly bruised at best, I prayed nothing worse. This was no time to get injured. I clambered to my feet and stood for a moment to catch my breath and steady myself.

'Nathan, are you okay?'

'I'm fine,' I lied. 'That water's colder than I thought. Took me by surprise. I'm on my way down now. Watch out.'

I fetched the rope and took a deep breath before I straddled the notch wide-legged and began my descent. At least that was the plan. What happened was the water took my breath away again just as I eased myself out over the cliff and my numb fingers scrabbled at the rope in a futile attempt to get a firm grip on its slippery fibres.

I lost my grip and fell like a stone into the mist.

[41]

I was too terrified to scream. Instead, as I fell, I made a deep huff, huff, huffing noise that matched the beating of my heart. It jumped inside me as if trying to leave me and escape its fate of being smashed on the rocks hundreds of feet below.

They say your life passes before your eyes when you're about to die, but that's nonsense. Trust me, in my mind's eye I watched while my imagination relentlessly rehearsed how I might have made the descent without killing myself in the process.

It says something when even your own brain is accusing you of being a hapless idiot and insists on showing you how things could have been so much better. What satisfaction it was deriving from it I couldn't say. Like the rest of me my brain would soon be a bloody pulp smeared across the rocks.

I twisted in the air trying to grab hold of the rope and halt my fall. I scrabbled at it but could no more get purchase on it than I could find purchase in the air. I howled in frustration. Even Preacher wouldn't know what had happened to me.

I would fall and become the mysteriously vanished man in the mist, soon to be washed away by the fierce torrent of the Jinsha River. Nuo would never know where her new husband had gone. It was all so *stupid*.

I was violently torn from the air, then rammed bodily into the unyielding cliff. I went limp, all the air expelled from me. My battered frame crumpled in a heap and I wondered what fresh horror had been visited upon me. Could I not even be allowed to fall to my death in peace? My life had become far too eventful just recently.

Then I tasted cold metal against my teeth and my mouth filled with a fluid that burned up into my sinuses and my brain. I almost choked, and I fought hard against the hands that held me pinned to the ground.

'For Pete's sake, Nathan, stop wriggling or you'll have the two of us over the side. Calm down, man. Take a deep breath, will you?'

Preacher? How? Then I realised that the miracle had happened, I was saved. That was an interesting moment in my life. I needed a few breaths to help me adjust from my hopeless fall to certain death, to being plucked from mid-air and rescued by being slammed against a narrow ledge high up on a cliff above a raging torrent.

It would be a fine tale to tell our children if Nuo and I ever had any. If I lived that long, which on current evidence seemed unlikely.

I was soaked and frozen and trembling with shock. My whole body quivered uncontrollably, and my teeth chattered together like Spanish castanets. My knees sent shooting pains up my spine and I had collected even more scrapes and bruises after my sudden collision with the rocky ledge. And yet... and yet... I had to admit I felt fine. Never better. I started to laugh.

The Preacher gazed down at me as if I was a madman and that made me laugh even harder. I laughed until I was doubled-up with the pain of it, my belly hurt with laughing. And then I started coughing and whooping. It took me a few minutes to get a hold of myself.

The look of grave concern on Preacher's face was almost enough to set me off again, but I made myself breathe into my cupped hands the way my father had shown me, and I was soon calm once more.

'Sorry about that,' I said. 'My father used to say I had an over-developed funny bone. He called it my tickle feather. I'd start laughing at the smallest thing and then I couldn't stop. He would make me breathe into a brown paper bag or my cupped hands to help bring me to my senses. I'm all right now.'

He hauled me to my feet. My hands were bleeding and my knees a mortal torture, but I was alive and that was what mattered. Alive to fight another day. My head swam, and I swayed on legs suddenly weak as water. A pair of big hands gripped my shoulders and dark eyes peered curiously into mine. Then he held his hands out before me.

He said, 'Put your hands into mine, palms down.' I did as he told me. He continued. 'The worm will smell fresh blood and be ready before we are. We don't want that. Wait a moment.'

My palms began to itch. I tried to pull them away to scratch at them, but they seemed firmly glued into place. It felt like thousands of ants were crawling into my skin, burrowing under the flesh. I writhed trying to get away from the strange sensation, but I was rooted to the spot. I stared at Preacher, mutely begging for mercy, but he was lost in concentration, his eyes firmly shut.

The ant sensation swarmed through me, up my arms and into my body. Soon every inch of me was alive with the maddening, burning itch. It was the single most disgusting feeling I had ever experienced. I wouldn't have been surprised if the flesh had sloughed away from my bones. An army of tiny sharp feet scrabbled away inside me; even my penis sprang to attention, stimulated by the swarming creatures tickling and biting at it.

It wasn't painful as such, but it was excruciating in a very singular way. I felt I was being tortured from my bones outwards, as if every nerve, every cell, every single part of me, was being scoured and polished by minute

158

claws. I had been shuddering with cold before, but now I squirmed in exquisite torment.

All the while the Preacher stood stock still and my palms were cemented to his. My knees screamed when they became the focus for the army of ants. I felt the little buggers flood down inside my thighs and puddle where I hurt most. That pain was harsh and jagged, I saw light and colours flashing before my eyes when the knife-like anguish stabbed and stabbed again and again through me.

I heard a lament-like noise that sounded like an animal in pain. Somebody put that poor creature out of its misery, I thought. It's too cruel to let it live like that, listen to its suffering. I was distracted from my own woes for just a moment, and then I realised where the sound was coming from. It was me.

The pain was a mass of contradictions, it seemed to last for an eternity, but it also flooded through me like a fever and was gone in a flash. At the same time, it wormed slowly into every secret place, and it burned and itched there, wearing away my tissues with maddening intensity.

When it was finished I found it hard to remember what it felt like, but I knew I would never forget my time of torment.

Preacher lowered his hands away from mine. I turned my palms to look at them. I expected to see the skin burned raw and blistered. I expected to see my flesh bubbling as if it had been boiled and scraped to bloody ruin. The memory of my horrible experience crawled through my mind with nauseating clarity, I shivered with revulsion.

I had been penetrated and invaded by a crawling swarm of something vile. I had felt them plucking at my body from the inside, tearing at me with busy, tiny teeth. Take the feeling of sandpaper on your skin and multiply it by a million, a trillion, more. Now send it scouring throughout your entire body. Feel that? It doesn't come close to what happened to me on that ledge.

I wanted to be sick. I felt as if every tendon in my body was humming like a plucked harp string. My scalp itched, and I pushed my unmarked hands through my hair. Then I straightened, waiting for the plangent agony from my knees to smite me again. The memory of pain was still acute, but my legs were whole once more. Every bruise, every scrape was gone. I tingled with health.

'What did you do to me?'

Preacher smiled, 'I know, it felt terrible, and I'm sorry for that, but I needed you fighting fit. Both your knees were partially dislocated and one of your kneecaps was cracked. A fair amount of the skin had been torn from your fingers, there was no way you could hold a gun, let alone pull the trigger.

'Add cracked ribs and a slipped disc to the list and you were in a sorry state. So, I shared some of my body with you. Call it Nano biotech, call it friendly science, hell, call it magic if you like, but just now you're set up like new. Better than new. How do you feel?'

I stretched like a cat in front of the fire. I unclipped its leather strap and pulled my Colt out of its holster then checked to make sure it wasn't damaged in any way. Satisfied I pressed it back and strapped it tight. I grinned.

'Preacher, I never want to go through that ever again, and that's a stone fact. But, right now I'm ready to kill me a mother worm. Shall we go?'

[42]

My enhanced sense of wellbeing added an eerie, dreamlike layer to our progress along that narrow ledge. I felt almost drugged by health, drunk with it. I kept flexing my knees and rolling my shoulders in disbelief. Over the years I had picked up a few injuries and one or two scars, plus I had aches and pains that I lived with on a day-to-day basis, as all working men do.

But now I was factory fresh and as clean as a new-born child. I felt as if I could run a mile and jump fences at the Grand National. I was light on my feet and giddy with energy. I couldn't remember what Preacher had called his treatment at first, nanny something, but 'friendly science' sounded good to me, even if my skin still crawled at the memory of those 'ants'.

But a part of me was still sober as a soldier on the front line. The mist was thicker than ever, and it billowed around us like pearl-coloured silk floating in water. My eyes ached to see into the distance, or even pick out a detail, any detail, of the landscape beyond the few feet afforded us by the weather.

Our isolated stretch of ledge kept providing proof that it was part of a much larger, living landscape. Some parts of it had been eroded and narrowed by trickles of icy water, or partly torn away by a rock fall. On one section the ledge was gone completely for several feet. I looked hard for finger and foot-holds we might use to scale the distance, all the while experiencing the pull of that invisible depth down to the river.

I didn't think Preacher would appreciate me falling again quite so soon and said so. He shook his head, turned to face me, said, 'Don't move a muscle,' and then locked his arms around me. Without another word he launched us both across the gap. I didn't dare breathe and tried not to look down during our flight. We rose on one section of ledge and descended to another. The process was as simple and as impossible as that.

But, as soon as our full weight pressed down on the stone again it crumbled away underneath us, and we fell a few feet before the Preacher managed to regain his powers of flight. I don't know how he did it, but I envied him his invisible wings. I wondered aloud why he hadn't just flown us down to the ledge earlier instead of using that rope, and he fired a few words over his shoulder at me.

'There are ways of doing things, my friend. I must abide by them, even when they don't seem to make any sense to you. I'm tied by them – I'm programmed that way, always have been. Since my fall from grace I can only fly in a crisis, that's part of what diminishes me. When I confront evil I must

161

have a human with me to defend or I'm forbidden to act. I'm a passive servant and a guard dog, nothing more, nothing less.

'To save a good man I would fight an army, but, to save myself I couldn't lift so much as a finger. Think of me as the servile genii but without his bottle. There's little to envy about me, Nathan. I envy you your immortal soul, I envy the least of mankind their spiritual immortality.'

I heard once more the weight of years pressing down on the man, for man he was in my eyes despite his godlike powers and strangeness. I heard the sadness wrenching at him with hungry fingers. There was nothing I could say to ease his sorrow or share his pain; his need was too great and too distant from anything I understood. All I could do is be the ward he needs care for. I provided the reason he was there, so he could act as my shield and strong defender.

If it hadn't been me I've no doubt Preacher would have found someone else. He needed his 'Parsifal' to protect in our war against the nightmare Sha-aneer. It made it more personal. Even so I was glad it *was* me; since meeting him my life would never be the same again. Thanks to the Preacher I knew things and had seen things that had changed me from guttersnipe to... What?

Yes, what was I? I had been the unfixed needle in a broken compass, a leaf in the breeze. The seeds from a dandelion clock had better foundations than me, at least one day they would put down roots and flower, I was the restless nomad who never called anyplace home.

But no longer. Now I was husband to Nuo and friend to a fallen angel. Yes, I was also the fool who was ready to follow that same angel into Hell. What was I thinking? Had I only gained a better life to cast it away on a fool's errand? Who knows? At least I was alive and knew it, that must be worth something?

I had found a purpose in life once more, something I had forgotten existed after mother died and then Grandfather had left me all on my own. I had stopped caring if I lived or died because life had lost its value for me. I lived my life wrapped in a blanket of dumb acceptance.

I was the lamb blindly entering the slaughterhouse, careless of its fate. If I was taken by the worm it would suck the life and soul clean out of me. I trembled at the thought, but at least and at last I was alive enough to care. That made it worthwhile.

'We're getting close to the cave mouth. Mind your step, Nathan, not far now. Be careful, stick close to the cliff wall, we've come too far to lose our footing at the last minute. Just a few more yards. Keep your eyes open for little black and red bugs. They look like thin maggots, don't touch them.'

162

'I remember, back at the militia compound. You think we'll find them up here?'

'Unlikely, they only get spread when the infected are at the mobile stage of growth and this creature don't move worth a damn. But we've been killing its calves, it may have evolved in ways I haven't seen before. Just keep your eyes and ears open, be ready for anything.'

I could hear the steel in his voice. He said he had been created to be a gardener planting the seeds of men – and had since grown from necessity to be a cold killer. What would he become if we succeeded in our mission? He was dedicated to destroying the beast, what would he find to do once it was gone? I know some people are only defined by their enemies.

I remember two shipmates who hated each other with such intense venom that they never sailed under the same skipper; until that last time when they both shipped out on the *Lucy Fair*. At first things were calm enough, but it couldn't last.

Nobody knew what sparked it off, but one calm evening there came a mortal hullabaloo from the stern and we ran to witness the fuss. The two men were facing off against each other with knives drawn.

The bosun shouted at them to show sense, but he didn't dare approach them. Those crazy men were slashing at each other with murder in their hearts and it was plain what would happen if anyone tried to separate them. We decided it was wiser if we waited until the fight was over then went in to pick up the pieces.

The end came quickly. One of the men lunged wildly, the other blocked the man's blade and stabbed at his opponent's belly. There was a confusing blur of movement, and then the first man stepped back with his guts spilling out into his hands. By the look on his face I knew he couldn't believe it was over, but the lifeblood was spurting from him in black gouts. He fell hard with a sound like a sack of iron and lay still.

His killer ran to him and turned him face up. He felt for the man's pulse and gazed for a while at the blood on his hands. Nobody said anything. Then the killer dropped his knife with a grunt of pain, and before anyone could stop him he leapt to his feet and ran to the side. He scrambled over the rail and was gone. Like most seafarers he couldn't swim,

The crew said the killer had drowned himself rather than hang, but I wasn't so sure. I thought he had realised he had no reason to live once his enemy was defeated. He had lived for just that one thing, to kill his enemy. Once the man was dead what was there to live for?

Would that happen to the Preacher once the worm was gone? Not if I had my way it wouldn't. I kept my eyes on him and followed him into the cave mouth. We had arrived.

[43]

How had those ancient soldiers managed to carry their mortally wounded general to this cave in the sky? The crumbling ledge would have dropped us into the river more than once if the Preacher hadn't had the power of flight in a crisis. The only answer I could find was that the ledge must have been a broader pathway back in their day. Easier to traverse.

Preacher was right about the difficulty of access to the cave from above, it would have been nigh impossible. There was a jutting overhang above the cave mouth and a wall of rock that folded around the entrance like a curtain. The cave was screened from every direction except the ledge. Without the map and Preacher's flying eyes we could never have found it.

As soon as we entered the cave I could smell the midden reek of the worm. It was faint but unmistakeable. We had found the right place. My mouth ran dry. By the faint silver light from outside I could just discern the walls of the cave. They opened out to create an airy space with a smooth floor. The walls near the entrance had been carved by a skilled hand.

Imperial dragons flew from the floor to the ceiling, in the centre of which Buddha sat in contemplation. His right hand was held up, palm outwards. I wondered if he was warning us to go no further. I for one was ready to listen.

'This first chamber must have been a place of pilgrimage and meditation, even though the Sha-aneer was secreted further down in the cave complex. See the buddha and bodhisattvas, those heavenly flying creatures? They were likely carved by a single monk over many years. The dragons probably came later, they look like the work of a different hand.'

Preacher spoke quietly. He pointed out the intricate architectural detail of the cave; which included carved arches and faux windows that opened onto delicate carved landscapes. He was even able to identify the Jade Dragon Snow Mountains and the Haba peaks.

'Priceless works of art, beautiful. And all this will be lost before the day is out, or we will have failed. Come on, Nathan. We're going in.'

At the limit of the light from the cave mouth we found a carved archway and waited until our eyes adjusted to the gloom. Gently the ghost light bestowed by Preacher's magic tincture came into play, and I was able to pick out a stone staircase. We followed it down. The walls closed in as we descended until we had to walk Indian file. The air became warm, moist, and rank. There were no sounds apart from our steps and my laboured breathing.

After an age we arrived at a second, smaller archway. We ducked through and entered a second chamber. It was immense. In phosphorescent outlines I saw two rows of giant carved buddhas in the huge room. I detected the sheen of gilding in their auras. They were beautiful and unearthly.

As we walked between them towards the far end of the chamber I was astonished by the peaceful expressions on the figures' faces. Was it remotely possible that an artist could carve such beauty knowing how close they were to the Sha-aneer and certain death? And then I reeled back from two nightmare figures crouched either side of the next entrance.

At first, I thought they were dogs or tigers, poised ready to spring. Preacher reached out and patted one of them on the head.

'Grave guardians,' he whispered. 'These are older than the buddhas. They warn visitors not to go any further into the cave on pain of eternal torment.'

'Would people take any notice?'

'Most would, some wouldn't. Chances are the ones who dared enter the next chamber didn't come back. Chinese legends are filled with stories of cave demons and monsters. Maybe this is where they started?'

The stink of the worm was much stronger. We walked cautiously between the guardians and entered the lair of the beast. The walls of the passage became raw stone, polished by time and the action of water but untouched by human hands. But man had been here. He had left his traces.

On a natural ledge to one side of the short stone passage was several long, thin, rusted objects that closer examination showed to be swords in their scabbards. On the floor nearby was a pouch from which spilled decorated discs with square windows cut into their centre, through which coarse string had been threaded to make a necklace.

With his mouth by my ear Preacher whispered, 'Han dynasty wu zhu coins. No one would drop them and leave them just lying like that. That pouch would have been worth a fortune.'

The silence was suffocating. Nothing lived in the cave, it was a dead place. I could taste the worm as well as smell it. I felt myself to be saturated with its foul reek. More of the trappings of men were scattered around underfoot. Scraps of rag that might have been a kerchief, a bag of tools, and a small dancing figure with long sleeves. I saw a squat little man playing his drum. He was grinning with joy.

There was so much life in those little figurines, so much verve and humour. What fate had left them so carelessly discarded in that eternal, stinking darkness? And that was when I saw him, laid out on a natural stone bier wearing a suit of armour that covered him from neck to foot. The general.

My first impression was that his suit was made from scales like those of a great fish, but as I drew closer I saw that his armour was constructed from strips of metal skilfully woven together with threads. It was magnificent, but it had failed to shield him from whatever had torn a gash in its side.

His desiccated, leathery skull grinned mockingly at me. It still wore a kerchief around its neck and a cap upon its crown – and it had a full head of hair tied back in a ponytail – but it was the most dead looking corpse I had ever seen. He had a sword by his side and the trappings of wealthy man about his person, but he was as dead looking as a mouse left too long in a trap.

Preacher pointed to the general's armoured left hand. It was resting on something the size of a full-grown, medium-sized dog. He leaned forward and carefully, soundlessly, lifted the general's arm. Then he took up the object he had revealed. It leapt and sparkled like a live thing in his hand. It was the five-clawed Fucanglong, the imperial dragon of hidden treasures.

Looking at that sculpture through ghost sight made it seem even more precious. It held a stone the size of a hen's egg in its jaws, and its eyes glistened with light, even in the darkness. Its body was lithe, every inch exquisitely carved and shaped. It was one of the most extraordinary manmade objects I had ever seen. I couldn't help myself, I reached out and stroked its long, lean belly.

And then Preacher shocked me to the marrow. He thrust his fingers hard into the dragon's mouth, squeezed them shut behind the stone held there, and pulled. With a slight squeak of tortured metal, the stone came free. He handed it to me. Then, one after the other, he plucked the dragon's eyes from their gilded sockets. These he also handed to me.

He replaced the defaced dragon where he had found it, and then put his mouth right next to my ear.

'Consider those to be your wedding gifts. That dragon's lost to history. It will never see the light of day again, and those jewels will set you and Nuo up for life. Put them somewhere safe and secure. Don't argue.'

I didn't argue. I had just finished buttoning them into one of my breast pockets when I heard the sound that made me draw my Colt from its holster. All around us grew the whispering of oily, sly voices. The worm knew we were there.

[44]

It was as if the fabric of the cave itself had come to life. The walls bulged and creaked under the worm's immense weight. The voices insinuated themselves into my ears like greased threads through the eye of a needle, underpinned by the rasping, creeping sounds of its massive, thick hide grinding against stone.

Who is that whispering? Is that the sound of living men come to visit the mother? You are welcome, most welcome. We see so little of you these days, little men. We shall take you and share you with the host, and you shall be ready and part of us when we calve soon. We must calve and go out to conquer the world of man and all his tasty beasts.

Wait, what is that creature there? What is this? One of the Eden things, here? I can smell you, filth. I can taste you in my flesh, and I have met your brothers. All of you, you, bastard creations, machine men cobbled together so very far away. Why are you here? Why did you come here? Have you come to die, Eden filth? Have you come here to be crushed and ground down into dust? Ground into the soil that never spawned you?

There is no escape, Eden spawn. This is my place, my home, the nest of the Mother Sha-aneer. See, I am all around you.

I turned back to look towards the hall of giant buddhas. The passage was blocked by a bulging curtain of pallid flesh. Things did not look good. I thought we had planned to catch the worm by surprise, but Preacher's whisper to me had warned it we were close. And now it was gloating.

There were two of you before, Eden spawn. Two of you, so very clever they were. They crept into the cave like silent thoughts into a sleeping head. They never made a sound. They were much quieter and cleverer than you, little Eden spawn. They didn't know where I was, but I knew them when they walked on me and I took them deep to my heart.

I heard it sigh with pleasure. *Crushed them to flints and splinters. I felt them die in my grasp. It was so, so sweet.*

The sound of that voice made me feel dirty. I wanted it silenced, I wanted it gone so that the world could become a cleaner, saner place once more. The floor rocked under our feet and the ceiling cracked above our heads. Dust and fine stone pattered around us.

Shall I make it fast? Or shall I make it slow for you? The human shall melt on my flesh and join us in the host, it shall add its spice to ours and feed us its delicious soul, hmmmm, so delicious. Do you know what a human soul tastes like, Eden spawn?

These dainty tidbits you spent so long pulling from the wombs of honest Earth beasts are the favourite dish in my larder store. And, you know, the whole world is my larder store. What does it taste like? I'll tell you.

The human soul tastes like despair, it tastes like loss. It tastes like the tears of a god left alone in an uncaring universe, and it tastes like arrogance turned to shit. Ahhhh, so sweet. And you made me so many of them. How can I thank-you? How can I ever thank-you? Ah, yes, by grinding you to pieces, by grinding you to DUST!

The floor and the ceiling began to close together. Preacher stood tall and spoke aloud.

'How did they walk on you, Mother of the wise worm? How did my brothers walk on you? Where are you in this cave? Do you not live deep in the belly of the Earth? How could they walk on you? Could *I* walk on your flesh? Could I touch you for the last time, oldest, greatest, and last of your ancient breed?'

The voices hissed and slunk all around us. We were completely surrounded. The worm must have pressed itself into every niche and crevice it could find. Even the narrowest threadlike seam was filled with the worm's elastic tissue. It had not yet digested me, but I already felt devoured by the beast. I stood in its bowels and waited for it to take me. I pointed my Colt in every direction.

Preacher whispered in a voice so low I barely caught it. 'Save your shells, Nathan. You'll know when and where to shoot. Bide me and be patient. I'll need you soon enough.'

What do you mean, oldest and last? I am not the last. I was the first, and I was fruitful. My calves are a multitude upon the face of the Earth and they shall rise to devour the children of men. They are ready to rise, and they shall come to me here. We shall plant seeds that will flower for the new age of the Sha-aneer. Our beautiful flesh shall sip the last flesh of men and it shall be once again as it was in the beginning.

Can't you taste the filthy smoke of man on the air. Can't you taste what he has done to our beautiful, clean home? He burns, and he hacks, and he destroys everything around him. Even here in the mountains his foul breath makes us sick with its filth. What have you done, Eden spawn, to bring such vileness to my home? Are you proud of your achievement?

'You are the first and the last, Mother of the wise worm. I have killed your multitude, hunted them down and burned them where they lived. I have burned the worm where it hid in the earth, and where its seed walked the lands. You are the last, and I would touch you before I kill you. Or, are you afraid?'

The silence that followed Preacher's oddly formal announcement rang for long seconds in the warm, still air of the cave. The floor stopped quivering and the ceiling ceased to pepper us with fine grit. I still couldn't see into the hall of buddhas, so I knew we were still surrounded by the worm, but I no longer felt under immediate threat. It was mulling Preacher's words.

When it spoke again it sounded odd, as if distracted. *I know you now, Satan Spindrift. I have seen your bloody footprints throughout history. You are the roots from which the Eden born have grown. You are the reason they have prospered. You fertilised the soil and tended the first buds of that foul offspring from an alien world. That foul offspring THERE!*

The worm's quill caught me full in the back and the shock of it sent me spread-eagled face down on the cave floor. I still had my pistol in my hand. I had hoped to use it on myself if all else failed. It was too late for that now. I was paralysed, all I could do was watch and listen.

Preacher ran to my side. He pressed something into my free hand, shut his eyes and said a single word. Then he stood tall again and spoke aloud.

'Will you let me walk on you, mother worm? The last of us and the last of you. Is it not fitting that it should be thus? I am your enemy, Mother worm, do you not wish to feel my touch for the last time? Do you not wish to make your goodbyes? While you still can.'

Last, you say you are the last? What of your great ship out beyond the red planet? Would it not send down more of you? You are not the last, merely the latest to die.

'The ship has gone, Mother worm. It has given up on mankind. It offered me passage to a new world, but I said no. I have been too long on this one to give it up. This is my home now, Mother worm, and I'm tired. It has been too long, and I want it done at last. I want it finished. Will you let me touch you in farewell?'

One of the walls of the cave fell away and lay flat. It undulated as if anticipating the print of Preacher's feet upon its surface. The stink of the worm became unbearably rancid. It was excited.

You are welcome to touch me for the last time, Satan Spindrift. Welcome. Walk on my glorious flesh.

[45]

I was astonished to find that I still had some limited control of my body. Although I couldn't physically move from my prone position, I could follow the Preacher's trek out onto the worm's body. Watching him was a gut-twisting experience. Before taking that lonely walk, he turned to look at me; and then addressed the worm.

'May I say goodbye to my friend?'

It hissed strangely, a vile bubbling sound I realised with sick horror to be laughter.

What is it to me? Say farewell to life, Spindrift, say farewell to all the hordes of Eden scum you seeded. It's a shame you will not be here to see the new world we shall create. All the humans we devour will help us populate the Earth with cleanliness and beauty once more; you should appreciate the exquisite irony of it all.

Say goodbye to it, then come quickly to me. I am awaiting our union with breathless anticipation. Shall I be the husband or the bride? I wonder?

It made that hissing sound again, and its volume grew until it was almost unbearable. For the first time I appreciated its immense size. Its laughter battered at me and rippled through the solid stone under me as if it was water. The thing must be the size of a mountain. What chance did Preacher stand against this gigantic mother of a beast?

'I guess this is goodbye, Nathan. You've been a mighty fine companion. Shoot the sack. Whatever happens to us we have that to be grateful for. Shoot the sack. Good luck, God's speed. I'm proud to have known you. Shoot the sack.'

He whispered the words with a fierce light in his eyes. Shoot the sack? What sack? And then he drew his pistol and he pulled the sack from inside his coat. He flicked a glance at me and then at the sack. It bulged as if it was filled with eggs. I nodded. Yes, I understood.

With that he turned his back to me and walked out towards the undulating flesh of the worm like a tightrope walker, his arms out like a crucified man. The laughter of the worm rippled and gurgled around us like slime pumped down a sewer pipe.

Wait, wait. Let us take a little time to savour this moment. This is history, Satan Spindrift, last of your kind. True history. This is where your few petty hours upon this Earth – this realm you and your kind invaded, unasked and unwanted – this is where your time comes to its end. Let us enjoy just a few brief seconds of contemplation before your little reign reaches its conclusion.

Preacher paused, and I saw him bow his head as if praying. He was still as a statue, and vital as a tree. I could not believe what was about to happen to him, and at that moment I would have taken his place. I wanted to scream at him to run, to forget me. He *must* live to continue the fight. I was nothing, I was nothing but a poor scrap of flesh. The world wouldn't survive without him, it couldn't survive.

He continued walking his tightrope. In one hand was his pistol, in the other that sack.

Satan Spindrift, welcome to my body. Please, take your steps upon me. Time for the wedding ceremony to begin. Ahhhhhhhhhh, yesssssssss. So, sweet a touch. Come now, don't be shy, don't be shy. And we shan't need THIS!

Faster than my eye could follow a sinuous rope of the worm's flesh lashed out and swept the Preacher's pistol from his hand. It slashed a deep V across the back of his hand and split his palm cleanly like the blade of an axe. Blood wept from him in a stream of darkness, ghost light could not see red.

And so it begins, the consummation of our union, Satan Spindrift. I have nothing to fear from guns, no more than you fear a grain of sand carried by the wind. But why bring weapons to our wedding? We have all we need here, you and I, and our wedding supper as witness. I shall take you, and then enjoy him. It is so long since I sipped a soul, but I don't want to rush things.

The flesh of the beast pooled around Preacher's feet and, at first, I thought it was rising up his legs, but then with increasing panic I saw he was sinking into its body. It couldn't subsume him the way it would me, but it could swallow him whole then crush him in its folds. It had crushed his fellows and ground them to dust. It had said so.

Preacher's legs were trapped firmly in its grip, and it slowly sucked him down, deeper and deeper. All the time I watched in helpless, fascinated horror. He was down as far as his waist now. All too soon it would take him into its depths, suffocating and crushing him in absolute darkness.

And then he leaned back and held the sack up high in his uninjured hand. He bellowed, 'Nathan! Now, for God's sake.' And I suddenly remembered, 'shoot the sack'. It had been his last instruction to me and in my horror, I had forgotten all about it. I used all my strength to fight my paralysis and I pointed my gun at the bulging bag. It leapt at me as if I was using a telescope.

It seemed close enough to touch, I could see the very grain of its fabric. I squeezed the trigger, panting with exertion. Nothing happened. I squeezed

172

again. Nothing. All the while I had been flapping that gun around like a wild man I had forgotten to pull back the slide and prime its hammer.

Panting and whimpering like an exhausted dog I turned the gun upside down and pressed it against the hard rock. I pushed it forward and was rewarded with the sound of it priming. I was so pleased with myself that I lost my concentration for just a second, I swear, just a second, and I dropped the blessed thing.

Preacher had sunk to his chest, he bellowed my name again and again. All the while I was fumbling with numb fingers, scrabbling to pick the gun up and get my finger to the trigger. I was sobbing with the effort and my chin was slick with drool. I lifted my arm and with an impossible effort I took the pistol's grip in my hand, looked up, and aimed.

Preacher was gone. I couldn't see him. I had failed him in his final hour of need. He had sunk down into that nightmare creature's foul embrace. I felt cold and sick. I tried to turn the gun onto myself. At least I could do one last thing properly in the heart of the nightmare.

And then I saw it, a flash of darkness against the grey expanse of the worm. The sack thrust up, still gripped in the Preacher's hand. It was his last-ditch attempt, his last forlorn hope that I could finally do something right. I didn't hesitate, I poured every shell I had into the sack's bulging belly.

The world exploded in a frenzy of actinic white light. I couldn't shut or shield my eyes from the glare, and soon the phosphorescent glow of ghost light was replaced by a burning sheet of redness. I could see nothing, but at least I knew I had hit what I aimed at. Poor, paralysed, blind creature that I was, I had saved Preacher from his terrible fate.

He must die in that conflagration, but at least his end would be quick and clean. And I knew I must also die, awash in a sea of flame and rendered to ash in the death throes of the mother worm. I didn't want to die, I had so much to live for, but at least I had helped rid the world of the last of that vile breed, the Sha-aneer.

My world was red as blood and hot as a furnace. I took a breath and heat scorched my throat and lungs. I could hear screaming as if from a million lungs and I praised God that the worm's injuries were mortal. I heard stone crashing and falling around me, and the floor was bucking under me like a live thing, but I still lived. I still lived in the inferno.

But my luck couldn't last, and I felt myself lifted into the air on a final wave of heat just as darkness descended. It ends, I thought, at last I had escaped the nightmare and found peace – and oblivion.

Pack up your troubles in your old kit-bag,
And smile, smile, smile,
While you've a lucifer to light your fag,
Smile, boys, that's the style.
What's the use of worrying?
It never was worthwhile, so
Pack up your troubles in your old kit-bag,
And smile, smile, smile.

I'd had a Lucifer to light my fag, that was for sure. Or at least a Satan. We'd done it, we'd killed the sly bastard, killed it and died in victory. A clean death in the white flame of the worm's funeral pyre. On the ships we used to wonder what was best, a watery tomb in Davy Jones's locker, a box six-feet under the sod, or cremation? The first two would see us as meat for the maggots and fishes, the last turned us to ash.

At least I hadn't had to choose. Cremation it was and from ashes to ashes I went. I supposed I was in limbo, or in some sort of antechamber to the afterlife. The worm hadn't sipped my soul, so I still had my passport to immortality. Would mother meet me? Would my father?

Or would I be greeted by a stony-faced Saint Peter and made to wait while he ran his finger down the page with my name on it and tutted in disappointment? I doubted it. I had little time for the traditional Heaven and Hell, but Preacher had told me I had a soul and I must end up somewhere. Surely? Somewhere?

Then I smelled a warm, seductive scent that I knew could not be from any angel. But equally it couldn't be from any demon. That scent was fresh and feminine, it was grounded in the mortal world. For the first time since coming to my senses I believed, impossibly, that I had once again somehow survived. But, I was blind. Alive, but blinded by the intense glare of our weapon.

A familiar voice breathed close to my cheek. 'Get ready, Nathan. Shut your eyes. We're going to remove the dressings and, at first, the light may seem a little bright. Are you ready?'

I tried to say yes but all I managed was a painful croaking sound.

'Don't try to talk. Your windpipe was damaged by the fire. One thing at a time. You know what they say about running and walking? Well, just now we're still working on the crawl. That's it, here we go.'

The air on my naked eyelids felt cool and pleasant to me. I had to know if I still had my sight. I opened my eyes. Rowan looked down on me, concern writ clear on her glorious features. I smiled at her. The skin of my face felt tight.

'They had to regrow your eyeballs, Nathan. The fire had burned them out of their sockets. Are they okay now? Just nod if yes.'

I nodded. Her face brightened. 'Good, that's good. Now we can work on the rest of you. Time for a little more sleep. See you soon.'

Sometimes I was awake, and I talked with Rowan or Colin, mostly I dreamed the hours away. There were too many odd visions plucked from fantasy to remember them all, and some were nightmares I'd rather forget. The few I could remember had their own strange logic.

In one I was the figurehead of an old navy man-of-war from Nelson's time, a fine three-masted frigate. All that remained of my body was my head and torso. My eyes had been carved as huge orbs with an oriental tilt to them. Gulls nested in my gaping mouth. No wonder I couldn't talk, I thought.

Then in another dream I was walking down the hall of great buddhas and as I passed them each serene face bent towards me and smiled. I apologised for destroying them, tried to tell them I had no choice. Each of them answered with my father's voice, 'That's perfectly all right, old lad. You only did what you had to do. Well done, you're a very good boy. Proud of you.'

The last was Nuo at the range in the mission house, busily juggling pots and pans like a cook in a soup kitchen. Duck carcasses hung overhead from hooks set into the ceiling. Off to one side Junjie was washing dishes like his life depended on it. She flashed me a look filled with pride and anger.

'You know this the busiest time for lunch. Don't stand around like a lemon just because we own the place, go do something useful. You get in the way there. Shoo!' I turned to scamper away and look after our diners in the refectory. 'Hey,' she shouted at my back. 'I love you.'

'I love you,' I said out loud.

'I'm flattered, but don't tell our wives. They might find it difficult to understand.'

My eyes flew open to find Colin seated by my bed. He grinned at me.

'I think I'm one of the few people alive who can honestly say they have an idea how you feel, Nathan. You're doing great, my friend. They say you should try to sit up. But first, Rowan has something for you.'

His wife appeared from behind him. She held out a simple pottery cup to me and indicated that I should take it. It was icy cold to the touch.

Rowan nodded at me. 'Drink it all down in one go. It's cold but it evaporates quickly. Go on.'

I drained the cup. The liquid seemed to instantly bloom from my mouth and throat and flood out with a warm buzzing glow to all my extremities, and I mean *all* my extremities. It reminded me of the Preacher's nanny technology, and it had the same effect on my most personal part. I was painfully aware that my old chap had become as rigid as a broom handle.

Rowan took the cup from me and made to pull my bedclothes down. 'Time to get up,' she said. I grabbed at the sheets with furious strength.

'Not just yet,' I told her. 'Your infusion has had an... effect. In the name of decency may I have a few minutes to recover? A gentleman shouldn't, ah, you know? Not in front of a lady.'

Rowan gazed at the bedclothes around my waist with an arch look in her eyes. 'Oh my,' she said. 'You're one of those! It takes some men like that.' She grinned with a face filled with mischief, like a cat loose in the birdcage. 'Lucky Nuo. Very well, I'll wait outside to save *all* our blushes.'

Colin and I waited until she had flounced out and closed the door behind herself. He burst out laughing and slapped me on the shoulder, then stepped across to a tallboy affair against the wall and fetched out some clothing.

'After what you've been through you've earned the right to a little privacy. You'll have to forgive Rowan, my friend. Something about you brings out the worst in her. I think she likes you. You get dressed while I go spank some sense into her, not that it'll do any good. Never has yet, not even using a hazel switch. I'll be right outside if you need me.'

I didn't believe he spanked his wife for one minute, but it made a pretty picture. Whatever was in that cup took a while to wear off and I rushed into my underpants as fast as I could in case Rowan burst in to surprise me in my state of undress. I nearly fell over with both feet down one trouser leg, but at last I was satisfied that I was fit for mixed company.

I felt a little numb at first, but otherwise fit as a fiddle. Then I felt something hard in my trouser pocket. I dug out three gems, a ruby big as a walnut and two cut diamonds, each the size of my thumbnail. An emperor's ransom. And I remembered the Preacher handing them to me before the worm began talking with us. *The Preacher*.

Holding those gems in my hands I relived his last moments, heard him bellowing my name. I saw his hand thrust out from the enfolding flesh of the worm, the sack held clear one last time. Shoot the sack, he'd said, shoot the sack. I remembered my clumsy fumbling with the pistol, priming the hammer, dropping it, scrabbling for it.

And then I remembered aiming, firing, and my world turning white, whiter than the heart of a star. All the while I was holding Colin's calling stone in my left hand and I hadn't even known. That was what saved me. At the time it seemed everything took hours, but it must have been much faster than that. In one of my rare lucid moments on my road to recovery, Colin had told me he had heard the call and responded within minutes, finding me alone and dying.

Long, long, minutes. Time enough for the Preacher to be lost in the inferno. And thanks to him I was still alive. I looked down at the stones. He had even ensured my future happiness. My eyes blurred, and I saw tears splash onto the gems. I clenched my fist and gripped the stones so hard they stung my hand. I slumped into a chair and wept until my throat felt raw once more.

[47]

I guessed it must be Sunday. The prettily made-up, bound foot wives tottered along Square Street like wind-up dolls, their husbands displaying them as brightly coloured trophies. I wondered if making the practice illegal would have any impact on the Sunday promenade, and whether new husbands would resent not knowing what it was like to sleep with a crippled woman.

But I'm getting ahead of myself. Before arriving back in Lijiang, I had to say goodbye to Scytaer Faehl and the people who had nursed me back to health. And I had one more place to see before my mind could finally rest.

Rowan told me I had recovered faster from worse injuries than anyone she had ever known. I didn't tell her about Preacher's nanny technology, I didn't understand it anyway, I just shrugged and told her I was from good stock.

I also bantered breezily with her that my family's menfolk were so well endowed that they had been used as breeding studs by aristocrats, so I might be related to royalty all over Europe. She just gazed at me as if I'd crawled out from under a rock.

'You must be feeling better,' she said. 'Takes a healthy mind to come up with something as sick as that. Better get you home to your wife before you say something worse.'

I *was* healthy. I was spit dandy, light on my toes, and ready to 'cut a rug' as the American fellows say. Damn – I felt ready to climb Nelson's Column – blindfolded. But I didn't want to go home just yet, not then. I had a special request before heading back to Shuhe and the American mission, and Nuo.

I wanted to be back with Nuo so hard it felt like a physical ache in my bones, but there was something else I had to see first. I had to find out what happened at the Tiger Leaping Gorge.

Colin told me that the French worm's death throes had destroyed much of a small town and blown a convent to smithereens; and that beast had been smaller! What had the Mother worm done to her nest?

When we got to the gorge we would be flying, and I had been strapped to Colin's body using a belt arrangement that put my legs just in front of his. Rowan had kissed me goodbye like she meant it, and she didn't laugh when I made a mess of getting into step with Colin when we walked to the portal. She just looked sad.

Colin slapped me on the shoulder and told me that if I couldn't march in step it was for the best that I hadn't gone for the career of a soldier boy, but I could also hear hesitation in his voice. Once I was home I knew I'd never see either of them again.

Colin took me to the gorge through one of those temporal portals elementals use. We arrived about a mile in the air, at least that's how high it felt when I opened my eyes in the sky above China. I had never seen anything from that high up before. It was like looking down at a map.

Over there to the west was Tibet, but everything else under me was China. Any time you start feeling like you're the biggest thing in your universe you want to get up that high and take a good look around. That should give you a better sense of perspective. The world is HUGE! And we're small. I could even see the curve of the Earth outlined in a kind of milky light.

And all the while I was fighting against terror. Those straps felt firm enough on the ground, but all that changed when I found myself dangling from Colin in mid-air at a point higher than the mountains. And it was mortal cold up there. I was wearing the street rig my friends had provided because I would be going home after we visited the gorge. It was not fit for flying. I was freezing.

I distracted myself by concentrating on what had happened when the worm burned in its nest. It was quickly obvious that it had changed the landscape beyond recognition.

Tiger Leaping Gorge had been a narrow series of curves cut through rock by the Jinsha River. It had been a playful tributary of white water carving its way across jumbled boulders towards the west. From up there in the blue bell of the sky we should have seen a delicate vein stretched across the immense landscape like a pencil drawing.

It wasn't. Not even close. It looked as if an angry giant had punched and gouged and torn at the ground, attacking it with insane fury. The delicate vein was now a gaping wound still filling with water, water that shone an impossible blue under a cloudless sky. It was shockingly ragged and was evidently the result of violence so extreme that nothing could survive. No, nothing could have survived.

I yelled, 'Can we go down?'

Colin answered, 'Yeah, okay, but keep an eye out for baffled geologists.'

'Why baffled?'

His answer was lost in the howling wind of our rapid descent. We landed in a copse of trees on the outskirts of the crater and I unbuckled myself from Colin with a sense of relief. The flying was fine – the views were amazing – but to be strapped so close to another man felt... uncomfortable.

179

I was in western dress, but Colin was in elemental robes. He wore trousers, and a long, light-coloured jacket over a soft collared shirt, the ensemble was finished with fine leather boots that would suit an Oxfordshire hunt Master. He looked exotic, foreign, and yet, undeniably human. Or, perhaps, what a human might wish to look like – in their dreams.

I had seen residents in his city who would raise an uproar among human society; real mermaids I once watched swimming *up* a waterfall, and strange, tall, albino apes that met any comment with an unsettling, silent smile. There were others with the frost of centuries settled like glittering jewel dust on their shoulders and hair, and rare fellows with barely contained fire in their eyes.

Colin could pass muster as human, and he treated me amiably enough, but I had to remind myself that he was Prince Pel-osen of the royal house of air elementals. He was no more human than the Preacher.

Colin wrapped the straps that had been holding me around his own chest and waist and then straightened his jacket. I asked him again what he meant about baffled geologists. He grinned at me.

'When Satan and I blew the top off that scarp and scorched the town we blamed a German secret weapon we called "Dragon's Breath". You guys punched a hole in China big enough to swallow New York City, maybe more. Scientists are going to want to understand what did it, and they don't have the Sha-aneer in their vocabulary. They'll need to come up with something else, but what?'

The hillside was eerily quiet once we left the trees. However, I could see a small, tented encampment off in the distance to our right. Faint voices and the clinking of hammers drifted to us on the light breeze. Colin nodded towards them.

'A lot of hard thinking and likely some harder drinking will come up with some blue touch paper to make their pet theory fly. Can't be volcanic because this isn't a volcanic area. Can't be a meteorite because the evidence shows this crater was blown out from underneath. Eventually somebody will come up with some nonsense and publish it in a learned periodical, and that will make it the truth.'

He chuckled, 'If you went over there and offered to put those fine folks out of their misery by telling them what really happened, they'd likely chase you away with their little hammers. Giant worms as old as time ain't in no text book *they've* ever seen, and now never will be. The threat of the Sha-aneer is finished, and the last servant of the GODS went with it. I guess it was worth it.'

'It was what he wanted, he planned it all the way there. Even after I was struck down Preacher knew my treatment after the previous quill toxin meant I still had limited movement, at least, enough to point a gun and pull the trigger. He put himself where he could do most damage and I fired that last shot. But, will you look at what we did!'

We came to the edge of the crater and were silenced by the sheer scope of the devastation. We were standing over eight thousand feet above sea level and wispy cloud drifted across the miles of torn rock at our feet. We had punched a hole in the ground even Everest couldn't fill, and its walls were lined with waterfalls. It held a desolate beauty.

Colin leaned forward and gazed down with intense concentration.

He said, 'Can you see that, down there?

'What? No, I can't see anything. It's too far down.'

'Come with me.'

He lifted me off my feet and threw us both into the abyss.

[48]

We fell like stones. And as we fell my ears began to ache so much I was afraid they would burst. We whipped through the cloud layer and still we plummeted towards the distant crater floor at incredible speed. Colin angled us away from the split and buckled walls and targeted the pool of water at the heart of the ruin.

As we approached it the pool grew to be a lake, and then kept expanding in my sight until it was more like a great inland loch enclosed by black cliffs. It was majestic and a fitting monument to God's warrior who had died there.

And then I saw what Colin had spotted from that impossible distance so far above us. He must have the eyes of a hawk. Reposing on a flat slab of broken, glass-like stone, was Preacher's dog. She looked like an Egyptian sphinx, patiently waiting for her master to come home. She gazed bleakly across the water, a picture of misery.

We touched down lightly just a few feet from the hound. It turned to regard us blankly, and then cast its stare back towards the still waters. It was a heart-breaking and yet noble sight.

I stumbled across the fractured stone until I was by her side. I ran my hand down her neck and teased the silky fur between her ears. I realised that in all the time I was with them I had never heard the Preacher call her by name.

'He's gone, girl,' I said. 'This time he's not coming back. You can wait forever, but he's gone.' I patted her shoulder. 'You've nothing to gain by waiting here. Why don't you come home with me? You'd be welcome.'

I looked around the vast space littered with fractured rock and slowly filling with water. With Colin's help we could climb out of there, or perhaps he could fly us out one at a time. I pushed at the dog's shoulder as if to lever her from her seat. She didn't budge. I might as well have tried to lift the slab she was sitting on.

'Come on, girl. He's gone. We miss him too, but he's gone.'

I pushed at her again. With a deep and ominous growl, she warned me away. Her lips pulled back to give me a good look at her powerful fangs. But I wasn't going to surrender her to the abyss. I stroked her neck as if trying to sooth her and spoke gently. They say music has charms to soothe the savage breast, I hoped soft words might achieve the same end. They didn't.

The dog closed its powerful jaws around my arm and growled again, squeezing me with its teeth. The threat was plain as words. *Leave me alone or I'll hurt you.* Colin came up and ruffled her fur.

'It's all right, girl. He understands. You can let him go and we'll leave you in peace. You want to stay here with your friend. That's fine. We'll go now.'

The dog released me and returned to its vigil. The lightest vesper tousled her midnight coat and she lifted her head as if she was listening to a familiar voice.

'We can't leave her here,' I protested. 'Preacher wouldn't want us to. It's the least we can do in his memory. We must take her to the American mission. She deserves a good home, somewhere to sleep, someone to feed her. We can't...'

Colin held up his hand to silence me. 'She's not going anywhere if she doesn't want to. Surely you can see that. She's like Greyfriars Bobby, that little terrier who guarded his master's grave in Edinburgh for fourteen years until he passed away too. And I for one am not going to force her to leave. I can come back and check on her if it makes you happy, Nathan, but she thinks she belongs here, and that's all there is to it. Let her go, okay.'

I stood and regarded the beautiful animal standing guard over her master's grave. In my mind's eye I could see her making a home with Nuo and me, imagine us taking her for long walks through the streets of Lijiang, throwing sticks for her to fetch. In a single fantastic moment, I lived my life as her owner. And then I saw her with fresh eyes and realised it could never come true. She had only ever had one master.

With a heavy heart I said, 'You're right, Colin, you're right. Please, take me home.'

And so, I found myself back on Square Street watching the pretty women promenade, teetering like badly controlled puppets, with dainty, silk-clad hooves where their feet should be. Colin had dropped me outside town and shook my hand. He smiled.

'I'll let you know if anything happens to the dog, Nathan, I promise. Be happy, my friend. Give our love to Nuo. God be with you.'

And with that he turned, shimmered in the air, and was gone. The world seemed suddenly less real. Despite the late spring sunshine some of the brightness had gone from the day. I felt heavy for a moment. Lost. Directionless. And then I remembered where I was and who I was going to see; Nuo, my wife.

I had a half-hour walk to get back to the mission and I threaded my way through the streets of the Big Ink Slab in a daze. I resisted the urge to pat the package buttoned into the pocket at my thigh. I didn't want to tell the light-fingered street scoundrels around me that I had anything worth stealing. Nor did I adopt the walk of a man of means. I didn't want to draw attention to myself.

And yet I *was* attracting glances from many of the women and girls in the town. Appraising glances, sometimes accompanied by bright smiles. One or two of the men I passed had also looked me over. This began to unnerve me to the point that I breathed a hearty sigh of relief when I finally reached the Black Dragon Pool and knew I was nearly home.

My belly was already quivering with nerves by the time I walked past Junjie's house and saw the gnarled stone bridge he loved so much. Every step I took brought me closer to my future, but my past dragged at my heels with sticky claws. Then I remembered my dream of the soup kitchen and Nuo at the range. It had been so real I still recalled the delicious aromas. My stomach rumbled.

Even so my head was whirling. Did I want the responsibility of my own household? Did I want a life of hard work and decision-making? Was Nuo truly happy to be the centre of my universe. Was she still waiting for me? I didn't even know how long I had been away, I'd forgotten to ask.

I knew the elemental portals could adjust time. Nuo had been gone for months but returned to me in an hour, but I didn't know what they had done for me. I was *meant* to be away with the Preacher – when was I due back? My mouth was dry, and my spine turned to water. I was a mess.

Then I turned a corner and there was the mission just a few hundred yards away. A slight figure was crouched on the doorstep polishing the brass door furniture. She was fragile as a flower and indomitable as a Dreadnaught under steam. She blew on a smooth doorplate and then looked closely at what she saw reflected there.

Nuo dropped her polishing cloth and leapt upright. She turned. I heard her gasp and saw the look of amazed delight blaze from her sweet features. She ran into my arms and I lifted her from the ground, our mouths pressed together. All feelings of doubt vanished in that one glorious moment.

A dry cough brought us both to our senses and we turned to see Junjie beaming at us.

'Word of advice to young lovers,' he grinned. 'Dogs have to do this in the street, but we have a house. Come on, come on, get inside with you.'

I discovered I had been away for just over a week, Nuo time.

For the next week or so Nuo and I made up for lost time while Junjie acted like an indulgent grandfather, giving us space when we wished to be alone, but there if we needed him. Then, one evening, a taller shadow filled the study doorway when I was alone in there. Nuo and Junjie were out shopping for dinner.

Colin walked towards me and, smiling with delight, I leapt to my feet, thrusting out my hand. He shook it right gladly, but his eyes looked grave. His expression wiped the smile from my face.

'Colin, what is it? Is Rowan okay. Are you all right?'

'Nathan, I promised to stay in touch. She's gone, Preacher's dog, she's disappeared. There's no sign of her.'

[49]

I watch our grandchildren play in the garden behind our house and I think about the river of time that has flowed away from me, like the river flowing under Junjie's stone bridge. Those long-ago adventures with the Preacher seem as real and fresh to me as yesterday, yet sometimes I forget what I had for dinner the night before. More recent memories flow away like water too.

We have lived a blessed life. Lijiang and Shuhe went unnoticed during the communist revolution so we escaped all the disruption and political upheaval that scarred China's history for long decades. Even party officials enjoy a good meal and we looked after them like princes when they came to Nuo's Diamond Flower Restaurant.

Junjie never asked me where the diamond came from. He weighed it in his hand and whistled low with admiration. 'Big as a dragon's eye,' was all he said, with an arch expression on his animated features. He sold the jewel for a king's ransom but refused to take any commission for the transaction.

'Young lovers have a long life in front of them, an old man treasures friends more than dollars. Friends bring sunshine to the twilight years, that is ample reward. And anyway, Nuo can pay me in dinners.'

'And kisses,' Nuo said, hugging him.

I insisted on paying him for negotiating the purchase of the mission house and overseeing its conversion to a restaurant. We kept the upper floors as accommodation for us, making Junjie's bedroom into an en-suite studio. We had two modern bathrooms built into our quarters and the roof space converted into spare rooms.

The Diamond Flower was always popular, and for some reason we were never approached for protection money. We prospered. I never needed to sell the other two gems. One day our children will have to decide what to do with the things they find in a locked security box in a Swiss bank.

Junjie said he had two things he wanted to do. The first was to see if our children could possibly be as beautiful as their mother, and the second was to live to be a hundred. He did both. He lived long enough to coo over all three of our children, and he celebrated his one hundred and third birthday with yellow wine and sticky chicken.

Some of my soup kitchen dream came true, we did have ducks hooked to the ceiling and Nuo did the cooking when her swelling belly allowed. But I was no good with customers in the dining room. Junjie was out at front of house, running the bar and flirting with everyone. I stayed back in the kitchen, helping with the washing-up and learning to cook.

Junjie was the solid foundation upon which we built our fortunes. I only saw him angry once, when he caught a waitress stealing scraps from customer's plates. He came to me, his eyes blazing, and took me into the garden where we wouldn't be overheard. Through gritted teeth he told me what he had seen.

'This waitress is a hard worker,' he said. 'Why is she stealing food meant for the pigs? Something is wrong here, you pay well enough that she can buy food. I want to take the afternoon off. Can you do front of house for me? I'll be back before evening and we can talk then, okay?'

I agreed readily. Later Junjie told me how he went to the woman's street and did what he did so well, he gossiped with her neighbours. When he returned after a few hours he poured himself some yellow wine and drank it down in one, then he poured another.

What happened next taught me a lesson about people that I never forgot. The evening rush hadn't started, and the bar was fairly quiet. Junjie called over the woman in question and asked if she could take over behind the stick because we had to go talk some business. She took off her apron and settled herself behind the bar, beaming happily.

Out in the garden Junjie told me about the woman's squalid life. Her husband was a pathetic wastrel who never lifted a finger in the home and didn't do a day's work. Neither of the two sons had an ounce of self-respect, and they treated their mother like a drudge.

When she left the restaurant at night she would cook for her men and clean the house after them. In the morning she got out of bed early to make rice for their breakfast and prepare their lunch before coming to work.

'She's stealing the customer's scraps because the boys eat everything on the table and she is expected to wait until they finish before she eats what's left. There's nothing left for the poor woman. It is medieval. I want to horsewhip the bastards. She supports them, and they treat her like a slave. May I have your permission to get involved with this conundrum?'

'Are you sure you want to stick your nose into someone else's family business? I don't want you getting hurt and I don't want to lose a good hard worker. What are you planning, old fox?'

And he told me. I was so astounded by the simplicity of his idea, that I laughed out loud and hugged him, actually lifting him off his feet. I was surprised at how solid the old man felt in my arms, and how light. I put him down and apologised. He leant forward and kissed me lightly on the cheek.

'You're a good boy,' he said. 'A very good boy.'

He went out again and I joined our problem lady at the bar. Her name was Daiyu, which, she proudly told me, means 'Black jade'. When I asked if I might talk with her she looked guilty and afraid. I smiled and tried to put her at her ease.

I asked if she was happy in her work; she insisted she was, very happy. I asked if she had any plans beyond being a waitress. She told me she was very happy and 'waitress was very suitable job for simple woman'. She smiled nervously, and I saw she was still pretty in an exhausted fashion. But her life was wringing the juice out of her. Time to put Junjie's Plan A into action.

I apologised but told Daiyu she could no longer be a waitress in the Diamond Flower. Her face crumpled, and I quickly took her hands telling her not to worry, please, don't worry. She wasn't going to lose her job. I told her I was so pleased with her that I wanted to give her a better job, that I needed her to help Junjie with front of house.

It would mean more money, of course, but it would also mean greater responsibility. Was she willing to give it a shot? Her smile lit the room. She was. Then I delivered Junjie's masterstroke. Meals were included as part of the package, was that okay with her? She was speechless, all she could do was nod and grin. I nodded and grinned back.

'Starting now,' I said, 'go get something to eat. I'll watch the bar for you.'

She protested, but I insisted. After that night it became policy that all staff should have at least one meal during or at the end of their shift. We called it Junjie's Law in his honour.

That night the man himself came back to the restaurant with a sullen, sour-faced man in tow. It was Daiyu's husband. Now we started plan B. Junjie had called on the man saying he was looking for a hard worker and had heard that he, known as Feng, was the ideal candidate. He told him it was an important position that required a person of great dependability.

Such flattery worked like a charm, and thus I ended up with an assistant dishwasher I didn't know I needed. Turned out Daiyu blossomed in her new role and Feng proved a sterling plongeur. I think having Nuo to look after him helped, and Junjie kept him flattered by praising the quality of his work.

Later, through the neighbours, Junjie learned that the sons had been told to 'shape up or ship out', that their parents worked together to put some spine into the pair of them. Junjie was a true magician with people, and he had a heart bigger than all China.

Our old friend never missed a day's work and was as bright and lucid as a twenty-year-old right up until the day he died. It was very sudden. One early morning he came into our lodgings looking pale as a ghost and sat in the chair he preferred.

'Nathan, Nuo... Thank you, for your love for an old...'

And he slumped down in the chair, gone. That big heart that had never let anyone else down beat its last. He had left us his house and all its contents, but more importantly, memories time has never erased.

Now I sit in our garden and I watch our grandchildren. I think of Preacher, Colin, Rowan, and Junjie. I think of Nuo, and as if she's heard me my beautiful wife comes to sit with me and takes my hand.

'I love you,' I tell her.

'I know,' she answers. And she stretches out her unbound feet and smiles like a happy cat. 'And I love you, too.'

[50] (Afterword) Spindrift

My system was badly damaged. It was almost terminal. Once the worm began to burn I had slid down into the belly of the beast and the conflagration raged around me like a firestorm. I was lifted, thrown around and buffeted mercilessly by the winds of flame. I felt things break inside me.

Nathan had managed to shoot the sack full of phosphorous bombs, that was all that mattered. I briefly wondered if Colin had rescued him in time, and then I stopped wondering about anything. After the cataclysm of the great Sha-aneer's death I was left shattered and broken, buried deep down amid the rubble and thick dust of its nest.

I had shared my Nano biotech with Nathan, but still had enough to use what remained of my original body – plus whatever I could mine from my surroundings – to begin repairs. The technology started working with what I shall loosely describe as my 'brain', a woolly term for a device both more complex and less wonderful than that beautiful organ humans take for granted.

The first thing I did – when I was able – was to contact my companion. She was overjoyed to hear from me, and I was just in time. Finding no trace of me at the worm blast site she was ready to follow GODS' protocol, which would have seen her power down and allow her body's molecular bindings to dissolve. My loyal friend would have become nothing more than a puddle of minerals and water.

Through her eyes I saw Colin and Nathan come to her, saw Nathan's attempt to 'rescue' her. She would never have harmed him, not really, but she had to stay where she was and wait for me. I was pleased to see both my friends looking so well. Nathan had taken on something of an elemental's 'glamour'. Nuo was getting her husband back looking much better than new.

Eventually I was ready to claw my way up to the bed of the lake that had formed since my burial. The water was murky and thick with silt, but it grew fresher and cleaner as I swam to the surface. I had chosen my time well. It was a pitch dark, starless night when I climbed onto the shore of that lake. By ghost light I saw her waiting for me.

'Hello, old friend,' I said. She sniffed at my naked body, backed away, and whined a question at me. 'Yes, please.' I answered. 'I couldn't find all the raw materials down there.'

I lay down and opened my mouth. My companion squatted carefully over my face and urinated copiously down my throat. The stream of rare elements she donated were instantly fixed into my neurological pathways. I woke up – and was fully myself once more.

What had stretched out on that barren shore had been the shell of GODS' servant. What stood up was Preacher Satan Spindrift. And now I needed clothes, and a gun. We headed for the geologists' camp.

...

I saw Wang skulking around the American mission, spying on the inhabitants, and then I followed him and his henchmen into the narrow back streets of Lijiang. For a fat man there was a lot of the ferret about Wang, but only if the ferret was oily, unpleasant, and sly.

I frowned at the picture and mentally I apologised to ferrets everywhere. Wang was not a ferret, just the incomparable Wang. A singular – and a singularly unpleasant – work of his own devising. Nature had given him his basic framework and as soon as he was able he had started shaping it to his liking.

Every day the fat, dish-faced man pulled the shabby tatters of his false pride around his corpulent shoulders and performed his petty acts of banal cruelty. He was a pathetic balloon filled with malice who didn't have enough imagination to be truly evil, but he was the willing puppet for others who did. I hoped that they were the people he was going to report to that afternoon.

Wang and his cronies had robbed and killed innocent travellers in the Jade Tiger Guest House. With Mrs Zhou they had been part of the gang who fed the worm calf under the guest house's foundations. They had betrayed their own species for their share of the spoils they took from the victims. The world would be a better, cleaner place without them.

The fat man wobbled down a side alley and squeezed himself into a doorway, his thugs hulked either side of him. He rapped on the door. A panel slid aside.

A voice asked, 'Donata?'

Wang answered, 'Sore wa watashi desu.'

The brief exchange in Japanese told me everything I needed to know. 'Who is it?' 'It's me.' It proved what I already suspected – Wang was reporting to his gokudo bosses. I needed to get into that building. Arrogance is a terrible failing in those who believe themselves powerful. It makes them blind to their weaknesses.

There was a guard on the street door but an open window on the second floor led me to an empty room and then out to a well-lit corridor. I made no pretence of stealth when I walked through the house and down to the ground floor. I wanted them to know I was there, and I wanted them curious.

I soon had a following of strutting, heavily tattooed men. Their faces were all stamped with identical, sneering grins. They asked each other who I was, and then answered the question with the same witty riposte 'A dead man', 'Yes, a dead man.' The questions and answers quickly became wearisome, but I knew I wouldn't have to listen to them for very long.

By the time I reached the building's reception hall – which sported a genuine golden throne for the kumicho, the gang boss – I had amassed more than forty curious gokudo cockerels, all armed with knives, swords or cleavers. My roving eyes and ears told me there were perhaps thirty more in this cohort of crime. I planted myself before the throne and waited.

The foot soldiers, or 'kobun', circled around me like snarling hyenas, all the while firing questions at me. Wang stepped forward to try to break my silence.

'I know him, he's one of the American Fathers from the mission house in Shuhe. He was at the Jade Tiger House when it was destroyed. He killed Mrs Zhou and two of my men. He's dangerous.'

An incredulous hiss went around the room, punctuated by sarcastic laughter. A white-haired, slender man in fine robes strode into the room at a fine clip. He slapped Wang hard across the belly as he passed him, which made the fat man wince in fear.

'Just because he has bigger balls than you, Wang, it doesn't make him dangerous to real men.'

His men laughed, and I knew he was the kumicho, the father of that gang of animals. He climbed onto his throne and sat regarding me, legs splayed wide. The image was so medieval I almost laughed aloud at the man's mock regal posture. I held his gaze.

'I admire a man of courage, American,' he said, grinning. 'No need to run to your death so eagerly. There is the door to the street. Close it behind you on your way out, we'll find you and your household when it's time. And that will be soon, never fear.'

He barked at the guard to unlock the door and told his men to stand to one side and let me pass. A path opened between me and escape to the alleyway. The guard drew the bolts and offered me a little bow. I walked through the gang and up the broad flight of steps to the door. Very precisely I bolted it again.

I heard that incredulous hiss once more, I turned to face them. My roving eyes and ears had told me that I had them all in front of me now. I bowed, slightly less than the guard had done, which earned a snarl of disapproval from the room.

'Kumicho,' I said. 'A man has the right to know who is killing him...' I paused. The white-haired man climbed out of his throne and made to speak. I held up my hand for silence. There came that hiss.

'So, I'm going to tell you,' I continued. 'Some people are good, and they make the world a better place. Others are evil bastards who take advantage of the good people just because they can. They are wicked, cruel cowards, who think they are powerful because they can count on overwhelming numbers to crush any opposition, as *you* plan to do now.'

I swept my glance around the room to encompass everyone in it, pausing to smile briefly at Wang, and then I returned my gaze to the kumicho.

'Between the good people and creatures like you,' I said, 'there stands me.'

I killed the guard first.

Author's note

The beautiful ancient town of Lijiang and the Tiger Leaping Gorge are real places, as is the Black Dragon Pool with its broken stele that rings like a bell when struck with a stone. Junjie's gnarled stone bridge is also real. Other places are fictionalised for the sake of my story.

A hole the size of New York City has never been punched into the gorge by a massive explosion, the snarling tiger cave is still there, as is the Stone Lotus Temple. Wives with unbound feet still take a colourful Sunday constitutional along Square Street.

Lijiang's position on the Silk and Tea Road has preserved it from everything history might otherwise have thrown at it: the end of colonial rule, the short-lived republic, invasion by Japan, and the rise of communism. It is an idyllic spot in the mountains where the Naxi people have maintained their gentle, hospitable ways for centuries.

The famed terracotta warriors and Great Wall draw visitors from all over the globe, while Lijiang is not so very busy, and perhaps that's for the best. By remaining off the well-beaten tourist tracks Lijiang retains the air of a restful, venerable place. Perhaps it also helps maintain the illusion that if such places survive in the world, the true Shangri-La might one day also be discovered in the mountains of Tibet.

A sweet thought.

...

Preacher Spindrift will return in *GODS' Scourge*

Other works by Derek E. Pearson

Preacher Spindrift series (prequels to GODS' Warrior)

Both volumes are Foreword INDIES Book Of The Year Awards FINALISTS in Fantasy

2017   **2016**

Soul's Asylum trilogy (2016 to 2017)

Star Weaver (book #2)
Foreword INDIES Book Of The Year Awards FINALIST in Science Fiction

Soul's Asylum (book #1)
The Sun ☆☆☆☆ :
"a weird, vivid and creepy book, not for the faint hearted. But its originality and top writing make for a great read."

Body Holiday trilogy (2014 to 2015)

T V PRESENTER JULIETTE FOSTER:
"Pearson's galactic-sized imagination delivers, with veiled gallows humour, a compelling image of a chic, high-tech society infused with a toxic strain that feeds on extreme violence."